A NIGHT OF THUNDER

BOOK TWO OF THE ZAKYNTHIAN FAMILY SERIES

CHRISSIE PARKER

FOSSEND
PUBLISHING

A Night of Thunder © Chrissie Parker 2025

Cover Design © CCBookDesign 2025

Cover Illustration © Susie Newman, Susie's Art in Greece 2025

This novel is a work of fiction. Names and characters and events are fictitious and a product of the author's imagination and any resemblance to actual persons, living or dead, is entirely coincidental.

All rights reserved. No part of this publication may be reproduced, stored in a retrieval system, or transmitted in any form or by any other means, electronic, mechanical, photocopying, recording or otherwise, without the prior permission of the copyright owner.

ISBN-13: 978-1-9164025-8-4

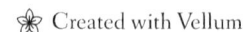

❋ Created with Vellum

To my wonderful Great Aunt Doreen, who packed parachutes whilst the bombs fell. We may always have been thousands of miles apart, but you were always close, in my heart. Love you! xoxo

PROLOGUE

Zakynthos, Greece, 1953

The early morning sunrise was washed through with hues of pastel orange and the occasional bright thread of purple and pink resembling an artist's palette. The eclectic streets of Zakynthos Town were virtually empty and most Zakynthians were still in their beds. The small guest house in Zakynthos Town was eerily silent. Too silent. It was almost disturbing.

He pushed back the loose bedclothes and quietly padded to the wooden dresser where he quickly washed and dressed himself. Twenty minutes later, he left the room without a backwards glance.

Walking downstairs, he passed through the abandoned entrance hallway and stepped out into the brightening morning sunshine. The town had a semi-abandoned air to it as he walked the streets. The earthquake of the previous day had damaged many of the surrounding buildings.

Cracks crept up walls, and old structures now had gaping holes in them. Rubble lay scattered at their feet. It hadn't seemed to faze some of the locals, though, who were now acting like it was just a normal day. Most Zakynthians had already begun to clear up, as though the earthquake had just been an ordinary occurrence and nothing to worry about. Earthquakes in Greece, it seemed, were just part of everyday life.

He had time to waste before he could board the next boat to the mainland. He chose to explore the town. Maybe he'd relax in a taverna – if any were open – or visit the much talked about castle standing high on the towering acropolis, overlooking Zakynthos Town. In the meantime, he traversed the main semicircular harbour towards the large imposing church and bell tower; a surprisingly close replica of the one in St. Mark's Square in Venice.

It was a pleasant walk despite the ever-present signs of earthquake damage. Sea water gently lapped the harbour wall and a lone turtle bobbed amongst the moored boats, searching for food. He marvelled at its beauty. It was a truly deceptive scene.

The sun continued to shine, and the pastels of sunrise finally faded, replaced with the brilliance of blue sky. For the first time, despite the surrounding chaos, he felt relaxed. His thoughts briefly turned to home, England, the place he had escaped from to try and make things better for all of them.

Now he was here in Zakynthos, it was proving harder than he ever thought it would be. Coming here had been a nice idea, a dream he'd had many times. Something he needed and wanted to do. The past needed fixing, and on the Greek mainland it'd felt like anything was possible, but now he was on Zakynthos, things were just as confusing as before. More so, even.

A NIGHT OF THUNDER

As he neared the church, he stopped to take in the incredible view. The harbour swept in a large semicircle from one prominent outcrop to another. To the north, the acropolis topped by the castle. To the south, the craggy mountain called Skopos. He wondered how many people had stood here on this spot over the centuries and taken in the same view?

As the heat of the day increased, his decision to visit the castle changed. A hot, sweaty climb to the top of the acropolis was something he just didn't want to do. Instead, he moved on to explore the damaged back streets of the town, sidestepping rubble, dust and broken glass as he went.

The town was growing busy, and despite the slightly uneasy air and the damage, he enjoyed watching the hustle and bustle of life carry on around him. Greeks, it seemed, were incredibly resilient.

He'd barely walked halfway down the main street before everything changed. It was as though a switch had been flicked. The air became intense. A sudden and unusual change in atmosphere. His sense of foreboding grew; it wrapped around him with dark tentacles, smothering him, making him want to turn and run. To escape.

He had no idea why, and yet it became stronger and more intense with every passing second. Abruptly, the ground beneath his feet began to vibrate and shake. Just like the previous day, a great rumbling and jolting swarmed its way through Zakynthos Town. It knocked him from his feet in its intensity. He landed hard on the still vibrating ground. Pushing himself up, he managed to scramble to his feet again.

This sudden earthquake was much stronger than the one that had occurred the previous day, and it struck violently with an explosive bang. The air was filled with frightened wailing and screaming. People ran from already crumbling buildings whose remains had given up and were falling to the ground in handfuls of loose stone and mortar. Dust rose and swirled into the sky making visibility difficult. Flames suddenly erupted and licked at ruinous structures around him.

He'd never experienced anything like it before, and he had no idea what to do. Whichever direction he turned, things were grim. It was an impossible situation that was becoming more deadly by the second.

Another fire broke out close by and a large group of people ran towards him. Their distressed cries fell upon him in waves. Without hesitation, he joined the throng, following them, hoping, and trusting, they knew where they were heading. It was hard going, and the ground was covered in ever-increasing rubble; shattered glass, masonry and wood. Trying to avoid it was hopeless. His feet tripped and slipped as he tried to run.

It was impossible to stand upright due to the earth's violent actions, and he fell to the ground again, becoming covered in dust and dirt in seconds. His right wrist hurt having landed heavily on it, twisting it. His palms were bloody and full of grit; his trousers were dirty and ripped at the knees. The fires around him increased, the smoke becoming dense and making him cough.

With a final hefty jolt, the earthquake ceased, but it wasn't over. As he tried to stand, he realised too late, his life would end there, in that disruptive and frightening moment.

Above him, the remains of a large building was unable to stay upright. It finally gave way to nature. It crumbled and fell in great chunks leaving nothing but a pile of masonry. As the rubble landed on him, it pinned him to the floor and crushed the life from him. His final thoughts were of Athena and what might have been, if only she had been given the chance.

ONE

Bristol, England, 1940

"Wait for me!" Lissy laughed as she ran through the trees. The wind brushed tendrils of hair against her cheeks, and leaves of burnished gold and yellow fell to the floor as she knocked the branches.

"Come on, Liss!"

"I'm coming!" She ran after him and grabbed his hand, finally catching up with him. Her beloved Richard. He slowed and turned to face her as she melted into his arms. "You're mine, Lissy Cook."

"Always?"

"Always." Richard lifted her and spun her around before kissing her deeply. As she succumbed to the kiss, the air around them was punctuated with a high-pitched wailing sound that permeated everything.

"I must leave you Lissy. I'm so sorry..."

"Please don't, Richard. I need you here with me. Please, stay..."

As he melded into the woods, becoming invisible, the trees disappeared too. They were replaced with the inky blackness of night and the continuous high-pitched wailing of air raid sirens, accompanied by the drone of aircraft engines growing ever louder.

∼

"Why is it always the same dream?" Lissy whispered as she hastily sat up and flicked a match to light the candle on the bedside table. Lissy pushed back the bedcovers, pulled on her dressing gown and grabbed the small black and white photograph of Richard from the bedside table. Stuffing it into her pocket, she got out of bed and slid her feet into her slippers.

Carefully, with one hand on the wall, Lissy made her way out of the bedroom, along the hallway and down the creaking stairs to the front door. With just enough light to guide her safely, Lissy grabbed her gas mask from the hallway shelf, then blew the candle out before opening the front door. She didn't want to break blackout rules.

The wailing siren continued, and the street was already busy. Families and couples quickly scuttled along in the darkness, all heading towards the nearest shelter. Lissy shut the door behind her and joined them. All around her, the throng of people was growing. Across the road a lit lamp caught her eye, but before she could speak, a shout rang out, "Put that light out!" Within seconds they were plunged back into the gloom. The siren wail became louder as she neared the shelter. The heavier mechanical throbbing of distant planes now joined the wail, and Lissy picked up speed. This time it was real, and she didn't want to get stuck outside when the bombs fell.

The air raid shelter was located at the end of the road and Lissy could've walked the route blindfolded if necessary. She'd passed the wall of entrance sandbags so many times she'd lost count. Picking up speed, Lissy arrived at the shelter as the planes reached the outskirts of town, dropping their first bombs. There was no time left; she had to get into the shelter. She hurried down the steps into the dusty, cramped space, pushing her way through the jostling crowd to find a seat. The wardens were still frantically trying to get everyone to safety, and it was difficult to get everyone inside.

Taking a seat along one of the rough wooden benches, Lissy tried not to let the panic overwhelm her. "You've done this before. You'll be okay," she whispered, trying to reassure herself.

"Are you okay there, Miss Lissy?" Mr Jenkins from the corner shop asked as he squeezed past with his wife and two young children.

"Yes Mr Jenkins, I'm fine. You take care of the little ones and your wife. They need you now."

"Well, you can always sit with us if you need the company."

"Thank you."

Mr Jenkins and his family pushed deeper into the shelter to find a seat. Lissy preferred to be closer to the doors. The claustrophobia of the shelter overwhelmed her, and as much as she knew it was for her protection, each minute stuck inside was an eternity.

The doors finally closed as planes flew overhead. The shelter shook as bombs landed close to their street. The atmosphere was tense and the vibrations of the impact shook the shelter's occupants, who silently prayed, cried, rocked in their seats or talked to their neighbours to try and drown out the noise of the bombing.

Wrapped in her dressing gown, Lissy looked at the

photo of Richard she still clutched in her hand and remembered the good times. It was all she could do. Keep remembering the good times.

She closed her eyes, his face imprinting on her brain as she blocked out the crowded shelter and concentrated on Richard and him alone. Lissy thought of the times they'd borrowed bicycles from Richard's friend. They'd ridden through the city streets and up to the green expanse of The Downs. Both had been hot and out of breath as they reached the top of the hill. They'd cycled alongside each other, across the open parkland, before sitting on the grass to enjoy a picnic.

The sun had shone brightly, and they'd enjoyed their day together. They'd talked about the future and everything they hoped it would bring for them: a life together, children and a house of their own.

After their picnic, they'd ridden back towards town, over the Clifton Suspension Bridge, into Ashton Court where they'd left their bicycles and wandered through the beautiful woodland. Richard had proposed to her under the green canopy, making her so happy.

Afterwards, they'd cycled back into town and said goodbye to each other: Lissy to go to work, Richard to tell his parents the good news and to say farewell to them and ready himself for war. They'd both known as young eighteen-year-olds that the war would become an influential part of their lives; little had they realised just how much.

"Oh Richard, where are you? Are you safe...?" A tear slid down her face and she brushed it away with the back of her hand.

As the shelter continued to rock and shake through hours of incessant bombing, Lissy's mind wandered through memories. Born in Bristol, Lissy Cook was the youngest of two children. Her real name was Alice, but as a young child she'd struggled to say Alice. Instead, she'd continually stumbled over the word saying *Liss* instead. In the end, it had stuck, and Lissy became her family nickname.

Alice now sounded alien to her, and she rarely used it except for official documents. As far as she was concerned, she was Lissy and always would be. Lissy's parents had run a haberdashery shop that the family lived above. She had gone to school and helped her mother in the house, and had expected to live at home with her parents until she met a man she could marry. It'd been a simple life and one she'd loved.

Her parents had been surrounded by great friends, and it was how she met Richard, a friend of her brother, Tom. The three children had grown up together. Summer fetes, Christmas nativities and family celebrations. They'd always been there together, playing with the other children as their parents enjoyed the festivities.

The families shared the highs and lows of life, and important events which would test them all. Their friendships spanned years, and those years slowly joined Lissy and Richard at the hip, and their childhood friendship blossomed into love at the age of sixteen.

It all changed when the Second World War began. Lissy's brother, Tom, left the family home as soon as conflict began, and Richard followed soon after. They'd been full of excitement at being able to join up to fight against an enemy who was slowly creeping through countries and swallowing them whole. Many other men had done the same, and England was now left full of lonely, anxious mothers, wives, girlfriends and sisters, desperately waiting for news of their loved ones.

Meanwhile, Lissy had continued living with her parents

and helping them in the shop, something she enjoyed. Her favourite thing had been exploring the stock room to see what interesting items she could find, and helping her father ring things up on the large metal till.

In early spring, 1940, Lissy's parents both suddenly died from influenza. Lissy had caught it too, but her body had been stronger. She'd fought the illness and survived. The country had been on war rations for almost a year. Even before rations, her parents hadn't eaten properly, instead putting food back for Lissy and her brother, insisting their children needed it more than they did. It hadn't helped them, and they'd paid the price.

Lissy missed her parents dreadfully. They'd worked hard keeping the shop going, and they'd loved Lissy and Tom devotedly. Even after a long, hard day at work, they always had time for their two children.

When Lissy's parents died, the rented shop went to someone else. Lissy had sat in disbelief as a solicitor tried to explain that her parents were penniless. Years before, they'd sold the shop that had once belonged to Lissy's grandparents to someone else.

Her parents had wanted to continue working in it, so a deal had been agreed to allow them to rent the shop and live above it. They'd wanted stability for their children. They'd wanted somewhere to live, work, and bring up their children in a happy environment, even if it didn't belong to them. The owner had agreed, happy to take the rent each month for little work, building their empire in the process.

Unfortunately, the Cooks had never told Lissy and Tom that once they died, the two children would be left with nothing. Lissy had been distraught to discover her much-loved family home and business no longer belonged to the family. Since losing her parents, Lissy couldn't bear going in and seeing someone else serving behind the counter. It would always be her parents' and grandparents' shop, no one else's.

Lissy didn't just lose the shop that day. Her family home, above the shop, became someone else's too. With Tom away, Lissy was alone, homeless, with little money.

Before her death, Lissy's mum had tried to instil a little independence into her children, and Lissy had started nursing training. She'd become a quick study and very adept at what was demanded of her. Lissy had been forced to give it up after her parents' death, needing to get a better paid job to pay for somewhere to live. Lissy was lucky to get a job in an office at the local corset factory, and she left nursing training without any hope of being able to do it again in the future. With her factory earnings, Lissy moved into a two bedroom rented house, sharing it with a fellow factory worker called Betty. The house wasn't far from the factory and several streets away from where she grew up; she was finally settled.

Six months after moving in, Betty married and moved in with her new husband, and Lissy was living alone, again. The landlord agreed she could live there alone, paying the same rent, until he found someone else to rent the room, but no new flat mate had materialised. Some of the older neighbours frowned upon a woman living alone, but whenever she was questioned, she ignored it. Lissy was her own woman, she liked her own company, and she'd do as she pleased.

When the war arrived, Lissy's life changed again. The factory was commandeered for the war effort, and Lissy was moved to the factory floor to help pack parachutes.

Lissy's new life had come at a huge price. Her parents were dead. Her brother and fiancé were fighting for the country's freedom. Despite trying to ignore it, loneliness crept in, and she wished things could be different. It didn't help that Lissy had few friends. There were lots of women at the factory she could've become friends with, but they weren't her sort of people. Instead, Lissy accepted life as it was, got up each day, went to work, paid her rent and ate what food she was able to get hold of.

Now the country was beset by war, and families were fractured. Sons were fighting for their country. Some were already dead. It was a difficult time for everyone, especially for Lissy and Richard who found their blissful relationship tested when he'd enlisted. Now she spent every day alone, staring at the small black and white image of him, praying he'd eventually make it safely back to her.

A bomb struck close to the air raid shelter, pulling Lissy from her reverie. Violently shaking the shelter's occupants, it made the dim electric lights flicker, and dust swirled around them. Children cried, women wailed and men tried to stay strong and comfort those around them. All Lissy could do was clutch her photo and think of Richard.

"Come back to me. Wherever you are, come back. I need you."

The relentless bombing of Bristol lasted long into the night, and it was hit hard. When the sirens finally stopped and the bombing ended, Lissy and her neighbours left the shelter. As they stood on the street in the growing light of dawn, they were shocked to see the landscape of their city, the place they called home, had changed, and in some places was almost unrecognisable.

TWO

Zakynthos, Greece, 1943

"Angelos Sarkis! Do not go to the Kafenion again! You are needed here, at home." Pigi glared at her son and threw her hands up in frustration as he silently shrugged his shoulders. Undeterred, she continued. "Your daughter, Sophia, needs *you*. I need you. There are things to do in the house! I know you are sad. I know life took a turn none of us wanted, but you still have responsibilities here, with us."

"I do what I can..."

"It is not enough! You lost Maria, your wife, you hurt, but I lost my husband too!"

"Pah! Wife? Maria was a traitor. I care nothing for her. She got what she deserved when the Nazis executed her. My other daughter, Athena, would still be here if it was not for my wife. Elena would still be alive too!"

Pigi sat and buried her head in her hands, releasing a long sigh. She raised her head and stared at her son. "Maria had her faults, Angelos. I never agreed with your father and Stelios matching her as your wife, but it was their decision. You know how things work here! I had to do what they thought was best for you and for her. I am sorry she betrayed you. She betrayed us all. What she did was despicable. Elena should not have lost her life because of that woman, but Angelos, you must understand that Maria is still Sophia's mother. Dead or alive, it is a fact that will never change. Do not ever talk about her like that in front of the child. We are forced to live with the hateful burden of what Maria did, but Sophia deserves better."

"Sophia is a baby! What does she know of her mother's crimes? Nothing! As for her mother, Sophia is better off without her. We all are. Maria betrayed everyone: me, you, Sophia, Elena and Athena. Our lives have been turned upside down. I will never forgive her. Never!"

As Angelos stormed from his home, his mother's words whirled about his head. He should've stayed and helped Pigi. She was right; his daughter Sophia needed him. Pigi needed him. She couldn't do everything on her own. Instead, the anger had coursed through him and Angelos had lost his temper, ignored his mother, and headed to the Kafenion to sit in his favourite chair, alone.

The air around him was now tinged with the smell of coffee and the fog of cigarette smoke. Other tables in the Kafenion were occupied by men talking and drinking, but Angelos remained alone with his thoughts. A cup of coffee sat untouched on his table and his eyes were closed. As the other men continued to talk, Angelos remained quiet and still, lost in his own world. Unable to draw himself back to the present.

It was December and another year was almost over. His life, however, was in limbo. The past refused to shake him free. He was trapped, still standing at the edge of Xigia beach, watching helplessly as Elena and Athena were torn apart and both taken from him.

A NIGHT OF THUNDER

Elena, the woman he loved, was dragged away by Nazis. Their daughter, Athena, floated out to sea on a boat with a stranger. It was a devastating loss. Angelos was taunted by memories that constantly twisted around each other, and he was forced to relive it all. He was unable to move on. He didn't know how. It was only his Greek pride and a promise he'd made about his remaining daughter, Sophia, that made him get up each day and carry on with what was left of his life.

"Your daughter Sophia needs you, Angelos! You say she is only six months old, but you are her father, and you have responsibilities!" his mother had raged at him one day. "I cannot continue to hold this family together without your help. I know you hurt; we all hurt. This war damaged us all, but it is not fair to do this to Sophia, or to me!"

Angelos swirled the coffee to the background Kafenion noise. He hated to admit it, but his mother was right. Sophia was important too. The loss of Elena and Athena cut deep, though, and he was a failure for not saving them. How could he explain to neighbours and friends that he was falling apart because of his loss? It was wartime. Many people had died. Even more had gone missing and still were every day. It was how it was.

Why should Angelos Sarkis be any different? He was just another person in the world who was lost in a sea of grief. He'd never forget what happened. There was no coming back from it, and whilst he tried hard to remember the good times of his short life with his beloved Elena, to cherish the happy memories, it was hard. This wasn't the life he wanted, but it was all he had left.

"Bastards. Bastards!" Angelos slammed his fist on the table, jolting himself from his reverie. The Kafenion owner wandered over and pulled out the seat opposite Angelos.

"Is my coffee that bad today, Angelos?"

"No. Your coffee is always good. I just have many things on my mind."

"Do not let the enemy see you weakened, Angelos. They want us to be weak. You have been through a lot, what they did... it was unspeakable." The man paused for a moment. "You must go on living. You have a lot to live for."

"You sound like you have been talking to my mother."

"No, but I see the hurt you have been through reflected in your face. Stay strong, Angelos. It will get better one day."

"When? When will that day be?"

"That I do not know. You must keep hoping. It is all any of us can do. Enjoy your coffee, and try not to damage the table."

Angelos withdrew into himself again and finished his coffee. His mother and Sophia needed him; he could not stay here all day. Leaving the Kafenion, Angelos walked through the lanes towards home. As he reached his olive grove, he climbed through a hole in the stone wall and wandered through the trees. As he neared the house, a wave of grief washed through him again, and he placed a steadying hand on a tree to stop himself from being transported to the past, but he failed.

"Not again. Why do you torment me?" he raged, falling to the floor and curling up at the foot of the olive tree.

His mind was taken back to the day that hurt the most, when Elena was taken from the Nazi headquarters to Keri. Angelos had followed them, hoping to try and save Elena somehow. He had lay in the grass, spying on them from a distance. Elena had stood on the edge of the Keri cliffs, surrounded by soldiers, scared but defiant. Angelos had been proud of her for holding her head high, despite her dirty appearance. It had shocked him to see her hair was matted, her clothes torn, her limbs bruised, scratched and covered with dirt. She was still beautiful to him. She would always be beautiful to him.

Angelos stayed hidden as the Italian soldier, Pietro Cipriani, took hold of Elena's arm and walked her to the cliff edge. It was then Angelos knew he couldn't save her. He was just one man, and they would shoot him before he got close. If Angelos died, Athena, wherever she was, would be completely alone in the world. Fighting against what his heart was telling him – wanting to save the woman he loved – Angelos listened to his head and became a coward hiding in the long grass.

Unable to look away, Angelos forced himself to watch as Elena shook with fear. Angelos forced himself to watch as Pietro Cipriani placed the gun to the back of Elena's head. Angelos forced himself to watch as the bullet punctured Elena's head and her lifeless body tumbled over the cliff edge to the ocean below.

Angelos had wanted to scream. Instead, he pushed his fist into his mouth, stifling his cry as the tears slid down his face. In fear of his life, a shaking Angelos continued to watch as Pietro Cipriani was duped by the Nazis and joined Elena at the bottom of the cliff with a bullet to his head too. It was over. They were both gone.

Angelos might have survived by being a coward, but he'd received his punishment too. It was a horrific scene that would forever be imprinted on his mind; to be recalled every time he closed his eyes. Angelos had rolled onto his back and lay on the dusty ground staring blankly up at the sky. The ground had rumbled as enemy vehicles passed heading to Zakynthos Town.

For the first time in his life, Angelos had truly cried.

The tears that fell were for the woman he'd always loved and for his daughter, Athena, who was now lost to him. He had no idea how long he'd lain in the undergrowth, but eventually Angelos staggered to his feet. He had dusted down his trousers and wiped the salty tears from his face.

Slowly, Angelos walked to the cliff edge, stopping for a moment next to a lone poppy growing in the dirt. How it had survived he had no idea, but it was like his beautiful Elena: bright, defiant and brave to the last. Angelos stooped to break the green stem and took the final steps to the cliff edge. Peering down to the sea below, the two bodies lay at the foot of the rock face washing back and forth, slowly being taken by the ocean. Soon they would disappear, lost forever.

Angelos sat on the cliff edge, a dangerous thing to do, but he didn't care. He continued to watch the movement of the bodies in the water below, not wanting to tear himself away.

"You were always the love of my life, Elena. I will never forget when we first met. You, sitting there singing your heart out. Then you saw me and said *Hey you! Sing with me!* No one had ever spoken to me like that before, and I fell in love with you instantly. I wish the world had been different for us, Elena. I wish I had been stronger and braver. I wish I had stood up to my father and stuck by you and Athena. I wish this war had never happened. Most of all, I wish you had not died like this. You have only just left me, but I already know I will feel the hurt of your loss for the rest of my life."

Angelos threw the poppy to the sea below and watched as it floated down to join Elena. As it landed, he knew he couldn't bear to go on without her. He put shaking hands on the ground either side of himself, preparing to push forward off the cliff to join her in the sea below. Taking a last look out across the flat deep blue of Ionian waters, a sudden glint of sunlight on the horizon caught his eye and it momentarily stopped him. It was then he heard Elena's voice in his head.

"Love, Angelos, is when you care deeply for someone. Love means you will always be there for them. Love means you would protect them, fight for them and even, I suppose, die for them. Do not die for me today, Angelos. I do not want you to die for me. Live instead. Live for me, Angelos! Live for Athena! Whatever you do, keep my memory alive by living."

Angelos knew it was his subconscious fighting through the grief. Elena wasn't there, but the words hit home. He couldn't do it. Elena may be lost to him, but their daughter, Athena, was out there somewhere, and one day she would need her father. Angelos couldn't leave Sophia fatherless or to the mercy of his father-in-law, Stelios, either. She mattered too. Placing his dusty palms together, Angelos looked out across the sea before closing his eyes.

"St Stylianos, Protector of Children. Please hear my prayer. Find my beloved daughter, Athena. Bring her back to Zakynthos. I promise to visit you often at church and light a candle in honour of the bravery of her mother, Elena Petrakis. Let me find Athena and bring her back to her home, Zakynthos. Let me bring her home to the place her mother was born. I promise to honour you, St Stylianos, if you will grant me this."

Instead of throwing himself to the water below to join Elena, Angelos stood and turned his back on the precarious edge and went to find his abandoned motorcycle.

That fateful day and the prayer he made to St Stylianos remained with Angelos through every waking and sleeping moment. Now, sitting at the foot of the olive tree back in his grove, he stared at his home and uttered his prayer to St

Stylianos again. It was a prayer he found hard to honour as his grief continued to overwhelm him, but he had to keep trying.

Angelos stood and dusted himself down. His life had never been perfect, but once, for a brief time, he'd had the love of a beautiful, fiery woman. He'd had a beautiful daughter who had been like her mother in so many ways. Now, here he was on this island he called home, alone, still surrounded by the enemy, not knowing when the war would end, or if it ever would. There were still some positives in his life, though. His mother was still alive, and his other daughter, Sophia, needed her father too.

He must try and live his life for all of them: the dead and the living, but it was incredibly hard and he often wondered if he should've chosen the easy way out, joining Elena in the sea that day. Maybe if he had, Angelos would've found the love of his life again, and they would both now be at peace.

THREE

Ionian Sea, Greece, 1943

"It is okay, little one," Richard whispered as Athena momentarily stirred in his arms. "It will not be long and then we will be safe."

A sliver of moon danced on the surface of the water surrounding them. It was the only light in an otherwise dark night. There was no way of telling where land and sea began or ended. The small wooden boat glided silently and softly across the water. Its owner as quiet as the vessel. Oars gently dipped the sea, rose into the air, and then dipped again, pushing them further away from Zakynthos.

At night, the inky waters could surprise even the most competent sailor, and every minute they were at sea, the boat's occupants were at risk. The sea between Zakynthos and the mainland was as deadly as land, full of patrol boats, submarines and mines. Silent killers that bobbed in the water sneaking up on unsuspecting vessels. Before boat captains knew what was happening, these death traps would wash against a boat hull, giving them no chance to escape. Once contact was made, the deadly explosion that ensued often sank the boat and killed its occupants. Anyone lucky enough to survive such a blast was left to the mercy of the water, likely to drown, or if the enemy spotted them, they were shot.

Local fisherman knew these waters well, though, and so far, they'd made it unscathed. Richard continued to pray for luck to be on their side.

Glancing over at the Greek fisherman, Richard was silent in his own thoughts. He'd expected to be rescued; it had all been explained to him. Being given the child, though, hadn't been part of the plan. Events on the beach in Zakynthos had happened so fast, there was nothing they could do other than get away as quickly as possible to save their lives.

Richard had sat with the child on his lap watching in horror as brave men fell, the beach becoming their final resting place. Elena had been saved death, and was instead hauled up the beach at gunpoint to a fate unknown.

He'd been surprised when the Nazis hadn't followed the boat. Two soldiers had attempted to run into the sea, wading as far as they could into the water. Their guns pointed into the darkness at the fleeing boat, firing indiscriminately. Richard had flung himself and Athena into the bottom of the boat, covering her, protecting her with his body. The enemy's bullets had missed them, landing in the sea, falling to the ocean floor. As the boat had rounded the headland, the darkness of night and sea had shrouded them in a protective shield; one they were still safely riding under.

It was a frightening thing to witness. Richard had held the young child, Athena, tightly, her face to his chest. He hadn't wanted the three-year-old's last sight of her mother to be one of Elena being dragged away by the Nazis.

A NIGHT OF THUNDER

"I wish I could have helped your mum, little one. I do not know if she will be okay. I am so sorry it is my fault. If I had not crashed on your island, your mum and her friends would not have been forced to look after me and help me escape. Maybe I should have got out the boat to help her? But what would I have done with you? I would never have forgiven myself if you or your mum had been killed too. I promise I will do my best to reunite you both one day. I need to get home first, though. Then I can work out what to do. I know I cannot leave you here in Greece alone or with strangers, and I made your mum a promise. I will not break my promise."

"Shush!" The fisherman put his finger to his lips and shook his head. Richard nodded and fell silent. He reached into his pocket and pulled out the locket and letter Elena had given to him on the beach. He stared at them. They were the only thing connecting Athena to her family and Zakynthos. A place she may not see again for a long time because of the madness of war enveloping them.

It seemed Elena had prepared for every eventuality. He'd do all he could to protect the child and her precious memories, but it wasn't going to be easy, and he couldn't do it forever. He had his own life and loved ones to consider, and Athena didn't feature in it.

Richard put the locket safely inside the envelope and folded it up, secreting it safely in a pocket. The sleeping child stirred and gently moaned. The fisherman momentarily ceased rowing, but she didn't wake. She merely turned and shook off the fitful dream. Silently, the oars dipped and powered in the water again pushing them closer to the mainland. All Richard could do was sit in the blackness and think.

He was still young, barely twenty-two years old, and

like many of his fellow RAF crew, he'd left family and a fiancée back home. War had changed so many lives. One thing was certain, he'd never fly a plane again. His crash landing and subsequent broken leg had seen to that. His time on Zakynthos had given him a different perspective on life and shown him how quickly things could change. He still had no idea if he'd ever see his home again; it wouldn't be easy getting out of Greece and back to England. He also had no idea if Lissy still waited for him. She had promised she would, but then again, some of the promises he'd made to her before he'd left England had been broken.

War had changed them all and life was no longer simple. He'd promised to write to her every day. He'd promised to let her know how he was, and that he was well. The situation with the war meant he couldn't write as often as he wanted and much of what he did write was censored into oblivion. It made him feel guilty. He loved Lissy, and wanted to get back home to marry her, but he was still thousands of miles away, surrounded by war and now responsible for a child that wasn't his.

Occasionally, a small wave crest caught the moonlight and Richard's senses heightened, expecting the enemy to appear and overwhelm them, but each time it was nature and nothing more. Eventually, the boat slowed and approached a small beach on the Greek mainland. Richard's nerves heightened again. He was expecting another boat. This was land, not a rescue boat. Neither was it Malta; they hadn't been at sea long enough. On the way to Xigia Beach, Elena had told him that a local fisherman would take him to meet allies on a boat at an undisclosed location at sea. The boat would return him to the airbase in Malta, where he'd been stationed. Then he could be repatriated home. There was no other boat to be seen, and the sight of land made him dread the worst.

"Where are we?"

"Between small village Kalamia and port Kyllini. Mainland Greece," the fisherman grunted.

"Why? What happened to the boat?"

"Plan change."

"Why? A boat was supposed to take me to Malta. There is nothing here except for a scrap of beach and rocks! Where are we supposed to go? The Nazis are here too!"

Richard was panicking. If it was just him, he could defend himself, but he'd have no chance of doing that with a small child in tow. He couldn't look after them both if they were attacked.

The fisherman put his finger to his lips, before leaning in and whispering, "Different plan. Mine hit boat. Boat sink. Many dead. Resistance here. They look after you. Nazis in town, drunk. You be safe."

Richard tried to read the man's face, but it was too dark. "How can I trust you?"

"If I want to kill you, I throw you both into sea already. You both still here."

The man had a point, and Richard had no choice but to trust him, but he didn't like it one bit. He was alone with a child that wasn't his own, in the middle of Greece as war raged around them. Richard just hoped it wasn't a trap. As the boat finally beached itself with help from the gentle swell of waves, the fisherman jumped out. The splash of him landing in the water combined with the scraping of the boat being pulled onto the shore echoed around them. Richard held his breath expecting to see stealthy uniformed figures emerging from the darkness with their guns trained on him. Instead, their luck held, and all was quiet, save for a lone Greek couple, who furtively appeared from the shadows. Fingers to their lips, the couple beckoned him forward. The fisherman nodded, indicating they could be trusted.

Richard passed the sleeping Athena to the fisherman and climbed out of the boat. On the beach, Richard took hold of Athena again, cradling her to him, hoping his arms would be all the protection she needed if anything went wrong. Nodding his thanks to the fisherman, Richard took one last look over his shoulder in the direction of Zakynthos to say a final goodbye, and followed the couple into the safety of the shadows.

FOUR

Bristol, England, 1940

"That were a long one. I hope me house is still standing."

Lissy was buffeted by hordes of neighbours and residents leaving the air raid shelter.

A weak winter sunrise greeted them, and the air was filled with the acrid smell of smoke as fires across the city burned. Lissy followed the chattering women along the street towards her house. She was glad to be back outside. During the air raid, stuck inside the shelter, she'd become numb to the chaos outside. The first handful of times a bomb landed she'd been petrified. Dust had fallen, swirling about them, coating everything in a fine film. Everyone's stress levels had risen and hers had followed suit. Everything in the shelter had shaken: the ground, her seat, the walls. Several times she wondered if the structure would hold. The closer the bombs landed to them, the more she feared it would be her last day on earth. The thought of being killed or buried alive in piles of rubble had frightened her. Air raid wardens had constantly reassured them that the shelters were well built, and they'd be okay, even if a bomb landed next to it.

Eventually the raid had ended, and to the relief of its occupants, the shelter was still standing, unscathed. When the sirens finally stopped, the doors opened and they were all allowed to return home. They weren't only thankful, but some were defiant in the face of an enemy who'd once more failed to get them, shaking their fists at the sky and yelling for the enemy to try harder next time.

Lissy stopped for a moment to survey the damage. Smoke rose on the horizon in many directions and the smell of burning singed her nostrils. Families hugged each other gratefully, talking with neighbours, thankful to be safe and have a home to return to instead of a smoking pile of rubble like those less fortunate in the city.

In the distance, the sky was tinged orange, sunrise melding with fires that were still being brought under control. A distant clanging of bells punctuated the air as more fire engines and ambulances made their way through the city to help people whose homes or businesses had gone up in flames. It was heartbreaking for Bristolians. Many had lost so much; their possessions and memories lost to the raging fires caused by an indiscriminate enemy.

By full daylight the sites would become smouldering craters, ugly pockmarks on the face of the city. Stark reminders of the vicious war still being fought. A war that was changing the city's landscape forever. Beautiful buildings and churches that had stood for centuries hadn't fared well and were now either badly damaged or gone completely. History destroyed in a couple of hours.

Exhausted, Lissy headed home again. She turned the corner into her street and stopped. Dust and rubble were strewn everywhere, and a cordon was in place across the road. There was no way of getting past. She pushed her way through the crowd of people that had gathered. Whispering met her ears and rumours were already rampant. This was what Lissy hated the most. The lack of information during the war. Secrecy for protection was understandable, but it also made wild rumours spread, which worried and scared people even more. No one was to blame, it was just the way things were, but it was frustrating, and there was nothing that the bored housewives of Bristol liked better than a good gossip. It filled long uncertain days, when they had little else to do.

"I 'eard it were old Thomas Wright's house what got hit. Nuthin' left, just a pile of rubble and three walls. Poor mite," an old lady in curlers and a dressing gown proclaimed loudly to anyone in earshot.

"Nah, tis that Mrs Holloway's house innit?" another woman said.

"What's happening?" Lissy knew Thomas Wright; he was a kind man who lived across the road from her. If his house had been hit, then hers probably had too. She hoped not, but they all knew it was a risk none of them could control. They'd all been warned. The Nazis had dropped so many bombs that it was potluck where they landed.

"One of them bloody Jerry bombs hit lovie, but it didn't go off. Them bomb men is down there now, we ain't going home 'til they disarm it or it blows 'em up tryin'," the old lady said.

"Did they say how long it would take?" It wasn't the news Lissy wanted to hear.

"No, it'll takes 'em as long as it takes, or they'll be corned beef on the walls tryin'. Guess we'll find out soon enough."

Lissy nodded at the old lady who was far too gleeful

with what was taking place for her liking. She left the women to gossip and pushed her way through the crowd to the cordon. Scanning left and right, she searched for a policeman. Catching sight of one, she waved to get his attention.

"Yes miss? How can I help you?" the constable said.

"How long will it be before we can get back to our homes?"

"I'm not sure, miss. The bomb disposal men are trying to make safe the bomb, but it's a tricky job. It takes time. We all need to be patient."

"I understand. Do you know which houses are affected? The road bends and I can't see anything from here. I can't see my house."

"Which one is yours?"

"Number thirty-two."

"Well, you're lucky, it's further up at number forty-eight, so even if it goes off, your house should be okay. There might be a broken window or two, but other than that you should hopefully be alright. You never quite know with these Luftwaffe bombs, though."

"Thank you." She shivered. She hadn't realised how cold the night had become, and she pulled her dressing gown tighter around her shoulders.

"You look like you need to warm up, miss. The café round the corner is open. They're serving free tea. I'll come and get you when the cordon lifts if you like?"

"Thank you, Constable."

"It's Constable Perkins, and it's no bother."

"Thank you, Constable Perkins." She nodded her thanks and headed for the café.

Lissy found a table in the corner of the café and sat with a hot, weak cup of tea between her hands. Tea was a rare commodity nowadays since the introduction of rationing. Some wasn't even tea at all, but somehow this little café always seemed to manage to have real tea in an emergency, even if it was still on the weak side.

As she sipped the hot drink, Lissy looked at the photo of Richard again and her mind wandered. She missed him terribly and wondered where he was. Hopefully, he'd fought some of the planes heading towards them and shot several of them down before they could drop their bombs. Would he know that Bristol had been hit? Would he now be worrying about her as much as she was worrying about him? It seemed that whenever she thought about Richard nowadays, her mind continually raced with questions, most of which she was unable to answer.

Lissy thought about Richard's parents. She hoped they were okay and had come through the night unscathed. She liked his parents, and she knew they'd been so proud of him when he'd joined the RAF. Mr and Mrs Hobbs understood their son's need to fight for his country and they supported him despite any concerns.

A loud explosion shook the café, pulling Lissy from her thoughts. Dust and small slivers of plaster fell from the ceiling, covering her, but the building stayed upright. They were safe. Lissy clattered her teacup onto the saucer, shoved Richard's photo into her pocket and sprang to her feet. She ran out of the café towards her road. A pall of thick, black smoke rose high in the air.

As she reached the cordon, Lissy battled her way through the crowd, pushing her way to the front. She scanned the area for Constable Perkins but couldn't see him. The loud clanging of a fire engine grew ever closer. Two policemen appeared, opened the cordon, pushing everyone back, forcing Lissy to move too.

"What happened? Where's Constable Perkins?" she asked as one of the Policemen motioned for her to step back.

"Why are you asking about Perkins? A bomb went off, we're busy."

"I was talking to him earlier. He was so kind. He said he'd keep me updated with what was going on. I live here."

The two men looked at each other, a look she'd seen before when volunteering at the hospital.

"He's hurt isn't he?"

"Leave it to the professionals, my love. Now move along."

"I was training as a nurse; I was accomplished before I had to get another war job at the factory. You know as well as I do, the ambulance may not be here for ages, if at all. From the amount of bombs that fell last night there must be lots of city damage. If I'm right, then who knows how many roads are blocked? Let me help. A trainee nurse is better than leaving a man to die!"

The policemen shrugged at each other, and one of them took her arm. "Come on then. Head towards that house with the red door and ask for Sergeant Radley. Tell him you're a nurse and that I sent you."

Without a second thought Lissy ran along the road towards the carnage. Passing her own house, she was relieved to see it standing. The tape she'd stuck across her windows had held and none were broken. It seemed she'd got off lightly.

She found the sergeant and told him who she was and why she was there. Sergeant Radley simply nodded and guided her through the ever-growing rubble. Shredded pieces of wood, bricks and other unidentifiable items littered the street. Someone's home. Someone's life. The piles were small at first, and she was easily able to sidestep them, but they became larger and more difficult to walk through the further they went.

Rounding the corner, she reached the fire, the smoke and the badly damaged houses. Lying on the ground were three bodies, one already had a sheet over it, a sure sign someone was dead. On the pavement, she saw the still body of a uniformed man. Constable Perkins. She shook herself and ran towards the injured man.

Kneeling on the ground, Lissy put her finger to his wrist and studied his chest to check the constable's breathing. She was relieved to see Constable Perkins was still alive. He had a faint heartbeat and was floating in and out of consciousness, but he was alive. She carefully checked him over and discovered his head covered in the sticky ooze of blood: a large cut to his head likely to cause concussion. There were other minor cuts and bruises to various other parts of his body from flying shrapnel. The worst injury was a bone protruding from his left arm; something that only a hospital could fix. There was no other damage immediately apparent, and Lissy hoped he would be one of the lucky ones.

With the sergeant's help, and a few bandages from a local first aid kit, Lissy tried her best to patch up Constable Perkins. Shrugging her dressing gown from her shoulders, Lissy laid it over the man, tucking it in around him to keep him warm. He needed it more than she did. She'd just have to be cold in her flannel nightgown.

Whilst waiting for the ambulance to arrive, she sat and kept the constable company, talking about anything and nothing. Even though he was barely conscious, she wanted to reassure him he was being looked after. If the ambulance didn't make it, she'd need to persuade the sergeant to put together a makeshift stretcher and get someone to drive him to the hospital. She looked up at Sergeant Radley, who had been patiently standing next to them.

"What happened? Last time I saw Constable Perkins he was at the cordon. Why was he down here?" Lissy asked.

"I've no idea. Sometimes the bomb disposal men ask for extra help, but we've all been told to stay away from the inner cordon. I don't understand it. Will he be alright?"

"I hope so. His arm's broken and there's a nasty cut on his head. He's in and out of consciousness and probably has a concussion. He's breathing okay and comfortable, but a proper doctor will need to look at him and confirm it, though. It looks like he was probably knocked off his feet by the blast and hit by flying debris," Lissy said. "I'll stay with him until the ambulance arrives."

"That would be good. There's so much going on here, and I must make sure my men can cope, especially now we're a man short. You look a bit cold in your nightdress, though. Take my cloak." Sergeant Radley removed his policeman's cloak and gave it to her, insisting she put it on.

"Thank you." Gratefully, she wrapped it around her, feeling the warmth from the heavy garment. "I'm happy to stay and look after Constable Perkins. Do you need to tell his family? I can tell the ambulance men who to contact."

"He doesn't have any family. It's just him. We joke he's married to his job. He's a good policeman, though. One of the best."

"That's sad."

"Yes. It's this war. We're all stuck with it. I wish it would end. I'm sick of it. We've got to keep going, though." The sergeant shook his head, looking around him at the destruction that surrounded them. "We've got to keep going or bastard Jerry wins." He pulled at his collar with embarrassment. "Pardon me language, miss."

Lissy laughed. It wasn't the first time she'd heard it during the war. "You're excused, Sergeant. Don't worry about Constable Perkins, I'll stay with him and make sure he's taken good care of."

Sergeant Radley nodded his head and walked away. Lissy sat on the cold pavement next to the constable, occasionally checking his pulse and talking to him. All the while, she anxiously waited for an ambulance she desperately hoped would arrive.

FIVE

Zakynthos, Greece, 1943

The stars were bright as Angelos sat under a canopy of olive tree branches. He stared out across the darkened grove and the land beyond. His family's land, still occupied by the Nazis. It made him angry. The invaders had taken everything from him. His home, his land, his child, Elena and his father. Now he was forced to live with his father-in-law, Stelios, which made him sick to the stomach.

Stelios was an unscrupulous man, a Nazi sympathiser. Angelos hated that he, his mother and daughter, were forced to live under the same roof as Stelios Makris, in the shadow of the enemy, but he had no choice. Stelios controlled everything they did.

Everyone in Angelos's life had been affected by this horrific war. His wife Maria had also been a Nazi sympathiser like her father Stelios. Maria had not only betrayed Elena, but she'd also betrayed Elena's entire family, sending them to an early death. Angelos would never forgive the betrayal, and yet he was forced to live with them. It was why he spent hours in the Kafenion or sitting in the dark under a tree.

Angelos looked out across the gloomy olive grove. *His* land. The shadows of old, twisted trees resembled a line of bent and gnarled old men. Men who were barely able to stand, holding the weight of life upon their shoulders.

"How strange that nature can imitate life so much," Angelos muttered to the night air.

Even though the war had taken everything from him, these trees still existed. Angelos had made himself a promise that once the Nazis had been defeated, however long that took, Angelos would reclaim his house and his land, and he would make it his home again. The Sarkis house and these olive groves were *his*. He *would* get them back. He would tend to his trees and make a business from what was left.

In Greece, especially Zakynthos, it was always possible to start again. The island had shown its residents that many times throughout the centuries. Even the sympathisers and traitors would be shaking hands with new friends in years to come.

As well as regaining his family home and business, Angelos would find Athena and bring her home too. He had no idea how, but he would. He would then sit Sophia and Athena down and tell them both about Elena. They would all then live happily together with Pigi.

A deep rumbling alerted Angelos to a passing Nazi truck. He ducked down behind the tree trunk to avoid the sweeping headlights. In the darkness, he lay silently as it passed. Angelos knew he'd be punished for breaking curfew if he was caught. He had to stay out of trouble for Sophia's sake. As the rumbling faded and the truck disappeared, Angelos knew he couldn't put off going back to the Makris house any longer, so he stayed in the shadows and made his way back as quickly as he could.

As Angelos pushed open the front door of the Makris house, he heard raucous laughter. Kyriakos Avgoustinos. The preening Greek idiot. Angelos sneaked past the room and placed a foot on the stairs. It creaked loudly.

"Here *it* is. The Romeo of Zakynthos. The man who lost his gypsy to a bullet!" Stelios's drunken voice carried into the hallway. Angelos ignored him and took another step upwards.

"In here, Sarkis! Do not ignore me in *my* house!"

Angelos had no choice but to do as he was told.

"You are drunk, Stelios. You should keep your voice down or you will wake your granddaughter. Talk of bullets is something she does not need to hear."

"Pah! The child is young. She will have no clue what I am saying. She will not remember." Stelios stood unsteadily and walked towards Angelos pointing his finger at him. A drunk Kyriakos sat in the corner laughing. Angelos took a step back, preparing to leave the room again, but Stelios was too quick and gripped his arm.

"Are you still sad, Sarkis? Are you still crying? Are you still pining for your traitorous little **πουτάνα**? You do know she never loved you. You do know she spread her legs wide for any man who wanted to take her? That is what peasants do. How sad you are pining over such a woman, still."

Kyriakos laughed again. "And what a **πουτάνα** she was! Half the Italian army had her, and half the Nazis too! I considered taking her myself, but knowing where she had been... no, she was not worth the risk. The Nazis did the best thing for her. She is better off at the bottom of the cliff."

Angelos knew Stelios and Kyriakos were goading him.

They wanted a fight. They wanted to belittle him, hurt him and make him attack them. He stood strong, not wanting to lower himself to their level. Shaking himself from his father-in-law's grip, Angelos stood his ground.

"You will be sorry one day, Stelios. One day you will get what you deserve, just like your traitorous daughter, and you *will* lose everything."

Stelios struck hard and fast despite the alcohol swimming in his veins. Angelos backed out of the room holding a hand to his bloodied nose, the pain reverberating around his head. Quickly, he climbed the stairs as vicious taunts and fading laughter rang in his ears.

∽

The following day, a tired Angelos opened the door to find Pentalis Avgoustinos, the younger brother of Kyriakos, on the doorstep. The men were so unalike, no one would've known they were brothers. Whereas Kyriakos was vicious and a Nazi sympathiser, Pentalis was a kind soul, who hated the shame his brother had brought on their family.

"Angelos, my friend. I am looking for my brother."

"Come in, Pentalis. He and Stelios are snoring like filthy oxen in the front room. They drank a bar full of *Tsipouro* last night. Where they get it, I do not know."

"Probably from the same bastards that killed my brother, Damiano."

Silently, Angelos led his friend to a small back room, away from Stelios and Kyriakos, and took a seat.

"I know we are a strange family, Angelos. Three brothers with such different views. Damiano the brave resistance fighter is dead, and I miss him greatly. It always made me smile that he called himself *Dionysios*. He was the brother I loved the most. I respected his strength in fighting for Zakynthos, even though I do not agree with this war and did not always agree with his tactics. In the end, though, I know he was trying to save us all. It has been such a hard war, Angelos. For all of us. I understand your loss. We are brothers linked by grief. Despite being a pacifist, I wish we could rid the island of the Nazis and their sympathisers. People like my brother Kyriakos and his friend Stelios. I despise my brother for his allegiance to those who would do us such harm. None of them deserve what they have. Their wealth, food and alcohol come from evil men who are rich off the backs of poor islanders who lived a true Greek life. True Greeks would never treat another Greek the way some of *them* have. You and I are unfortunate to have had such traitors in our family Angelos. It is sad that the brave souls die in this war and the traitors continue to live."

"Thank you, Pentalis, you are a good friend. They are becoming harder to find."

The two men sat in contemplation for a while, enjoying the silence of comfortable friendship, until the door banged open.

"Pantelis! What are you doing with this idiot? Have I taught you nothing? Take me home, now!" Kyriakos turned on his heel and disappeared. Reluctantly, Pantelis bid Angelos farewell and followed his brother.

Angelos stared out of the window as their footsteps retreated and the house fell silent. So many families had been torn apart by this war and there was still no sign of it ending. How much more would they endure before freedom finally came?

SIX

Kalamia, Greece, 1943

"We resistance. You, be quiet," the Greek man instructed, beckoning to Richard. "Come. This way."

With a restless Athena in his arms, Richard followed the Greek couple. Protected by the cover of trees, they stealthily wound their way through winding lanes. Occasionally, the Greeks motioned for Richard to crouch behind a low wall or thick tree trunk. He obeyed and held his breath, praying Athena wouldn't wake as the sound of wheels on rough ground passed by. It would only have taken one cry from her, and they would've been discovered. When it was safe to move again, they continued.

Knowing Nazis were close unnerved Richard. He'd left one battleground only to land deep inside a worse one. There were more Nazis on the mainland, and a chance encounter with them would only end in Richard and Athena's capture. He had to keep his wits about him, and stay alert for anything unusual, all whilst looking after a young child.

Richard had no idea where they were heading. The

original plan had dramatically changed and now he had to put his faith in the Greek couple. If he'd been alone, he'd have made a run for it, but his primary concern was no longer himself. His primary concern was Athena and the promise made to Elena.

Looking back now, it had been a foolish decision, but in a split second, at the height of war, he'd made a promise to take care of the child. A child that wasn't his own. Many would've refused. Many would've left mother and daughter together on the beach to the luck of the gods. He wasn't that sort of person, though. Leaving the child behind would've signed her death warrant, so he'd taken her. Without thinking, he'd scooped her into his arms and made a solemn promise to her mother. Now he needed to honour that promise any way he could, however difficult it may be.

Athena was *his* responsibility now, and his life had changed immeasurably. Now they needed to find somewhere safe to ensure Athena survived long enough to get to the end of the war and for him to get home. It was a huge burden to bear, but bear it he must.

A rustle in the trees brought his heightened senses swiftly back to the present. Richard shifted the sleeping Athena over his other shoulder. She was heavy, but his determination to protect her was all the strength he needed to continue. He was incredibly tired and hungry. His healed leg ached with the weight of carrying the child and it compromised his mobility.

All Richard wanted to do was hole up somewhere, rest and come up with a plan of what to do next, but he had to keep going. He had to keep following the silent Greek couple. He had to trust in them. It was his only option, but his hope of getting home seemed further away than ever. There was no boat to take him to a safe port. There was no travelling to Malta and then home to England, and there would be no emotional reunion with his parents or fiancée Lissy. He was still stuck in enemy territory and that worried him greatly.

Thirty minutes later, they'd turned off one of the dark lanes into a large olive grove full of old, gnarled trees, their twisted, aged branches reaching skywards. The trees were like old men, lamenting the sorry state of their country, crying out to the heavens in sorrow for all that had befallen Greece. It was darker amongst the trees, and it made Richard feel momentarily safer, but he knew the enemy was close. He could feel it.

Pulling Athena tighter to him, she stirred, opening her eyes and looking up at him. He stroked her head gently, doing his best to get her back to sleep. He didn't want her to fully wake. Her cries would bring the enemy running quicker than they would be able to stop them. Athena yawned and her eyes fluttered closed again. She rested her head back on his shoulder and drifted to sleep.

In the depths of the groves, they reached an old run-down stone building. Whilst the walls were sturdy, parts of the roof had fallen in, and had been hurriedly patched up for continued use.

The Greek man put a key in the door lock and twisted the handle. The door swung open with a creak and a groan. He stepped inside and motioned for Richard to follow. Richard obliged and took in the dusty and gloomy surroundings. The building was bare save for two mattresses on the floor and two old wooden chairs; basic and only just functional.

The Greek woman pushed the door closed behind them. She swung a bag from her back and pulled out a thick blanket. Laying it on the mattress she motioned to it and then for Richard to sit. He walked over to the mattresses and placed Athena on the blanket allowing her to continue her sleep. The Greek woman dropped the bag onto the floor. She pulled out another blanket and placed it gently over Athena.

"Sit," the Greek man said, motioning Richard to one of the chairs.

Grateful to take the weight off his leg, Richard pulled the chair next to Athena and sat.

"Where are we?" Richard asked, glancing at his grim surroundings.

"Kalamia, Greek mainland."

"What happened? We should be heading to allied shores not deeper in to enemy territory."

"Plan change. Ship hit mine. Many in sea. Boat sink. No more ship. People dead. You safe here."

"But for how long? Where will we go next? It is not just me. I have her to look after." Richard motioned to Athena. "This place is cold and damp. The roof barely covers the building."

"Nazis everywhere. Maybe you here one week. Maybe longer. We bring food and water."

Richard sighed and rubbed his fingers at his weary eyes. He was exhausted. He also knew there was no choice, at least for now. Here, he and Athena were relatively safe. If they started walking, they would be at risk of being seen or reported and ending up in the enemy's hands. He was forced to trust this Greek couple. They were bravely risking their lives for him just as Elena had.

The Greek woman pulled food and water from her bag, putting it on the mattress. She handed Richard a candle and matches before swinging the bag back over her shoulder and heading to the door. The man joined her. "You eat. You

A NIGHT OF THUNDER

sleep. Only use candle for emergency. Do not leave her. Keep her quiet. You need toilet, outside but quick. You piss by tree. You shit in hole, cover it. Smell bring animals. You have this." He leaned a rifle next to the front door. "We come tomorrow."

With that, the couple were gone, and Richard and Athena were alone. The small farm building only had one way in and out: the door they'd come through. There were two small windows. One was boarded up and the other, next to the door, had old material hanging from rope to cover it.

Richard sat on the other mattress and ate. He knew sleep wouldn't come. Every snap of twig under animal foot, or shriek of bird overhead, heightened his senses making him wary. By the time daylight arrived, he was even more exhausted. All he wanted to do was close his eyes and sleep, but he couldn't. Athena had slept well and was now awake. He tried to keep her quiet by talking to her in low whispers, keeping her attention. He fed her and gave her water to drink, but he'd no idea what else to do. She was a young child who needed space. She needed to play, but there was nothing here for her. There was nothing here for either of them.

The day dragged on endlessly and eventually, his body fought against him, and he fell asleep on the mattress with Athena cradled safely in his arms. As night fell and the dark crept in again, Richard awoke with a start. The farm building was silent, and they were alone. They were still safe.

Richard ate the remainder of the food and gave some to Athena before washing it down with water. A noise outside caught his attention. Richard sprang to his feet and grabbed the rifle. At the window, he carefully lifted the curtain corner to look through the glass. It was the Greek couple from the previous night. They approached, stopped and looked around them. Richard opened the door for them, and they silently entered, shutting it behind them.

The woman went over to Athena and sat on the mattress next to her. She lifted Athena onto her lap, singing to her in hushed Greek. It made Richard smile. He wished Athena still had that life. The simple pleasure of a heritage she'd been born into. Normality.

"We have new home for you. You come with us. We take you to people who help. You go to the mountains. You stay there until you leave Greece. You travel at night. Two nights. Resistance go with you."

"Can I not get a boat to Malta?" Richard didn't want to go to the mountains. He wanted to go home. The mountains were further inland, dangerous territory.

"No. Sea bad. Mines everywhere. You lucky to come Kalamia. Many die." The man shrugged. "You go to mountains. She stay with us." He pointed at Athena.

"What? No. She stays with me."

"Why? She Greek." The man glowered at him. "She yours?"

"No. She is not mine." Richard looked at Athena. How could he explain? He motioned to the man and lowered his voice. "Her mother saved me. She was resistance and saved my life. When the Nazis arrived on the beach, the child's mother told me to take the girl and look after her. She made me promise. I must keep that promise."

"Ah. You make promise." The Greek man shrugged. "Okay."

The Greek man turned to the woman and spoke rapidly. They descended into a frantic argument, their voices growing louder. Richard stood next to them, allowing them. Eventually they stopped, each shrugging at the other.

"Wife not happy. She say you leave child. We argue. She okay. Take child. Come, we start journey. You keep child quiet."

Richard lifted Athena from the woman's lap, hugging her to him. "Okay. Let us go."

They left the dilapidated building, creeping out into the darkness. Turning their backs to the coast, they headed inland.

For hours they walked through fields, olive groves and through tiny, deserted country lanes. Just before the sunrise, they stopped at a small house in the middle of nowhere. A different man and woman greeted them with a nod. The Greek man from Kalamia pulled Richard to one side. "Wife and I go now. You safe here. You still have choice. We can take child."

"I know you want to help, but I must keep my promise."

"You honest man. This do you well. Be safe, trust this couple. They take you on next part of journey."

"Thank you."

The Greek couple from Kalamia slipped quietly from the house heading out into the remainder of the night.

Richard and Athena were taken into the new resistance house and led into a small room. There was a bed, with a side table holding a pitcher of water and a wash bowl. The woman motioned to the bed and passed Richard some clean clothes. She took Athena from him and headed to another room.

Too tired to complain, Richard washed the grime from his skin before changing into the fresh clothes. He took his old stained and ripped clothes into the kitchen where the couple and Athena were sitting at a scrubbed wooden table.

The woman was feeding Athena and smiled shyly at Richard. The man took the old clothes and went outside. Richard had no idea where he was going, but in the greater scheme of things he didn't care. The man returned a couple of minutes later and sat again, speaking as he placed some food on the table.

"Tonight, you eat. You sleep. Tomorrow night, we go to mountains. We walk at night. Safer to travel then. Sit."

Richard obeyed and gratefully tucked into the food in front of him. Since crash landing in Greece, he'd been treated well by so many good Greeks and was eternally thankful the resistance had found him and not the Nazis.

Things would've been so different if he'd been captured.

It hadn't been easy, though. He'd been holed up in a cave for so long he'd lost track of time. He'd spent many hours alone, but the one constant had been Elena, the resistance fighter who'd placed her life in grave danger to look after him.

War made everything different. In England it had all been so simple. His life had been about Lissy and their dream to marry. If he ever got home, then his life would continue where he left off. The war would become resigned to memories. Eventually, nothing that happened during the war would matter. There would be no guilt, no hurt, no looking back. It's how it had to be. He'd never tell Lissy that in one stupid moment, whilst feeling low, in pain and disillusioned about ever getting home again, he and Elena had lain naked on the floor of the cave and satisfied each other. Afterwards, he asked her why. She'd already told him about Pietro and Angelos. Elena had looked at him and shaken her head.

"Angelos was never mine and I can never have him.

A NIGHT OF THUNDER

Pietro says he loves me, but I do not love him. He is using me. My life is not my own. You looked sad. I feel sad. You do not love me. I do not love you. War is all around us and neither of us know if we will still live tomorrow. I wanted to lose myself in something. Something different and new. That something was you, Richard. I am sorry. It will not happen again."

Richard had understood what she meant. He'd felt the same at the time. But now he felt terribly guilty and knew it had been a huge mistake.

War had changed everything. The normality of life before 1939 no longer existed, and Richard didn't know if things would ever be the same again. Before the war, he'd agreed to marry Alice Cook, or Lissy as she preferred to be called, a girl he loved with all his heart and wanted to spend the rest of his life with.

Then he'd abandoned Lissy to fight for his country and it all went wrong. He'd been shot down in Greece and forced to hide out in a cave, his only companion a resistance fighter. Emotions in war heightened, and many lived for the moment, knowing life could change in an instant. Selfishly in that cave, he had chosen to throw everything aside and his future in Bristol with Lissy had been forgotten.

In England, Elena would've been called a common tart for her actions. A woman with loose morals, no better than a prostitute. Richard knew it would've been unfair, though. Elena was a brave resistance fighter. She'd lost the love of her life, Angelos, to another woman and been forced into having sex with an Italian soldier to gain information. Elena told Richard she hated it and wished she'd never agreed to it. She had never stopped loving Angelos, but knew that the happiness she so greatly wanted would never come.

In frustration, she'd chosen Richard as an outlet and

he'd willingly obliged. It had been a stupid idea and once they'd finished, she'd slunk away, leaving him imprisoned in his cave, alone with his guilt.

Richard's attention came back to the room, Athena's cries moving him to action. The poor child. She must be so confused. He'd no idea what their future held. How would he even begin to get home to England, let alone keep his promise to Elena and look after a child that wasn't his? He was in a dire situation, and it was one he just couldn't see a way out of.

Sitting silently with the family, he finished his food before Athena began to cry again. He took her from the Greek woman and held the child close, comforting her. She immediately stopped crying. It seemed she'd accepted him and trusted him. It was a heavy burden, and one that was going to be hard to bear, regardless of any promises he may have made.

That day, the Greek household slept well without being disturbed. As the sun began to set, Richard and Athena were awoken. As Richard washed his face and cleaned himself up, he stared at the man in the mirror he didn't recognise. His growth of beard and lengthening of hair made him passable as a Greek local to the enemy, if they didn't look too closely. Coupled with the help Elena had given him to learn Greek, Richard now spoke it well enough to converse with the resistance and Athena, which helped him blend in.

At the kitchen table, the four of them sat in silence as they ate and drank. Then, as the stars began to prick the darkened heavens, the Greek couple silently led Richard and Athena from the house, heading eastwards to the mountains.

SEVEN

Bristol, England, 1940

The hospital corridor was busy and overcrowded as Lissy sat and waited for news of Constable Perkins. She was now wearing her dressing gown again, which was covered in dirt. At the bomb site, Lissy had waited ages for the ambulance. Once it had arrived, she'd travelled in the cramped and uncomfortable vehicle with the constable, refusing to allow him to make the journey alone. The story of his loneliness had struck a chord with her.

The emergency bells had clanged noisily, telling other road users and pedestrians they were in a hurry, and it wasn't long before they reached the hospital. Staff had rushed the constable into one of the buildings and Lissy had followed closely behind. A stern matron had directed Lissy to a seat, instructing her to wait there until she was called.

That had been two hours ago, and Lissy was now tired, cold, and hungry. It had been a long night, but she couldn't leave, she needed to know how the brave police officer was. No one else had turned up to see him. No family or friends, not even his sergeant. How awful to be in such a position. Lissy couldn't leave him all alone. She didn't want to go back home to wallow in her own misery – that's if she could get to her house yet. No, she was better off staying where she was for now. At least she felt like she was doing something positive in all the chaotic madness.

The matron appeared, giving her the thinnest of smiles. "He's awake if you want to see him. Five minutes and then he needs to get some rest."

Lissy stood and followed the matron along the corridor and into a small ward. Everything was quiet, white and sterile. She felt out of place in her dirty night clothes. The matron stopped at a bed and nodded to Lissy.

"Remember. Five minutes."

Lissy watched the stern woman walk away before stepping closer to the bed. The constable was awake but pale and tired. His arm lay on top of a pillow next to him, encased in plaster.

"Hello, Constable. How are you?"

"Aren't you the young woman from earlier?" he asked slowly as if trying to place her.

"Yes Constable Perkins. I'm Lissy. We met at the cordon before the exploding bomb injured you. I helped nurse you before the ambulance arrived."

"Thank you, Lissy. Just call me George. There's no need for all that official stuff."

"Nice to meet you, George. May I sit?"

"Of course. I'd be a gentleman and pull out the chair for you, but unfortunately..." He indicated his arm and smiled. Lissy smiled back.

"Do you remember what happened, George?"

"No. I do remember speaking with you at the cordon

and helping keep back the crowds, though. Then I went up to help the bomb disposal men. Suddenly there was a big bang. A big rush of solid air lifted me off my feet. Next thing I knew, I was flying through the air. Then I hit the floor and nothing. All I remember next is being in here."

"They say you were very lucky. You hit your head and have some cuts and bruises. The arm's the worst of it, though."

"The doctor did say I was fortunate to only have a broken arm and end up with scratches. I've heard stories of what happens to people when the bombs explode. I could've ended up with my guts all over the houses. Gosh, sorry Lissy. I shouldn't be so vulgar. I hope I didn't upset you."

"It's fine. Trust me. It's wartime and I've heard much worse."

"Two minutes!" the matron ordered as she swiftly walked past.

"She's forceful that one," George said, laughing despite being in pain.

"She is, but they must be. This is a place of rest and healing, and it would do no good for it to be crowded with people at all hours of the day and night." Lissy stood and pushed back the chair and made to leave. "I'm glad you're okay, George."

"Me too." He paused. "Would you come and visit me again tomorrow?"

"I'd be happy to, if they'll allow it."

"I'll speak to Matron and tell her you will be back. Thank you, Lissy, you're a brave woman."

"I'd better be off; she's coming back and I don't want the wrath of Matron! See you tomorrow."

Lissy turned on her heel, walked back through the ward and out into the corridor. It had been a long night; she was exhausted and ready for sleep. First, she needed to find a way of getting home.

Eventually, Lissy returned home, helped by a neighbour she bumped into who was also leaving the hospital. It was all she could do to keep her eyes open as her neighbour chattered away about the terrible bombing. Back home, she was relieved to be able to crawl into bed to get some sleep, grateful to be back in her house. She awoke after lunchtime following a fitful couple of hours of sleep. It was a miracle she'd slept at all with all the noise in the street outside from clearing up the debris.

After waking, Lissy washed, changed her clothes and ate some food, unable to remember when she'd last had a meal. Once she'd eaten, she put on her hat and coat, closed the front door behind her and walked along the street.

Where there once was a long line of homes, a gaping hole now stood in the middle of the row. Someone's home and belongings blown to pieces, scattered across the road. Bricks, mortar and dust were everywhere, still being cleared away so locals could get the road up and running again. It was the same all over the city: homes and possessions obliterated, people killed or injured and roads full of rubble, all from an enemy above. Lissy hurried on; she needed to get to work. She'd already missed a morning due to everything that had happened, and she needed to get back to the factory.

Like many other women in the city, Lissy was doing her bit for the war effort. If their men could do it, then they

A NIGHT OF THUNDER

could too. They'd all seen the posters and adverts in the newspapers asking for their help. *"Come into the factories!" "We can do it!" "Soldiers without guns!"*

Factories, munitions and farmers needed them; the work wouldn't get done without them. So Lissy, like many other women in Bristol, walked, cycled or boarded the bus for shifts at the local factories.

Lissy's job was packing parachutes at an old corset factory for brave men who needed them. Lissy often wondered if one of the parachutes she'd worked on had ended up in Richard's plane. She knew how thorough they were when they packed them, and if Richard needed to use a parachute, Lissy knew it wouldn't be a parachute that killed him if he didn't make it home, it would be something else instead, and it was what worried her the most.

Even though Lissy only completed half a shift that day, she was exhausted, like she'd worked a twelve-hour day. Her concern about being reprimanded for not clocking in on time that morning had been unfounded, as a woman from a neighbouring street had recognised her at the cordon and told the manager what happened.

Back home Lissy wearily pushed open her front door and lifted a single envelope from the mat. She tore it open and read with delight. Finally, a letter from Richard! There wasn't much in it and some of the text had been redacted with thick black lines, erasing it, but it was a letter, and that's what mattered.

My darling Lissy,

You must think badly of me for not writing sooner. ~~Here in our base in Malta~~, *it's difficult to get news out. I've written you several letters, but I don't know if they ever reached you.* ~~My squadron's been stationed in Malta for a while now~~ *and* ~~I have been flying sorties across the Mediterranean towards Europe.~~ *It's hard work.* ~~Those Luftwaffe pilots fight hard and have no care who they kill. They bomb relentlessly and it's our job to stop them.~~ *Sometimes I feel I've the weight of the world on my shoulders. Other times* ~~we get up there in the sky and we can see the whole world. The adrenaline kicks in and we just fly!~~

When the adrenaline stops, there's sadness. Much of the ~~squadron have been shot down, or just simply vanished.~~ ~~I know us pilots can die at any time. I've lost many friends already, their planes hit, young lives lost~~*, but I'm doing my best to* ~~avoid the enemy and stay alive for you~~*, my darling.*

You're my best girl back home. Knowing you're waiting for me, keeping the home fires burning, keeps me sane.

I love you and miss you. Knowing we'll be married ~~as soon as this blasted war is over and I can come home from Malta~~ *is all I need to keep me going. I hope you're safe, my darling girl, and faring well through this nightmare we're forced to endure.* ~~I'm proud to be in this squadron fighting for my country~~*, but it's harder than I imagined it would be. I never thought* ~~fighting Jerry would be like this~~*.*

I must go now but I'll write again soon.
Forever, your loving Richard

Lissy read the letter over and over, grateful to have finally received it. It seemed previous letters had been lost, but this one had miraculously arrived. It was frustrating that so much of the letter was redacted, but she understood why. Innocent sentences to loved ones could easily give away information to the enemy.

In a warmth of happiness, Lissy hugged the letter to her.

Richard still loved her and still wanted a life with her. Those two sentences alone would have been enough. She placed the envelope on the mantelpiece in the front room next to his photograph. A reminder that he was still with her, loved her and would do whatever he could to come home to her.

EIGHT

Zakynthos, Greece, 1943

Twelve long, loud chimes reverberated around the room as the clock struck midnight, heralding the end of 1943 and the start of 1944. A new year should've been a time for celebration. There should've been a house full of people toasting good health and prosperity to each other. Instead, Angelos and Pigi sat silently, listening to the chimes as Sophia slept in Angelos's arms.

Stelios had left hours before for the Avgoustinos mansion. Angelos knew they would be hosting a huge party, and the island's remaining rich families would be in attendance alongside the highest-ranking Nazi officers.

"Traitor," Angelos mumbled under his breath as he thumped the arm of the chair with his free hand. "How can he be so callous?"

"You should take her to bed, Angelos. The new year is here now. You have shared it with the only family that matter. Change will come. It will not be like this forever." Pigi stood and gently patted her son's shoulder. "It is time for us all to rest."

Angelos stood and carried his still-sleeping daughter up the stairs and laid her in her basket. She was still so small, but some features were already beginning to morph from baby to young child.

"You are a good father to her, Angelos. You have been through so much in this war. Yet you are still here, and you are still getting up each day and being a brave man. You are taking care of the family you have left. I am proud of you. Do not ever think I am not."

"I know. I just wish things could be different. I know thinking of the past will not help me, but every time I close my eyes..."

"Our past is a cross we must all bear, Angelos. Sometimes all we can do is accept it and learn to live with it. You must find a way to do that."

"I know. But..."

"No but... butting is for goats! You are a man with a family to take care of. It is time you laid your ghosts to rest. Goodnight Angelos. Sleep well my son."

"Goodnight." The door shut, and he was left alone with his daughter who was still gently sleeping.

"There are so many things I want to tell you, Sophia. I am not sure if I will ever be able to. I do want you to know that you are not alone in this world, and whatever happens, I will always be the best father I can for you. I will always be here for you. I just hope I can do a good job."

He leaned forward and lightly kissed Sophia's forehead before settling back into the chair and pulling a blanket up around him. He didn't want to be alone tonight. The presence of his daughter was the comfort he needed, and he slipped into a light sleep. But it was filled with nightmares that kept jolting him awake. Eventually, he gave up, took Sophia up to her own bed and wandered back downstairs.

Opening the front door, he stepped outside and stared up at the dark sky. It was a clear night with nothing but the light of the moon and stars to keep him company. Sitting on the wall opposite the house, Angelos marvelled at the twinkling stars overhead. Being out in the dark after curfew was a risk, but he wanted to be outside. It was something Elena had loved to do, and it made him feel close to her despite no longer being with her.

His peace was eventually broken by the faint raucous laughter of drunken revellers. He stood to go inside, but as he did, Stelios and another man from town turned the corner, heading towards the house. Angelos slunk behind the wall and waited for them to say their farewells. Instead, they stopped, leaning on the wall of the house, their drunken voices carrying to him.

"It was a good party tonight, Stelios. Our German hosts know how to treat us well."

"They do. It is a shame that the ignorant pigs of this island do not embrace them. The Nazis are here to stay, and we must do all we can to ensure we win this war with them. There is no hope on the other side."

"You are right. What of your family Stelios? The rumours say your son is resistance."

"My son, Niko, is no resistance! He, like everyone else in my family, will do what I tell them to. By force if necessary." Stelios kicked the wall of the house venting his frustration.

"And your son-in-law, Angelos?"

"Pah! That man. He is a curse around my neck. I do not know why I ever agreed for him to marry my Maria. She suffered at his hands, and he embarrassed my family name when he carried on with that Petrakis peasant. At least she

A NIGHT OF THUNDER

is dead now. It is a shame I cannot say the same for him." The sound of laughter echoed in the darkness.

Angelos felt his blood begin to boil at the mention of Elena, but stayed still. A fight in the street with Nazi sympathisers wouldn't help him one bit, so he stayed hidden and forced himself to listen.

"You know, that Petrakis girl was feisty. She gave the Nazis a tough time after they captured her. She refused to tell them anything. They eventually beat her stubbornness out of her, and it took many beatings to break her. Even before she died, she refused to give them anything. Instead, they gave up and took pleasure from her!"

Stelios laughed loudly. "They fucked the bitch. Ha! Once a peasant *πουτάνα* always a peasant *πουτάνα*."

"She did not care where she got it from: Greeks, Italians and Nazis!"

"Ah but there was nothing left for her to give in the end, so they shot her and threw her over the cliff. The stupid Italian went with her. Good riddance to him. He was an embarrassment!"

The evil laughter and taunts reached Angelos and wrapped their tentacles around him, smothering him, bringing it all back. He placed his hands over his ears, unable to listen to anymore. The tears came, and he curled up in a ball on the ground trying to block out the vicious words.

It may have been New Year, but nothing had changed. The island was still full of evil, and his family were living under its roof. Something needed to change and quickly. Angelos wouldn't allow this to continue any longer. His family deserved more and so did he.

NINE

Greek Mainland, 1943

Dimitroula Papadoulia sat patiently behind a large rock. The dark night made it easy to hide and watch a group of village resistance fighters. She'd tracked them and knew they were waiting for something, but she didn't know what. Her parents had been furtive and anxious for two days now, and Dimitroula didn't know why.

The Papadoulia family lived in a small mountain village in the middle of Greece. With barely a handful of houses, it was so small and quiet that no one ever came to it, not even the enemy. She'd heard local stories about how the enemy had ravaged her country, but the enemy had stayed away from them, the only telltale signs of war was the occasional distant sound of guns and grenades exploring.

Her life in the village was a boring one. They lived on a mountainside farm where her father looked after the sheep and her mother made cheese and tended the food they grew. Dimitroula had always known that her life was going to be a simple one. And now, at the age of nineteen, her fears had come to pass.

Whilst others moved away, joined the resistance or married, she was still at home with her parents. Her day was full of cleaning, cooking and helping on the farm. Whilst some would've told her she was lucky to be far away from war and still be alive, Dimitroula was bored and wanted something more exciting.

A sudden movement to her left caught her eye, and she saw three figures walking towards the resistance fighters. The three figures stopped for a moment, before one of them let out a sound like the hoot of an owl. The resistance returned the call and stepped out to greet them. A hushed and hurried conversation took place; two of the people faded away into the background leaving one alone with the resistance. They walked towards her hiding place. Under the sliver of overhead moon, she saw a weary man carrying a young child who was asleep in his arms.

They continued towards her, and she slunk back into the shadows. As they passed, the stranger with the child looked towards her and she caught the startled look in his eyes. She smiled at him, before putting a finger to her lips. He bowed his head slightly as though agreeing not to give her away, and continued to follow the resistance along the rough pathway covered by overhanging trees.

Dimitroula slipped from her hiding place and stealthily followed them. She was curious about who the man was and why he was here. The resistance had never brought anyone to the mountain. Intrigue fizzed in her; finally, something to be excited about in her dull village life.

They walked for half an hour before stopping at one of the old shepherd huts in the mountain. She crouched down behind a tree, watching as they went inside. Ten minutes later, the two resistance fighters came out and walked towards her. Lying on the ground, she waited for them to pass by. Suddenly, a hand gripped the back of her dress, dragging her to her feet.

"You stupid girl. You do not think we know you are following us?" one of the men said.

"Your father would be angry if he knew where you were. Go home, Dimitroula. This world is not for someone like you!"

"Who says so? Because I am young? Because I am a woman?" Dimitroula stood with her hands on her hips, glaring at both men.

"Stop being ridiculous! Or would you rather I whip you like your father will when he learns of your disobedience!" The man pretended to undo his belt.

"*Γουρούνια*!" she spat, running away from them down the mountainside.

"She calls us swine! The stupid child will get herself killed one day."

Dimitroula stopped running and sank down behind a tree. She watched the men walk out of sight, and then slunk back up the incline.

∼

After a long and tiring journey, Richard had arrived at a small stone hut on a mountain in the middle of mainland Greece. From the outside, it was nothing more than an old farm outbuilding, enclosed by towering trees. Inside however, there was a bed, table and chairs all made from wood: basic but functional. Several thick woollen blankets were piled on the bed and there was food and water on the table. It was more comfortable than the first building he'd stayed in. This one also had a cleverly unobscured view down the mountain. A rifle was propped next to the only door in and out of the building, and a box of bullets was on the shelf above the table.

He set Athena down on the bed and covered her with a blanket. Sitting at the table, he cut a slice of cheese and savoured the taste. A sudden rustle outside caught his attention and he swiftly moved to the small window, moving the thick curtain. It was the young woman he'd seen hiding in the shadows.

Opening the door, he grabbed her arm and pulled her inside, closing the door behind her.

"Are you trying to kill us all!" he said in Greek.

"No. I was just interested."

"You were just interested?" Richard stared at her in disbelief. "Interested in what exactly? Do you think this is a game? Do you think war is fun?"

Dimitroula crossed her arms and glared at him. "You are English. You may speak my language, but you have a stupid English accent. You need *our* help. I do not need yours."

Laughter bubbled up, suppressing Richard's anger. He moved to glance out the window again before putting the curtain back in place. Confident they were alone, and no enemy had followed her, he motioned for her to sit. She glanced at the bed then shrugged, before taking a seat.

"She is your baby?"

Richard took a seat on the opposite side of the table, angling the chair to give a better view of the main doorway. He leaned the rifle against his leg. It was better to keep it at his side instead of propped up against the door. If anyone chose to enter, there was a fighting chance of shooting them if he needed to.

"What is your name?" he asked the woman.

"What is yours?"

"For God's sake. I am tired, I have walked halfway

across Greece carrying a young child on my back. I am hungry. I need sleep. Who are you and what is your name?"

"I am Dimitroula, but you can call me Roula." She sat back in the chair suddenly looking tired, as though her spark of fight had been extinguished.

"Roula. It is a nice name. Are you local?"

Roula took the compliment as intended and looked up, her combative nature all but gone. "Yes. I live with my parents. They farm these mountains. I know them well. It is only good for farming. It is steep, far from the towns."

"How old are you, Roula?"

"Nineteen."

"Nineteen. Still young." He was only three years older than her and yet he felt like an old man. War had aged him. "I am Richard. You are right, my Greek does have an English accent because that is where I am from. I am a little older than you, and no, Athena is not my child. It is complicated."

Roula smiled. "She is a pretty child. Her mother must have been beautiful. Where is her mother?"

Richard looked at Athena. "Another day I will tell you. But I need rest. It has been a long journey."

"I understand. I will leave you." Roula stood and walked to the door. "It was nice to meet you, Richard."

He gently grabbed her by her arm as she reached the door and turned her to face him. "You must not tell anyone I am here, Roula. Our lives depend on us remaining a secret. If the enemy found us, they would kill us both and maybe you and your parents too. Do not put any of us in danger."

"You may think I am a stupid young girl, Richard, but I will not put you in danger. Maybe one day I too will tell you a story, one that will explain why I am not as stupid as you think I am and why I am so desperate to fight for my country."

"Maybe, one day." Richard opened the door and Roula left, blending herself into the dark shadows of night. He closed the door and dragged one of the chairs across to it, wedging it under the handle. It wasn't the best of locks, but it would at least warn him if someone tried to get in. Eating the last of the cheese he'd cut, Richard removed his boots, put the rifle on the floor next to the bed and lay down next to Athena. Her slow breathing told him that she was fast asleep and he lay listening to her as he slowly drifted off.

TEN

Bristol, England, 1940

December arrived bringing another huge air raid with it. Lissy had scrambled to the shelter again under a sky filled with barrage balloons, brilliant bursts of gunfire and sweeping searchlights. Underground, she'd waited for hours whilst the enemy noisily destroyed more of her hometown. It was demoralising, but they had no choice but to sit and wait it out.

Christmas swiftly followed, and Bristolians made the best they could of it, but it was a subdued and lean festive season for many. The new year heralded typically cold weather, and the country continued to be at war with no sign of it ending anytime soon.

After the bomb blast that had injured Constable Perkins, Lissy had gone back to the hospital regularly to visit him, and they had found solace in friendship. He had insisted she call him George, and after being given the all clear by the doctors, George had finally been released to recuperate at home until he was fit for work again.

By Christmas, George had returned to desk duties until

his arm was out of plaster, and as the new year struck, he'd finally been allowed back out on the beat. Lissy often saw him whilst she was out and about and they would stop and talk about all sorts of things: the war, local issues and what they'd been doing lately.

There was an easy manner in their growing friendship as though they'd known each other for years. Each time they met, Lissy felt comforted that there was someone in the city she could talk to if she needed to.

Lissy's life continued with nights punctuated by ever-increasing air raids. Her days were filled with the monotony of factory work, which was increasingly important as the war gathered pace. Shortly after New Year, shifts changed and they had to work nights as well as days, leaving little time for anything else in her life. Even worrying about Richard and what was happening with him began to fade to the background, although it remained on the periphery of her thoughts, occasionally poking its way through.

It wasn't that she didn't miss Richard or had fallen out of love with him. Lissy still missed him terribly and wanted her old life back, but people were depending on her and so her life fell into a pattern of sleeping, eating and dedicating her time and energy to war work, and it left little time for anything else.

∼

It was a relatively calm and quiet day as Constable George Perkins walked his usual beat. During these hurtful years of war, Bristolians had begun to learn that when the ominous silence arrived, something more serious followed. It was easy to become complacent, and news reports indicated that things in Europe were escalating.

George took in the terraced houses as he passed. They were full of so many people: wives awaiting husbands, widows and younger people like Lissy Cook, working hard for the war effort. People who were trying to get through the worst time of their life, when they should be living.

His mind often came back to Lissy as he walked the beat. He knew exactly where she lived. How could he forget after their first meeting at the air raid cordon? Lissy was the epitome of the war spirit that people talked about so much. Although their friendship was relatively new, it seemed she lived her life for others, putting them first and herself last.

Lissy was an incredible woman who'd done an incredible thing when she'd stepped inside a police cordon, after a bomb explosion, to help treat him. Not many would've done that, and yet she hadn't thought about herself at all; she'd simply offered her help, used her nursing skills and put his life before hers. George would always be grateful to her. She hadn't saved him from the bomb, no one could've done that, but she had helped him get well again.

Spotting a couple of fly-posters ahead of him, he blew his whistle and rushed over to stop them before they could complete the job. Hearing the policeman coming, the fly-posters dropped what they were carrying and ran away before George could reach them.

～

Lissy got off the bus, shivering in the bitterly cold mid-January night. The faint smell of snow hung in the air despite the night being crisp and the sky clear. She pulled her coat tightly around her and walked towards her house. It had been another long night at the factory and her feet

A NIGHT OF THUNDER

ached. All she wanted to do was get home, eat something and fall into bed. Working nights was playing havoc with her. She longed for a break, but the work was endless, and she couldn't stop. None of them could.

Lost in her own world, she walked into Constable George Perkins.

"Constable. I'm so sorry; I didn't see you."

A smile crept up his face. "I noticed. You were a million miles away."

"I should've been paying more attention. I'm sorry, it's the new hours I'm working. I'm exhausted."

"Night shifts?"

"How did you guess?"

"You're not the first and won't be the last. It does get easier, though."

"It does?"

"Yes, it just takes a bit of getting used to, that's all."

"I'll take your word for it." She laughed, shifting from foot to foot, trying to ease the ache in her lower limbs.

"So, where have they got you working?"

"Constable Perkins, you should know better than to ask. Loose lips and all that!"

George smiled. He liked the easy manner they had with each other. "Of course. You're right."

Lissy glanced around and saw the coast was clear. She quickly mimed pulling a cord and floating along the street as George watched and laughed.

"I see. Well, that's a good description. Mum's the word."

Lissy turned to face him. "I thought so too."

"Any other impressions I should be aware of?"

"No, it's my only one I'm afraid."

"Right, I'd better make a move. This beat won't walk itself. It was nice to see you again, Lissy."

"You too." Lissy walked past him before stopping again. "Oh George, I'm sorry, how selfish of me. I should've asked. How are you now, is your arm okay? Are you feeling better?"

"As good as new. Everything's healed, and I don't have any problems other than a dull ache in my arm when it gets cold."

"That's good. I'm glad you're feeling much better. Please look after yourself." They were silent for a moment, then Lissy spoke again. "I'd better go. Goodbye George."

"Goodbye Lissy."

This time, Lissy continued walking and only stopped when she reached her front door. Opening it, she headed for the kitchen and ate a couple of slices of day-old bread before heading upstairs to sleep.

The next evening, Lissy boarded the bus and sat at the front. The light was dimming, the cold night drawing in. Soon she'd be at the factory for another night shift.

Factory work was hot and tiring, and at the end of each shift she felt like she'd been on her feet for weeks. She couldn't complain, though. The work she did was important. She was a much-needed cog in an extremely big wheel, and if it helped men like Richard in fighting the enemy, then her tiredness didn't matter.

At the factory, she clocked in, changed into her overalls and took her instructions: another long shift packing parachutes. It was a job that required incredible concentration because parachutes were lifesaving, and if it wasn't done correctly, it could be fatal for anyone using them.

Lissy walked into the large packing room. Long benches ran the length of the room. The waiting parachutes hung from the ceiling, airing. Lissy set to work and headed to the rows of hanging parachutes, checking they were aired and

A NIGHT OF THUNDER

ready to be packed. Lifting the first one down, she carried it to the long bench and hooked the parachute to the end of the table.

Carefully, Lissy stretched the length of parachute along the table, ensuring the rigging lines were separated and in the right order with the main pack at the far end ready to receive the folded contents. This was the bit she hated, the meticulous concentration needed to fold the fabric in the right way to ensure the rigging didn't twist.

Carefully, Lissy took the fabric in both hands and gave it a gentle shake before folding the chute material in the special way they'd been shown. Back and forth, left to right. When one bit was done, Lissy put lead shot weights on the material to enable her to concentrate on folding the next bit.

Once all the folding was done, the small pilot chute that had been attached to the top of the parachute was then checked, before Lissy moved back to concentrate on the rigging.

Picking up a crooked metal tool, Lissy lifted the organised rigging lines and used the tool to feed them through the small leather loops in the main parachute pack. Weaving the rigging back and forth, the nylon lines sat neatly in a uniform manner that would assist with easy release if the parachute was ever opened.

Lissy put the metal tool to one side before carefully pulling the folded length of chute material towards the pack. Carefully lifting it, she folded it in an S shape into the pack before finally tucking the pilot chute in the top.

Sighing and stretching out her back, Lissy passed the completed pack, that had taken a little under thirty minutes to complete, to a colleague. She walked to the rail, collected another aired parachute and started the process all over again.

Several hours later, they stopped for a fifteen-minute tea break. Lissy gratefully took a seat to rest her aching feet and legs. She was exhausted and just wanted to get through her shift and get home to sleep. Back at the folding table, Lissy was just working the rigging on another parachute as the clock struck three o'clock and the air raid sirens sprang to life. Work immediately ceased and they traipsed through the corridors, heading to the factory air raid shelter.

War work was a risk. Many air raids targeted munitions factories and airstrips, and they all knew the risk they were taking. Their factory wasn't a big target, but as many past air raids had confirmed, it didn't matter. Bombs landed where they shouldn't, and often innocent people lost their lives, homes and businesses.

As the air raid shelter door slammed shut, Lissy sat and closed her eyes, trying to block out the droning sound of approaching Luftwaffe planes. Normally, Lissy concentrated on Richard and how much she missed him. Surprisingly, today, her thoughts wandered to Constable George Perkins instead, and she had no idea what that meant.

ELEVEN

Zakynthos, Greece, 1944

The lilting Greek music was loud and cheerful as everyone danced a traditional Greek *Syrtos*. Food was plentiful, with fruit, olives and village bread, surrounded by traditional sweet treats. The sky was a brilliant blue and the sun shone high overhead.

Angelos had never seen his bride look so beautiful. They were surrounded by family and friends who had all gathered together for the celebration. Even the villagers had joined them, too.

The open courtyard was surrounded by fragrant bougainvillea and small vines that showed promise of abundance. Amongst the flowers, Elena shone brightly, brighter than the sun itself, if that were possible. She laughed, lost in her own world. Suddenly, she looked towards him and smiled. He was hers and Elena was his. Together at last.

Elena moved towards him, and he stepped forward to greet her, but as their fingers touched, everything changed, and the world turned grey and dark. Elena vanished and Angelos was alone. The guests and musicians had disappeared. Their instruments lay abandoned, strings had snapped and the wood had splintered.

The long table of delicious food had turned to mold and was covered in maggots and flies. The bread was hard and speckled green, and the wine, bitter. The sun was now hidden behind looming dark clouds, and the sky streaked with lightning as distant thunder rumbled. The rumbling changed to a vibration through the earth that grew stronger, cracking walls and knocking everything over.

∼

Angelos awoke with a start from the nightmare. His heart pounded and he was drenched in sweat. He sat upright. The night was still dark, and dawn was still hours away. He wouldn't sleep again tonight, though. The repetitive nightmare taunted him often, but however much he tried, he couldn't stop it.

The New Year celebrations had been resigned to the past, and they were still in the grip of war and the Nazis were still occupying the islands. The island's Jewish residents were still safe in hiding, and all were still alive.

Angelos hoped war would end soon, but as each new year arrived, the conflict still had a stranglehold on his country, and it seemed like the war would never end.

The overheard conversation between Stelios and the man's friend weighed heavily on Angelos's mind. Such hatred for a small island. He walked quietly downstairs, not wanting to disturb the household. Stepping out of the front door into the night, he jumped, seeing a lonely figure slumped in a chair. Stelios, his father-in-law. Angelos hated the man more each day, and yet his bravery seemed to elude him when he needed it the most, when he needed to stand up to Stelios.

"Angelos... Why are you awake?" Stelios asked, slugging back *Tsipouro*.

"I cannot sleep."

"Still chasing the ghost of the dead woman in your dreams, eh?" Stelios laughed spitefully.

"You find it funny? You find all this hatred, death, and destruction amusing, Stelios? Your own daughter got a bullet in the back of her head and was thrown down a well because she was a traitor! Does that make you happy too?"

Stelios sprung from his chair. He wrapped his hands around Angelos's throat, slamming him into the wall of the house. "You dare to talk about my Maria like that! My beloved daughter! She was your wife!"

"My wife. Pah! She was a woman you and my father forced me to marry. I did not love her. I did not even like her! She was a traitor. She did not care about me, and she did not care about her own daughter, Sophia. If she had, she would not have betrayed us!"

"You do not talk about my daughter that way!" Stelios's grip on Angelos's throat tightened a little more.

The harsh stone of the wall dug into his back and Angelos gasped for air. His voice rasped as he spoke. "So you can talk as you like about me and Elena? You are a spiteful bastard for fun, but you cannot take it when it is given back to you, Stelios. You pitiful man. I feel sorry for you."

Stelios's hands gripped tighter, and Angelos became lightheaded. "Do it," he rasped to his father-in-law. "Kill me. I am already dead inside anyway. Without my Elena and Athena, I am nothing. Do it! Kill me now, you bastard, and put me out of my misery. It is the greatest pleasure you seek Stelios. Take it. I will be out of your life forever."

With seething anger, Stelios threw Angelos to the ground. "You pathetic man. You already have a daughter. Sophia! Yet you pine for a dead peasant and a bastard child that probably is not yours. You are no longer welcome in this house, Angelos Sarkis. Take your pathetic, cowering mother and leave. Sophia stays. She is mine!"

"You will not take my daughter from me!"

"You do not want her! She is my blood, Angelos. Blood is blood!"

"No, Stelios. She is *my* blood. I am her father. She stays with me."

Angelos was now on his feet and the men squared up to each other, neither caring if anyone was out in the early hours and witnessed the argument.

"You and your partisans took my daughter from me!" Stelios spat. "So I now take your daughter from you. You have no say!"

"I am her father, Stelios."

"You are nothing. You are a peasant. It is a shame the Nazis did not put a bullet in your head too."

"You are a vile bastard, Stelios Makris." Daylight had begun to peek over the horizon as Angelos pushed past Stelios and stormed into the house. Stelios followed fast on his heels.

"This is my house. I no longer want you in it, but Sophia stays!" Stelios bellowed as he followed Angelos up the stairs.

Banging on Pigi's door, Angelos entered. "Get up. We are leaving, Stelios is throwing us out."

Pigi rubbed her eyes in confusion and got out of bed,

looking over at a still sleeping Sophia. "What is all this? You pair of idiots. You will wake the child."

"Get yourself and her ready. I will be back soon. Stelios is not to go near the child."

Angelos left the room and walked straight into Stelios. "I will be back to get my mother and child as soon as I have found somewhere to live. You are a spineless bastard, Stelios. I will never understand why my father was your friend."

Without waiting for a response, Angelos stormed from the house. His fleeting bravery fizzling away as soon as he turned the corner. He had no idea where they were going to go. Pounding the streets, he headed to the harbour to think.

"You are out early, Angelos," Niko Makris said as the two men walked into each other.

"You are too, my friend." It still puzzled Angelos how a son and father could be so unlike, but that was war, it split everyone apart.

Niko shrugged. "What my father does not know… Is he in a good or bad mood today?"

"Bad. His anger over Maria has consumed him. He tried to strangle me and demanded Pigi and I leave the house. He is throwing us out. We have nowhere to go."

"And Sophia?"

"Of course, he demands to keep Sophia. She is his property, not a beloved child. As always, he will get his own way." Angelos shrugged and wished it was not so.

"My father is a cretin. He spends his time with the island's enemy, Angelos. I am ashamed to call myself the son of Makris. Come, I think I have an answer for you, if you trust me?"

"You are the only one in that family I do trust, Niko. You are a good man; you always have been. You are fighting on the right side. You are fighting for us all." Angelos saw the look on the man's face. "Do not worry, Niko, I will not tell your father. If it was not for people like you, we would all be in trouble. You give us hope."

Niko nodded then smiled. "Come."

Angelos followed Niko through the back streets of town and out into the countryside. They met a man with a horse and cart and climbed aboard, carefully traversing back roads, avoiding the enemy, until they found themselves in Planos. The village was small, barely a handful of houses along a sweeping shoreline. Niko climbed from the cart, beckoning for Angelos to follow him.

"Ten minutes," he said to the cart driver, who flicked the reins, telling the horse to move on so as not to attract attention. Angelos stood next to Niko as he knocked on the door of a house and waited. It opened a crack, the occupant nervous. When the older man saw Niko, he pulled the door a little wider.

Angelos and Niko stepped inside and the door closed behind them. Angelos stayed silent as Niko spoke in rapid hushed tones with the older man. Ten minutes later, the older man turned to Angelos. "Tonight, nine o'clock. You meet us in Vanato. It will be dangerous. Nazis everywhere now. They are angry because they lose their precious war. Niko help you, though. We have house in the mountains, in Exo Hora. You stay there. We did not like your father and Stelios Makris. Niko is good man. We know about you and Elena. A sad story. We are sorry for your loss, she will be missed. Your child deserves a chance. We will help you. You must follow our instructions, though."

"Of course. What about Stelios?"

Niko laughed. "Kyriakos Avgoustinos and his rich friends are entertaining again tonight. Father will be there, so will most of the Nazis! With wine and women, they will not care about anything else tonight."

The man showed them to the door. "It is settled. Good luck."

Angelos and Niko left the house, climbing back into the cart as it pulled up to begin the perilous journey back to town. By the time they had returned to the Makris house, Stelios had gone. Pigi was pacing the floor, wringing her hands. Sophia was awake and Angelos took her in his arms. The poor child. It wasn't her fault her grandfathers both turned out as they had. She'd been born in a time when the world was a bad place, when people chose sides regardless of the consequences. Sophia wouldn't be punished for the sins of her mother or her grandfathers. One day, Athena would return to them. They would be reunited, and the two girls would be the sisters they were always meant to be.

As the day drew on, Angelos had packed up as much as he could. All they needed were the important things; they could get the basics again in time.

"How will we leave town?" Pigi asked, nervously glancing at the door.

"It is covered. Niko will take us. Wear your best clothes. Agree with what I say, nod and smile if we are stopped, but do not say too much."

At six o'clock they left the house, secreting their belongings in hidden compartments in the cart seats. The rest was in baskets, covered with sacks, for their journey from Zakynthos Town to their new home.

Slowly, they wound their way through the streets, nervous and worried about being stopped. At the edge of town, their brief luck ran out as they hit a roadblock.

"Halt!" The Nazi stepped forward. "Where are you going?"

Niko smiled. "I am Nikolaos Makris, son of Stelios Makris. We are joining him and his friend Kyriakos Avgoustinos for dinner tonight."

"All of you?"

Angelos and Pigi nodded as Niko spoke. "Yes, all of us. My father wants the family together. You know he is an important man. If you do not believe us, ask the Commandant, although I doubt he will want to be disturbed."

The soldier spoke to the other officer for a moment, before nodding, "You may pass. Heil Hitler!"

The Nazis allowed the cart through the roadblock and the occupants breathed a sigh of relief. The remainder of their journey was unhindered, and once they arrived, Niko stepped down from the cart, passing the reins to a member of the resistance who jumped up next to Angelos.

"This is where I leave you, Angelos. You are in safe hands. I must go and do something else. We still have a war to fight, and I am needed more now than ever. Look after yourselves, and remember, Stelios may be my blood, but he is my enemy and I consider you to be my family. I will visit you soon."

"Thank you for your help, Niko. We will see you soon." Angelos shook his friend's hand and the cart jerked forward, continuing in silence towards the mountains and their new home in Exo Hora. They travelled under the cover of night, and eventually, after some close shaves, they arrived on the outskirts. With help from local resistance, they gathered their belongings from the cart and quietly made their way into the village.

Angelos knew Stelios would be incandescent when he found Sophia gone, but he didn't care. For now, they had started a new life away from Stelios, were safe in a new home, and it was up to Angelos to keep it that way.

TWELVE

Mainland Greece, 1944

Roula was bored. It had been a tedious day of helping her mother. Cleaning clothes and bed linen. Sweeping floors and preparing food. She wanted to be out in the fresh air doing something that wasn't cleaning or cooking.

Sneaking to the back door, she tied a scarf in her hair and left the house, making her way up through the ground at the rear of the building. Her father would be at the Kafenion talking to the owner and villagers about all that was wrong with the world. Roula didn't understand how the Kafenion stayed open. It was wartime and hardly anyone lived in their village anymore. The men were defiant, though. It was their favourite place, and so they opened it for a couple of hours each day.

The mountains were a lonely place. No one ever visited, and the only people they saw were vehicles on the main road that passed through the mountainous area, linking local towns. It was a lonely place to grow up. Everyone was older than Roula, there was nothing to do and no hope of ever having a life outside of being the wife of a farmer. When she was able to escape her parents' watchful eyes, Roula ran wild through the hills among the trees. No one questioned it; it was just Dimitroula, it was what she'd always done. No one cared.

Now things had changed. She was nineteen, an adult. War had overtaken their world, and she wanted to fight for her country. She'd heard all about the resistance and begged her parents to become part of it. They'd refused. Her place was at home, looking after the house and doing her chores.

"The resistance is not for young women! Your place is here with your *Mana*!" her father shouted one day as they'd argued about it again.

Walking steadily uphill, Roula spied the shepherd hut ahead, nestled in the mountainside, surrounded by trees. She stopped to look around her. She was alone, and there was no one else for miles. She carried on, climbing upwards towards the building.

The man who spoke Greek with an English accent intrigued Roula, and she wanted to talk to him again. She had dreamed of seeing more of the outside world. Instead, the outside world had come to her, and she wasn't going to miss her chance to find out more.

∼

Richard had cleaned the inside of the hut and was just tidying away the last of the previous night's food when he heard a soft knock at the door. Grabbing the rifle, he went to the window and looked out.

Roula. Damn the girl. Hadn't she listened to anything he'd said? Pulling back the chair, he opened the door and swiftly pulled her inside.

"What are you doing here?" he demanded, kicking the door shut behind her and wedging the chair against it.

"I thought you might be bored."

Richard laughed. "You thought I might be bored. What on earth made you think that? I am stuck in a hut on a mountain in the middle of Greece with a young child. We have no change of clothes; she has no toys to play with and we cannot even go outside! Have you ever tried to entertain a four-year-old child? I am sick of this already. Boredom does not even come close!"

Roula ignored his rant and went to the bed where Athena was sitting. "Hello, little one. I have a gift for you." From her dress pocket, Roula took out a small bear. It had seen better days, but Athena's face lit up at the sight of it and she reached her little arms out to grasp it. Roula allowed her to take it, and watched as Athena gleefully played with it.

"See, not everything is bad." Roula pulled out a chair and sat. Richard sat opposite her and smiled.

"I am sorry, Roula. Thank you for the bear, it is nice."

"I do not need it anymore. Tell me, Richard. Is today the day when you will tell me more about yourself?"

He studied her closely. For the second time in recent months, he was relying on a Greek girl to get him through a tough time. Despite still being wary, his gut instinct told him he could trust her. "I am English, from a town called Bristol. My plane was shot down over Zakynthos Island and the resistance looked after me. They tried to help get me home, but it went wrong. There was supposed to be a ship, but I ended up here on the mainland instead. Resistance brought me here to the mountains. I do not know what happens next, but I do know I want to go home. I miss it, and I miss those I care about."

"Someone is waiting for you?"

"Yes, I was supposed to marry. I hope she is still waiting for me. But it has been so long since I have spoken to her. I am not sure if or when I will see her again."

"That is sad."

"And what about you, Roula? You said you may tell me something one day. Is that day today?"

Roula paled and looked suddenly scared, something Richard hadn't seen in her before. She gripped the table edge with her fingers as though she was trying to focus on something.

"I am sorry, I should not have asked." He looked over at Athena. "The woman who looked after me when I was shot down was a resistance fighter. She was Athena's mother. When the resistance put me on the boat that was supposed to take me to the ship, the Nazis found us. They took Athena's mother. Athena's mother begged me to take the child and look after her. She made me promise. I had no choice. I pulled Athena into the boat with me, and I ended up at sea with a child that is not mine. If it was not for the quick actions of the fisherman rescuing me, they may have got us too." He lowered his voice. "I have no idea if Athena's mother is still alive. All I can do is try and keep the promise I made to her and look after the child. I know to some it may seem a stupid decision, and I have no idea what the future will bring for either of us, but I could not leave her there."

"You had no choice; you did the right thing. Maybe now, Athena has a chance to live? I think you are a good man. I wish there were more good men."

"There are some," Richard said gently.

"This is a quiet place, Richard, but a bad road runs through it. Evil people use the road, and some Greek girls

A NIGHT OF THUNDER

are not so sensible. They pay for their stupidity and ignorance."

"What do you mean?"

"It does not matter." Roula stood and went to the bed. She sat and gently pulled Athena onto her lap, bouncing her knee, making the child chuckle.

"What happened, Roula? You obviously want to tell someone. You have heard my story. Tell me yours."

"I cannot." She looked up at him with tears in her eyes.

"Whatever happened has scared you. Please tell me."

"If I tell you, you must promise you will not tell anyone else!"

"I promise."

"There was one other girl like me living on the mountain, in the village. We grew up together. A week before you arrived, I found her."

"Found her? I do not understand."

Roula put Athena back on the bed, stood and walked to the window, beckoning Richard to follow suit. He stood next to her and looked out. The sun was setting and it was picturesque. On the image alone, no one would have believed that the world was gripped by war. But it was a deceitful scene and they were at war.

"See to the left, that ridge that runs by the main road? It was where she met the German soldier. It was months ago. She was there by accident, and she met him. She went back every couple of days, and they met up. I do not know if it was love or something else, but one day they were seen. The resistance, they saw her. A week ago, I was out walking and I heard screams. I went to see what it was and .." Roula was pale, and words failed her. "You need to be careful, Richard. There are enemies everywhere. There are enemies on all sides, even in the resistance. Even in the people we think we can trust."

"What happened, Roula?"

"I cannot say anymore."

"You need to tell me."

"If I do. You must promise…"

"… I promise."

"Thanasis. His name is Thanasis. He is a vicious Greek man. Thanasis found them together, the Greek village girl and the German soldier. Thanasis shot and killed the soldier, then he dragged her to the ground by her hair and…" She paused for a moment. "He forced himself on her and told her she was a traitorous peasant. He continued to violate her, calling her names until she could no longer move." Roula wiped her eyes, brushing away the tears.

"You saw this?"

Roula nodded.

"Did she tell anyone? Did you tell anyone?" Richard was appalled by what he was hearing.

"She could not. I have been too scared. After he was done with her, Thanasis threw a rope around the girl's neck, dragged her to the nearest tree and hanged her from it. He walked away leaving her to die." Roula's tears fell fast. "I tried to save her, Richard, after he left, I tried to save her. I ran to her and tried to cut her down, but I could not. I was not strong enough or tall enough. I had to watch her die, Richard. Thanasis is Greek resistance, and yet he violated and killed a defenceless girl. One of his own kind! I hate this war so much, I hate it!" Roula buried her face in her hands and burst into tears.

Richard sat back, shocked at what Roula had just told him. This war was a horrific beast that crept into all their lives, putting people in impossible situations, making them face things they should never have to. Roula had witnessed something so awful that would live with her for the rest of her life. He looked at her now and could see through all the bravado she'd initially shown. There was a frightened young woman hiding behind it and he wished he could help her.

"It was not your fault, Roula. War makes fools of so many. The girl put herself in danger by seeing the German soldier, and the fault for her death lies with Thanasis. He could have let her go. He could have let her walk away, but he did not. *He* is the one that committed the crime, *he* is the monster. You did your best. That is all we can do in this war."

"But I wanted to save her. I tried..."

"I know. And sometimes, in this life, that is enough. You tried your best. It happened because she chose to fraternise with the enemy. Thanasis saw it as going against all he believed in. He dealt with it badly, though. Thanasis should never have treated her that way. He should have spoken to her, but he was an animal and treated her disrespectfully. *He* is the one in the wrong, Roula, and he is the one who will have to live with what he has done for the rest of his life. You were brave and tried to help, and it counts for a lot. You were with her when she died and she knew someone cared about her. That is the most important thing of all."

Silence fell in the shepherd hut and was only disturbed minutes later by the sweet laughter of Athena playing with her little bear. What a tragic situation for them all, Richard thought. He was glad he knew what had happened, though. He would be on his guard. It sounded like Thanasis was a man not to be trusted.

Richard watched as Roula used the trees as cover as she ran back down the mountain in the fast-approaching twilight. It made him think of Lissy and the day they'd gone to Ashton Court woods in Bristol and walked among the trees. It had been a beautiful day and war had seemed so far away; the sunlight had dappled through the leaves, shining brightly on the world of nature under the canopy.

Lissy had run through the trees savouring every beautiful view, and Richard had smiled at her reaction. Later, as they reached her favourite area, he'd taken her hand and pulled her to him.

"I have something to tell you, Lissy."

"You do?"

"I know things are not looking great with the world, and neither of us know what will happen next week, but I do know that I truly love you."

"I love you too."

Richard kneeled before her and lifted a ring from his jacket pocket. "Alice Cook, my darling Lissy, I love you so much. I want to marry you. Will you be my wife?"

"Yes, Richard Hobbs, I will marry you!"

Richard had slipped his grandmother's ring onto Lissy's finger and stood. Taking her face in his hands, he kissed her and held her in his arms, before spending the rest of the afternoon walking and making plans.

∽

That day felt like a lifetime ago. Richard missed Lissy, but the war had changed so much. The life they'd planned together back in Bristol would never be the same. He'd been through a lot, and he had no idea if Lissy was still alive. From sparse information he'd gleaned, he knew England had sustained bombing raids and their city would look very different when he returned home.

He knew he'd changed as a person and no doubt Lissy would have too. It was going to be a difficult homecoming when it happened. All he could do was stay positive and hold on to the hope of seeing her again.

His immediate worry was Athena, though. He had no idea what to do about Athena. She wasn't his child; she was Greek, and her life was here in Greece. He'd been stupid to take her with him. He'd agreed to put Athena's life before his, and it was a huge burden to bear. He had to get her back to her family, but had no idea how to do that whilst war still raged. He couldn't abandon her here on the mainland with people he didn't know either.

Could he take Athena home with him? Was it even possible? The questions tumbled in his mind, and each one made him more confused than the previous one. Richard looked down at the young child. She'd curled up with the bear and fallen into a peaceful slumber. He hoped he would be able to reunite her with her family, but the reality was she would probably end up being a casualty of war like many others.

THIRTEEN

Bristol, England, 1941

Lissy had awoken early, unable to sleep. The morning was chilly and the previous months of air raids, rations and long hours working at the factory had begun to take their toll. Her routine had become sleep, eat, factory and repeat. The air raids were incessant, and much of Bristol had been decimated by the anger of German bombs.

Lissy was still packing parachutes, and it amazed her how many parachutes had been needed. Like everything in the war, citizens were only told what they needed to know, and she had no idea where they ended up or who was using them. Rumours swirled around factories and neighbourhoods of resistance fighters who were being dropped into France and sometimes other countries. Brave men, and maybe even women, who'd agreed to immerse themselves in foreign society to help fight the war.

Lissy had no idea whether it was true or not, but if it was, the job she was doing was now even more important. People were relying on her to keep them safe. She had to keep going, despite the continual exhaustion.

A NIGHT OF THUNDER

Making herself a cup of weak tea, Lissy pushed back the net curtain and stared at the street below. At times like this, when the world was quiet, no planes flew overhead, no sirens wailed and things were calm, the threat of war seemed a million miles away. It was still lurking, though, like a snake in the undergrowth waiting to strike.

As Lissy sipped her tea, a dispatch rider turned into her street and she watched them closely. It normally meant a telegram delivery containing bad news for the recipient. As they drew level with her house, the rider stopped and looked up.

Lissy dropped the net curtain and it swung back into place. With a shaking hand, she put the teacup on the side, steeling herself. A knock at the front door confirmed her fears. Willing her body to move, she went to answer it.

"Miss Alice Cook? Sister of Tom Cook?"

Glancing over the man's shoulder, Lissy caught curtains moving. Everyone would know why he was here; all of them would be grateful it wasn't for them. With a wavering voice she spoke, "Yes. I'm Alice Cook."

"A telegram for you, Miss Cook." He passed her the envelope before turning on his heel. Her eyes flicked up and she watched him walk away. Was that it? No other information? No stopping to see if she was okay? Standing on the front step, she opened the telegram with shaking hands.

Buckingham Palace

Cook, Alice, Bristol, BS5

The King and Queen deeply regret the loss you and the army have sustained by the death of private T Cook in the full service of his country. Their Majesties truly sympathise with you in your sorrow.

Keeper of the privy purse.

Lissy slid to the floor not caring who witnessed her anguish. "Tom, oh my poor baby brother. I can't lose you. You're my only family."

She reread the telegram, hoping it was a mistake. Hoping the rider had delivered it to the wrong person. But it was all there in black and white. Her baby brother had been killed in action. Where or how, she didn't know. He'd been so desperate to fight for his country, and he was now dead, and she would never see him again. The realisation hit her, and she sat leaning against the doorframe and wept.

"Lissy? Are you alright?" The calm, concerned voice of George Perkins wrapped around her and she looked up, wiping her eyes with the back of her hand.

"George?"

"Yes. Is everything okay? Has someone hurt you? Have you been robbed?" He peered into the hallway.

"No, nothing like that." With a still shaking hand, Lissy passed him the telegram.

"My condolences. Someone you knew?"

"My brother."

"I'm so sorry. This war always delivers such tragic news. Come now, let's get you inside and away from prying eyes." George helped Lissy to her feet and into the house, pushing the front door closed behind him. He guided her into the small front room where she sat on the equally small sofa. He placed the telegram on the side table and went to the kitchen, filled a glass with water and took it to Lissy.

"Drink this." He sat in the armchair next to her.

Gratefully, Lissy took the glass and sipped.

"Is there anyone who can sit with you?"

"No, it's just me. My parents are both dead, and Tom was the only relative I have... I had left. I've nothing at all now. I rent this house. My parents' shop went to someone else, and they're all gone. Everything's gone. All I've left is three pieces of furniture and some small mementoes."

"I'm sorry you're all alone. You're not married?"

"No, not yet anyway. My fiancé is away fighting, like so many other men. They always want to go and fight and leave us here alone to pine after them. I haven't heard from him in so long. Some news would be good. When the man arrived to give me this telegram... I..."

"You thought he was dead?"

"Yes." She paused to look at the telegram next to her. "I don't know what's worse. Losing my brother or losing my fiancé. Both are too heartbreaking to even contemplate."

"I understand. I've seen a lot of death and destruction since the war began. People injured and killed; homes destroyed. It's a terrible thing that's happening to us all, and I don't know where it'll end."

Lissy wiped her eyes again.

"I'm sorry, I didn't mean to make you cry." George passed her a clean handkerchief which she gratefully accepted.

"You haven't. You're right, the whole thing's horrible. I just want the war to be over. I cannot live like this anymore. I'm exhausted. I work so many hours in the factory, I barely have time to eat, my sleep's broken by nightmares or air raids, and I'm sitting here waiting for a man I hardly ever hear from, who may not even be alive!"

"It isn't easy, but you have to try and stay strong. We all do. If you ever need anything tell me, Lissy. I'd rather you talk to me than no one at all."

"Thank you, but I still don't know much about you. I know you're not married, but what about your family?"

"I'm like you. I've no one else. My parents passed. I'm an only child and I'm not courting either. Women in Bristol all want an Army or RAF man on their arm. People like me, unable to go to war because of their health, are at the bottom of the pile. We aren't exciting enough."

"Is that what you think? Oh George, people like you, air raid wardens and nursing staff, are just as brave and important! Without you looking after us here at home, we'd be lost. You all put your lives on the line for us to keep us safe here at home. My fiancé might be out there flying a plane to stop the enemy, but we need help here too. You keep the peace, help people in distress and stop us turning into a lawless society, and I for one am very grateful. You helped me today, when none of the neighbours did, and I appreciate it."

"Thank you, Lissy. It's not often people express gratitude for what we do. I know we are appreciated, but sometimes we need to hear it. I can't take away the pain of the loss of your brother, but I do hope you feel a little better?"

"I'll always miss Tom. I have to come to terms with the fact I'll never see him again, and I know it will take time, but he'd want me to live my life. It's going to be so hard, though, especially as I feel so alone right now."

"Things will get better."

"I know."

"Are you alright now? I should get back to my rounds."

"Of course. I've kept you from your job long enough." They stood and Lissy showed him back to the front door and opened it.

"Thank you again, George."

"My pleasure."

Lissy watched as the constable walked away from the house, passing another bombsite at the end of the road as he went. Yesterday, there had been a row of houses and a shop there, now it was only two houses and a pile of smouldering rubble a lone fire engine was still damping down.

Lissy watched as George approached a group of young boys sitting on a wall.

"Move along, young 'uns. There's nothing here for you," he reprimanded. The children moved off. The older one turned as they reached the corner. "We weren't doing nothing mister, unlike you! Lazy conchie what can't fly a plane!"

"Get out of here before I clip your ears!" George shouted, threatening to chase them. The children disappeared before he could get close.

"Cheeky young lads." Lissy shook her head and went back inside. In the front room she picked up the telegram and put it on the mantelpiece next to the photographs of her parents and Richard. She didn't know if her brother's body would ever be returned to her. The telegram was her last tangible connection to him, and because of that, it would stay on the mantelpiece. Collecting up the teacup and glass, Lissy took them to the kitchen. It was time to dig deep and find her *war spirit*. Whilst the war continued, she still had work to do.

Several hours later, Lissy was on the factory floor listening to the manager speak. Normally, they came straight in and got on with their work. Time was precious and every spare minute was needed to get the work done. After changing into their overalls, they were told to wait for the manager.

He now stood before them with his secretary, a grave expression etched on both of their faces.

"I'll remind you of some important things before we start work today. What we do here is for the war. We're here to support those brave men and women who're fighting for our freedom. We've had to let go two members of staff this week who were seen talking about the work we do out in public. Packing parachutes might not seem important, but it is. Whether it's parachutes, munitions, or some other vital war service, you cannot talk about what you do outside of this factory. War work is government work, and you all signed a secrecy act when you joined. Anyone else caught talking about what they do here will lose their job and could face prosecution."

There was a stunned silence and Lissy glanced around the room. One of the night workers called Dotty, who Lissy had known since school, wasn't there. She wondered if Dotty had been one of those who been dismissed.

"You must also follow your instructions clearly when packing your parachutes. Two men have died from twisted rig lines that weren't properly packed. The parachutes weren't packed here, and I'm happy to say that we still have a good record, but the government has asked us to remind everyone. They don't want any more deaths from poorly packed chutes."

The manager leaned over to look at the secretary's notepad. "Finally, we're changing shifts again. The new shift pattern will be on the noticeboards downstairs. Check it before you leave. If you're on the shift change list, you'll get three days off, between the end of your current shift and the start of the next one. That's all. Back to work."

Lissy snuck downstairs to check the shift rota before heading back to work. She was elated to see that she'd been moved back to day shifts from the following day and would have the next three days off. On the factory floor, she went to her table, grabbed a parachute and began packing. Whilst it may have been monotonous work, the manager's words had hit home. Men's lives depended on them, and she refused to have anyone's death on her hands.

FOURTEEN

Zakynthos, Greece, 1944

The Zakynthian wine had flowed freely at the Avgoustinos Mansion, and there had been willing women to do whatever Stelios wanted with. He had enjoyed himself immensely. He loved his life. Things might have been hard for the peasants on the island, but if you knew the right people, like he did, indulgence in the simple pleasures of life was still possible.

His house was quiet and dark as he stumbled through the door, and he'd gone to bed to sleep off the alcohol coursing through his blood. Stelios awoke late the next morning with a pounding head and dry mouth. Stumbling downstairs, he frowned. The house was quiet; it should've been bustling with life. He walked into the dining room expecting the table to be laid with food and Pigi fussing as she always did, but there was no food in sight.

The only person present was Niko, drinking a cup of coffee, with his feet up on the table. Stelios suddenly remembered; he'd told the ungrateful pig Angelos to leave.

A NIGHT OF THUNDER

Stelios grinned; the peasant had done as he was told for once.

"Get your feet off my table, Niko! Go and get Sophia. I would like to say hello to her. My granddaughter needs a big hug from her grandfather."

Niko swung his legs off the tabletop and did as he was told. Minutes later he returned alone. "She is gone. They have all gone. I do not understand it. I thought the house was quiet but..."

"What!" Stelios raged. "She cannot have gone. She is *my* granddaughter. I told the pig she was to stay with me! This is where she belongs! She is mine not his!" Racing from the room, Stelios tore through the house, calling out for the child who would never hear him. Quietly, Niko slipped away; he didn't want the brunt of Stelios's anger. As far as Niko was concerned, his father had it coming and deserved everything he got.

On the other side of the island, in Exo Hora, Angelos awoke in a strange bed. Then he remembered. They'd finally escaped Stelios. They were safe in a new home and could begin their lives again. It still wasn't the housed he wanted. That one was still being used by the Nazis, but at least he had somewhere safe for him and his family to live that was warm, dry and with a roof over their heads.

Slipping from bed, Angelos walked around the house. He hadn't seen much of it upon arrival in the darkness. Next to his bedroom there was another bedroom his mother and daughter shared. At the back of the house was a small kitchen and a storeroom. A small, walled, outside space would allow Sophia somewhere to play.

It wasn't much in comparison to the house he grew up in with his parents, or the Makris house, but it was somewhere they could call home, and it was far from his overbearing father-in-law.

Sophia was still soundly sleeping. She needed the rest after the tiring evening they'd faced. Pigi was back in the kitchen after hanging clothes outside to dry. She'd already cleaned everything and was getting food ready.

"You are awake, my son. I did not want to disturb you."

"I think it is the best sleep I have had in a long time. It is good to be away from the Makris house."

"You have been through a lot. We all have." Pigi looked away and continued with her cooking.

"I am sorry *Mana*."

Pigi stopped stirring the cooking pot and turned to him. After wiping her hands on her apron, she took his hands in hers. "Dear Angelos, you have nothing to be sorry for. This war, it has brought much hatred and upset to our island. So many families have been changed forever. I never approved of your *Baba's* ways. I loved him, yes. But he was a stubborn man with ideas too grand for him. Your *Baba* wanted everyone to live the life *he* expected them to live. That included you, Angelos. He treated you badly. He treated us both badly. I wish I could have been stronger. I *should* have been stronger and stood up to him somehow, but I was scared. He made me a stupid, pitiful woman. I am sorry he forced you to marry that miserable Maria. I know you and Elena were in love. I could see it. If I had been stronger, maybe..."

"It was not your fault. It was *Baba* and Stelios. They planned it all. We did not have a say in what happened; not you, me, Maria, or Elena. It was a business deal; that was all we were to him. To both of them. They forced us to do what they wanted. It was their stupid Zakynthian pride and honour, and they would not allow anything to get in the way of that. None of this was your fault. It was all theirs."

"I know. Stelios and your *Baba* were difficult men to talk to. They had their plans for each of us, and you are right; their pride made our lives unbearable. I am sad you lost your daughter, Athena, too. I will never get to see both of my grandchildren together. That is the saddest thing of all. They would have been wonderful sisters. They would have liked growing up together."

Angelos studied his mother for a moment and realised it wasn't just him who had been hurting all this time. Pigi had too.

"We are still a family *Mana*. We may be small, and part of us may be missing, but you, me and Sophia are still family. We always will be. That is what matters. Nothing can be done about the past, but we learn to live with it, eventually. I am trying, but I am not sure I can ever come to terms with what happened. It hurts too much. I know I must learn to try, for you, and Sophia."

"I know, my son. You must get up every day and tell yourself why you are still here..." She crooked her finger and then pointed to Sophia's bedroom. Pushing open the door, she revealed a sleeping Sophia. "Her... *she* is the reason you still live. *She* is the reason you get out of bed every day. You must remember every single day of your life, even in the darkest of times. A lot of bad things happened in this war, but she is one of the few good things. You remember that. You keep living for her. Sophia needs her father. She needs *you*."

Angelos gazed at the sleeping figure of his daughter. His heart filled with love for her. "I will *Mana*."

"Good, now enough with all this talking. She will be

hungry when she wakes. I need to cook!" Pigi left Angelos leaning against the doorjamb, watching his daughter sleep.

∼

Under the shady canopy of the olive trees, Sophia crawled unsteadily through the grass, stalking a lizard as it ran through the undergrowth. Angelos and Pigi sat on an old blanket in the sunshine watching her.

The quietness of the olive groves in Exo Hora was their favourite place. Sitting here always lulled them into a false sense of security. It was a deceptive veil of protection that cloaked them and shut out the rest of the world. The war always seemed far away here, in the sunshine, hidden away from Nazi patrols and roadblocks.

They were still at war though and Nazis still roamed Zakynthos, although patrolling in the northwest of the island was rare. Occasionally though, a patrol would wind its way up to the north of the island to remind Zakynthians they were still in charge. Villagers dreaded it, hiding away in their homes, tired and weary, remaining prisoners on their island.

Sophia squealed with delight as she found flowers under a tree. She sat on the ground among the blades of grass, playing with the brightly coloured petals. The lizard she'd been chasing scuttled up a nearby tree and sat on a branch watching her, thankful to be left alone.

"Look how she plays with the flowers, Angelos. She loves it here. We should bring her more often. It is good for her. She is a growing child; she needs to play!" Pigi tapped her son's arm to get his attention.

Angelos looked at his daughter and smiled. "You are right *Mana*. This place is good for her. It is quiet, there is lots for her to see and she is away from the anger and desperation haunting our island. It is good for us too. We can be a family away from the bad side of the war."

"It keeps you away from that Kafenion too!"

Angelos sighed. This was a repeated conversation he and his mother had had too many times in recent months. "You know I like the Kafenion, mother."

Pigi returned a hand to her son's arm, resting it lightly. "I know, son. As a Greek man it is your place to escape to. I know you like to sit with islanders, drink your coffee and listen to the illegal radio, but when you go there, I worry. That radio risks all of you. It risks us too. Look at what they did to the Petrakis family. The Kafenion is closer to the Nazis too, and they are getting ruthless and desperate. They are losing the war. They have already brought so much pain to the island. Look at what they did to old Takis. He was found wrapped to a tree, in barbed wire, shot through the head! He had been walking in the wrong place, at the wrong time. The soldiers challenged him and the stupid, drunk fool argued back. He called them names and he told them to leave the island. Now he is dead for his foolishness! I do not want that to be you, Angelos. You have so much anger and hurt because of Elena and Athena. You try to control it, and I know you would not intentionally cause a fight, but you are still angry. I see the shadow of hurt on your face every day, the pain of their loss is in your eyes. I could not bear to lose you."

"I know you worry, mother. Takis was an old fool. He thought he was invincible. He is not the only one. There are many old fools on this island. I am not one of them, though. Takis should not have died in such a horrible way. No one deserves that. I hate what is happening to our island. People are turning against their own families. Look at that bastard,

Stelios. He has already destroyed two families. How many more should suffer? I will not let anything happen to us." Angelos took his mother's hands in his own and looked over at Sophia and sighed. "When was it that Greek's lost their pride *Mana*?"

"Sometimes it is not pride, son. It is greed. With others, it is fear. Some on this island fear losing what they have. They long to keep their money and status. Look at the old Venetian families' history. It was a golden era of Zakynthos, but look how the nobles argued and cheated each other for money and status. It is in the blood. They call themselves Greeks, but they have the Venetian blood, and do not care who stands in their way. They think they are better than us. Some Zakynthians never change. It is a bad time and I long for it all to end. I pray it does soon." Pigi looked at her innocent granddaughter as the child played. She was crawling around the trees chasing another lizard.

"We all need a better life, Angelos. I just hope it comes soon."

"I will stay away from the Kafenion if it makes you happy, *Mana*."

"Thank you, son. It will."

FIFTEEN

Mainland Greece, 1944

Winter in the Greek mountains was harsh for Richard and Athena. Since their arrival months earlier in 1943, life had settled into a boring but steady routine. They were still living in the shepherd's hut, and Christmas had passed by in a blur of monotony and meagre food.

Days were bitterly cold, the nights even colder. Snow had slowly fallen in the early part of December 1943 and continued for weeks. It dusted everything white; icicles had hung from trees and the roof of the hut. Richard and Athena had hunkered down under blankets and animal skins to try and keep warm. Richard had hung whatever he could over the windows and doors to keep out drafts. He plugged up small holes in the walls with moss and old pieces of newspaper brought to him by Roula. It was a lot of effort, but it was essential.

Richard had grown weary as the days passed. They may not be Nazi captives, but he and Athena were still prisoners, confined to a freezing cold hut on a mountainside. It wasn't healthy for either of them. Athena had adapted to her ever-changing circumstances and was now talking. Richard constantly had to watch her and keeping her quiet was proving to be incredibly difficult.

Once a week, Greek resistance came to see them bringing provisions, and Richard was grateful to those who put their lives on the line for them. Roula visited often too, even during the coldest snowy days, and they talked of many things, but she hadn't mentioned Thanasis since.

A soft knock at the door pulled Richard from his reverie. He walked to the window and lifted the heavy curtain. It was the resistance with their provisions, but there was also a man with them he hadn't seen before. Opening the door, Richard stepped aside to let them in, swiftly closing it behind them to keep the icy air out. The resistance put down their parcels and patiently waited for the stranger to speak.

"I am Thanasis." He neither smiled nor extended his hand to Richard.

Richard assessed him. Finally, he was meeting the man of Roula's nightmares, and he understood why she was scared. At over six feet tall, Thanasis was a beast of a man. He had an air of ruthless determination about him. An ugly red scar ran under the man's left eye, his hair was wild and he had a lengthy beard.

"Thanasis. It is good to meet you." Richard neither meant nor felt it. He was, however, alone out here and sometimes it was better to keep enemies like Thanasis close.

"It is sad we meet in these circumstances. But that is war. Nothing is simple." Thanasis shrugged. "The Nazis, they have caused us trouble and we have lost many good Greek men. They invade our country, they steal our women and they leave us with nothing, but we fight back. We always fight back."

"You are right. War is a terrible thing."

"Now to business. We must move you. This hut, it is too close to the road. You must move to the other side of the village. Not that we can call it a village anymore. Many people have left. They have gone to fight, or they are dead. It will be better for you in the village. Warmer too!"

"Are you sure?" Richard wasn't sure moving was a good idea.

"Yes. You speak good Greek, you have long hair and a beard, and with the child, you blend in. It is like you are her father; a good honest Greek man with his young child. If Nazis come, they will not know any different. You will move in two days. We will go now to tell the owners of the farm. They will not say no to me. They will help us, and a strong man like you will help them on their farm."

"I will not put anyone in danger."

"We are all in danger. We must do what we can for our country. They will too. I will see you in two days."

Thanasis said no more and left the hut with the other resistance. Richard shut the door behind them and opened the food parcels that had been left on the table. He was always hungry, but he had to make sure Athena ate more than him and stayed healthy.

As a growing child, her health was more important than his. Putting the food on the shelf, he sat next to Athena, wiggling the teddy bear in front of her. She giggled and reached for it. The smallest of things amused her, and he hoped that when she was older, these were the things she'd remember about the war. Not the horrors and hardships.

As Roula walked into the small kitchen, she stopped, seeing Thanasis sitting at the table talking to her parents. She tried to retrace her steps hoping they hadn't seen her. Manos Papadoulia crooked his finger at her as his daughter tried to sneak out of the door.

"Dimitroula. Come sit! Can you not see we have a guest?" He frowned at her.

Roula obeyed her father and sat next to her mother, opposite Thanasis. She hadn't seen Thanasis since that awful day out on the main road, and now he was here in her house, talking with her parents. What he'd done was callous. Did he know that she knew? She hoped not.

"Dimitroula, you have grown into a beautiful young woman. It is a shame there are no suitable young Greek men to take her off your hands, Manos. If I was younger, I would have been pleased to have the opportunity. She is the sort of strong Greek girl who will bear many children. Unfortunately, I am already married and my wife would not approve. It is a shame…"

Roula shuddered as the men laughed. Thanasis wasn't a man to be trusted. The thought of him coming anywhere near her frightened her. If she'd been in the house on her own, she would've run and hidden. Thanasis turned his steely gaze away from her as if suddenly bored of her company and continued his conversation with her parents.

"I will bring him and the girl here in two days. We will move them in the night. It will be safer for us all. If the enemy visit you, it will be up to you to explain who he and the child are. He speaks Greek well."

Roula had zoned out, watching a lone beetle climb the kitchen wall. She snapped her attention back to the men with interest.

"We have someone coming to stay?"

"Not now, Roula. We will tell you everything later," her mother said.

"Maybe telling her now would be a good idea, Vivi," Thanasis said, leaning back in his chair. "It is time your daughter grew up and stopped running the local hills like an untamed goat. She should learn we are at war, and untamed goats often find themselves in trouble, some even get shot, mistaken for wolves..."

Roula's blood boiled at the veiled threat, but her parents seemed not to care.

"What is the big secret?" she demanded.

"The resistance rescued a man and his child. They need somewhere to hide them. They will live with us. He will help us on the land. Your mother will look after the child."

A small smile spread across Roula's face. Were they talking about Richard and Athena? Were they leaving the hut to live with them? It was a big risk for all of them. Roula knew her parents had only agreed to have them on their land until somewhere else could be found, but the man and his daughter had been stuck in the old hut for months. They'd endured a harsh winter and food had been scarce. Now, Thanasis was saying they would be coming to live in their home with them.

"Is that okay with you, Roula?" Thanasis's eyes narrowed at her. Defiantly, Roula stared back at him. Did he know she'd been visiting them?

"It is up to my parents. I just do as I am told."

Her parents and Thanasis laughed, and her mother spoke. "The day my Dimitroula does as she is told is the day the stars fall from the heavens!"

Roula crossed her arms and sat back in her chair. Pretending to zone out again, she listened intently as Thanasis and her parents made their plans to move Richard and Athena. It would put them all in great peril, but Roula was excited; in fact, she was looking forward to it.

~

Two nights later, in the depths of a cloudy, moonless night, there was a knock at the shepherd hut door. Richard opened it a crack after checking who was there. Thanasis and two of his men entered, and they gathered up the meagre belongings Richard and Athena had accumulated since their arrival.

Richard wrapped a sleeping Athena in an extra blanket and lifted her, cradling her in his arms. Carefully and slowly, they made their way out into the cold, dark night and made their way down the mountainside. Richard struggled in the darkness. Athena was heavy and the mountain was still icy underfoot. A member of resistance guided him from behind making sure he didn't fall.

As they reached the village, they skirted the edge to a farm on the far side. Everything was in darkness, as though the farmhouse occupants were fast asleep, but as they reached it, the back door swung open, and a man bathed in dull, yellow candlelight greeted them, pulling them inside.

With the door firmly shut, more candles were lit, and Richard surveyed his surroundings. It was someone's home, and even though it was basic, it was sheer heaven and much warmer than the hut.

"This is the Papadoulia family. You will be safe with them," Thanasis said, introducing them one by one. "Manos, and his wife Vivi, and their daughter Dimitroula."

Roula! He was staying with Roula's family? He nodded and said hello to each in turn, barely glancing at Roula. He didn't want to reveal they'd already met. Athena moaned in his arms, fitful in sleep. Vivi stepped forward and took her from Richard. "I will put your daughter to bed. She needs sleep."

"She's not..."

The woman had already left the room, and Richard had a fleeting feeling of anxiety. He glanced at the kind, smiling faces and relaxed, knowing he would be safe with this family. They were risking their lives for him, and anyone who did that for a stranger could be trusted.

"Sit." Thanasis motioned to a chair at the kitchen table. They all sat and were joined by Vivi moments later. "She is sleeping."

"This is a good family, Richard. They farm this land and keep to themselves. Nazis stay away and do not come here. This family will look after you and your daughter. You must remember, if anyone comes here or walks past, you are Greek. You come here from the north to find an uncle. When you arrive, they tell you he is dead. This family knew your uncle and took pity on you. They gave you shelter. You and Dimitroula fell in love and you married. You now live here with your daughter. If you want to be safe, and keep this family safe, this is the story you must remember."

"But how will that work? Surely people will guess?" Richard said. There was no way Roula could be Athena's mother. Physically it wasn't impossible, but she was so young. No one would believe it.

"It is war Richard. Nothing is normal. You and Dimitroula are close enough in age; no one will think anything of it. This is a quiet place. Nazis do not come here often, if at all. They pass by on the main road. You will be safe here. The resistance will watch and warn you of any danger. You cannot stay in that hut. It is a surprise you have not been found already or died from the cold! This is better for you. Welcome to your new family and wife." Thanasis laughed, but it was an uneasy sound.

Richard looked at the Greeks around the table and tried his best to smile. This group of strangers was now his family, and this was his home. For now. Roula, the girl he'd already met, her parents and the resistance fighter Thanasis, a man he didn't trust.

"How long will I live here?"

Thanasis shrugged. "We do not know. It is best to be comfortable. Your life might be here for a long time, or it could be shorter. We do not know."

The reality hit him. This would be his life for now until he could be rescued or the war ended. He never thought his escape would end up with him deeper in enemy territory, and it was a million miles away from Bristol.

Now he had to pretend to be a *husband* to a young Greek woman he barely knew to keep himself and Athena safe. The irony of the situation didn't escape him, and he wondered just how real his new life here in Greece would become. Looking over at Roula, she glanced up at him from under beautiful dark lashes and he realised his wayward thoughts might not end up being too far from the truth.

SIXTEEN

Bristol, England 1942

Lissy's feet throbbed as she alighted the bus to begin the short walk home. Tiredness seeped through her muscles and into her bones. What she was doing was so important, but the monotony of war was becoming tiresome. The repetitive folding of parachutes. Repetitive days doing the same thing over and over again until her body couldn't take anymore.

Two days earlier, she'd bumped into an old school friend, Eileen. Every day, Eileen waited for a special bus that drove a group of women to a secret location, where they would work for ten hours, before returning home.

"It's my duty to do this," Eileen said as she'd fallen into step with Lissy.

"I feel the same. I'm not supposed to say, but I'm at the old corset factory. It's monotonous, but I know it's for a good cause. Where are you? Where does the bus take you, Eileen?"

"I'd like to tell you, but we signed the Official Secrets Act, so not allowed to." Eileen grinned. "Maybe one day, when the war's over, I'll tell you. It's been an eye-opener. Got to run, my dear, the bus is here."

Eileen had waved at her fellow workmates and run over to join them. Lissy had pondered their short conversation. She'd heard rumours of the secret war work on the outskirts of Bristol where women worked 100 feet below ground in a disused stone quarry for the Bristol Aeroplane company. Lissy wondered if that was where Eileen disappeared to every day. She had shuddered, thankful she hadn't been given that job.

Lissy passed the bombed-out shell of someone's home as she turned into her street. Several local houses had been obliterated now, including the one destroyed by the bomb that had almost killed George Perkins.

George. If it wasn't for George, she didn't know what she'd do. He'd become a good friend and had supported her when she felt low. As she neared her house, she saw a dispatch rider knocking on her door and her blood ran cold. Breaking into a run, she was alongside him in seconds.

"Can I help you?"

"I have a telegram for Miss Alice Cook."

"Yes. That's me."

"I'm terribly sorry, miss." He handed her a telegram and left.

Lissy's hands trembled as she opened the front door, and she stumbled inside. In the front room she sank into the chair, turning the telegram over in her hands. She'd always known this was a possibility. Where there was war, there was bad news. Flying planes was risky, and Richard surviving the war was slim. Her hands continued to shake as she summoned the courage and read the telegram:

. . .

Miss A Cook, Bristol, BS5

Deeply regret to inform you that Flight Officer R Hobbs is missing from night air operations over Mediterranean. Letter follows pending further information. Please accept my most profound sympathy.

Missing? He wasn't dead! The elation was swiftly followed by confusion. If he was missing, what did it mean? Was it worse than him being dead? Had Nazis captured him? Was he stranded somewhere? Even worse, was he dead, never to be found, only presumed missing forever? The questions tumbled around her brain.

Why had the telegram been sent to her and not Richard's parents? Now *she* had the job of informing *them*. Why, she wondered, had he listed her as his next of kin and not them? They weren't married yet. She stuffed the telegram into her handbag. She needed to go and see them. It wasn't something that could wait.

An hour, and one slow bus later, Lissy had arrived and was sitting on the sofa in Mr and Mrs Hobbs's house.

"It's lovely to see you, Lissy. We've missed you." Mrs Hobbs poured three cups of tea, passing one to Lissy.

"I'm sorry. War work keeps me busy. I often work six or seven days a week, and I was moved to night shifts for a while, so I had no time to myself."

"Well, you're here now, my dear."

Mr Hobbs glanced at his wife as he spoke. "Why *are* you here, dear?"

Lissy opened her bag and passed the fateful telegram to him. "I'm so sorry. I've no idea why they sent it to me. You're his parents. It should've been sent to you, not me."

Ashen, Mrs Hobbs put down her teacup. "Is he…?" she asked as her husband read.

"He's missing in action," her husband replied quickly.

"Oh, thank goodness!"

"Yes, it's not as bad as it could've been."

Lissy looked at them both. "But he's missing. He could be anywhere. Isn't that worse?"

Mrs Hobbs leaned forward and took Lissy's hands in hers. "Missing is good Lissy; missing means there's still hope. It means he's hopefully still alive out there somewhere. You must stay positive. Richard, wherever he is, will be thinking of you and counting the days until he can come home. You must stay positive for him. He'll come back to us when he's able to."

"I know. It just seems, well, it's difficult to take, especially after losing my brother, Tom, too. It seems there's nothing but bad news. This war is going on forever with no end in sight."

"Everything will be fine. Come on, stiff upper lip." Mrs Hobbs patted Lissy's hand again. "Now, you'll stay for something to eat. We don't have much, but you're family, or as close as can be. Richard's proved that by making you his next of kin. It'll give us the opportunity to catch up. It's been too long. Please say you will?"

Lissy nodded, agreeing to stay for a short time, at least. She didn't want to go back home just yet and knew this was the Hobbs's way of some normality.

After tea at her future in-laws' home, Lissy caught a bus to the city centre and alighted. Crossing the road, she headed for the harbourside. As she walked the cobbled harbour

A NIGHT OF THUNDER

edge, the words *missing in action* came flooding back. What if Richard was lost and never came home? What if he *was* already dead? Everything would change.

Mrs Hobbs insisted Lissy must stay positive, that being hopeful was the only way to get them through this awful mess. Lissy wasn't hopeful, though. She was angry. Angry at this stupid war. Angry at the bombs that kept falling and devastating their city. Most of all, she was angry with Richard for leaving her to be a hero. His stupid bravado hadn't helped anyone.

Anger continued to swell inside her and tears weren't far behind. Sitting on an old iron mooring post, Lissy watched the still harbour water and allowed herself to cry. She cried for her parents, wishing they were here to hold her tight and take away the pain. She cried for her brother, a young life taken too soon. She cried for Richard because she missed him, but also because she was bloody mad at him. Finally, she cried for herself. The pitiful, lonely wretch that she was becoming. She was so lonely. She had no friends or family. There was no one for her to turn to when she needed it. And now she was waiting for a man who may never return.

"You shouldn't be here, miss. There could be an air raid at any time. Head home now," an air raid warden said, tapping her gently on the shoulder.

"Yes sir. Keep yourself safe tonight."

"You too, miss."

After a short journey on the local bus, she alighted and made the last part of the journey on foot. Turning into her street, she saw the lone silhouette of a policeman walking towards her. Her spirits lifted momentarily, and she walked towards him waving, but stopped when she realised it wasn't George.

"Is everything alright, miss?"

"Yes, my apologies, I thought you were Constable Perkins. He walks this way sometimes."

"Ah, sorry to disappoint you. He's patrolling the park tonight. Is there anything I can help you with?"

"No. It's okay, thank you."

"Well get home safely, young lady."

"I will. Thank you."

She watched the policeman saunter away. As he turned the corner into the next street, she crossed the road to walk down a parallel street, heading for the park. As she reached the entrance of the park, a deep reverberating sound of the air raid siren rang out. Followed by a large explosion nearby that rocked her on her feet.

"Damn you, you bastard Germans. You're not going to blow me to pieces in my town. Do you hear me!" she screamed at the sky, which was lighting up with searchlights and increasing allied gun fire. The sound of a falling bomb rocked the nearby streets. "You will not take me too!" She ran towards the nearest shelter. Turning a corner, she slammed into another police officer.

"You shouldn't be outside. Quickly, move along, this way!"

"George?"

"Lissy?"

"Was that a bomb?"

"Yes, we can't go to the nearest shelter, though. A bomb hit it."

"What do we do now, George?"

"Come with me. I have an idea." George grabbed her hand and pulled her along behind him as he ran. Lissy matched his step. They reached a set of brick railway arches and George squeezed past a pile of scrap metal at the entrance. Still holding her hand, he pulled her in under the arches.

"It's not the best shelter, but it's sturdy enough and better than being out in the street." Taking a small torch from his pocket, he turned it on, lighting up the dismal space. It was abandoned save for more scrap metal and the odd vermin scuttling into the dark recesses.

They were unlikely to survive a direct hit if a bomb fell on them, but it would protect them from anything that fell nearby. Grabbing two wooden packing cases, George turned them upside down, dusting them off and motioning for Lissy to sit. The sound of sirens, planes and whistling bombs continued, swirling about them in a cacophony of noise.

"Are you alright?" George asked.

Lissy nodded, "Thank you, George."

"I'm just glad I found you. If you had headed towards the falling bombs, you may not be alive now."

"I can't believe this is still happening. How long are these damn Germans going to attack us? This is our home, it's where families live. We've done nothing to them! Piece by piece, they're taking everything away from us." Lissy burst into tears, and George scooted the packing case closer to her and gently rested his hand on her arm.

"What's happened? I can tell something's upset you."

"Richard's missing. They sent a telegram today. He's not dead. At least, I don't think he is. The telegram said he's 'missing in action over the Mediterranean, and a letter follows pending further information'. I don't know what that means. It's confusing." She wiped her puffy eyes with a pink embroidered handkerchief. "Oh George. Missing is much worse than dead. Dead is final. We know the answer, and even if it's hurtful, there's an opportunity to come to terms with it, to move on. But missing? He could be anywhere! He could be a prisoner somewhere. He could be lying at the bottom of the ocean being eaten by fish never to be seen by anyone again!" The hysteria rose, and Lissy tried to calm herself, but she struggled. "There are so many possibilities, George. His parents said there's hope, but what hope? There's nothing to cling to."

Lissy leaned her head on George's shoulder and they fell silent. Night had fallen and dark shadows were creeping towards them. The noise of the air raid still continued around them.

"What can I do to make it better, Lissy?" The question was barely a whisper.

"There's nothing anyone can do. It is one of those terrible things war throws at us. Either we must accept it and live with it, or fall to pieces." Lissy sat up and picked at the embroidery on the handkerchief that lay in her lap.

A mechanical noise overhead, accompanied by a growing whining, interrupted their conversation. The ground shook as the bomb hit, covering them in dust and tiny pieces of mortar. Instinctively, George wrapped his arms around Lissy to shield her as they were knocked to the ground.

With George's arms around her, Lissy's heart thudded loudly in her chest. Instinctively, she wanted to sit up and push George away, but she was scared. She wanted to feel safe and secure. She wanted to feel his arms around her. She gave in and leaned her head on his chest, the sound of her own heartbeat melding with his softer one. It was the comfort and protection she needed.

"I wish life was different," George whispered.

"I think we all wish that, George. I wish the war had never come. It's changed everything."

"I don't mean the war." He sat up, brushed his uniform down and got to his feet. He held out his hand to help her up. She took it, and once on her feet, she brushed the dirt from her clothes and sat on the packing crate.

"What do you mean?"

"It doesn't matter."

"It must've mattered if you said it."

"It was nothing. We were talking about you before the bomb hit."

"I'm fine. I have my war work. I'll be okay."

"That's the brave war worker, Lissy Cook, talking. What does the real Lissy think? The Lissy who loves with all her heart and soul but is unable to because she's always alone. The lonely Lissy who's lost her family and just wants a normal life, instead of one where she works every hour of the day to forget about everything. The Lissy who's always exhausted because she fills her life helping others so she doesn't have to think about herself. The Lissy who always puts everyone else first, not considering what she wants or needs? What does the real Lissy want?"

Shocked at the bluntness of his words, she stared at him. "I..."

"Now is the time for honesty, Lissy. It's just you and me. I think it's time to tell the truth."

Lissy stood. The frank words had hit home, but she didn't know how to respond. She began to walk away from him, her mind whirling. She then stopped and turned around.

"You want the truth, George?"

"Yes, if you're brave enough to speak it."

"Fine. Then I will! I may be lonely, I may be a workaholic, but many of us are because of this bloody war. I hate it. It's taken everyone I ever loved from me. I've no life because of the damn war, and the only thing I really want right now, I can't have! And the fact that I want it scares me. It makes me more scared than I've ever been in my life!"

"And what is it you want?"

They stood staring at each other, neither daring to speak. "I can't..." she whispered.

"You can, Lissy."

"It will change everything."

"I know. But have things not already changed?"

"I can't, George." She turned and sat back down again.

George walked to the open arches and looked out into the dark street. The sirens still wailed, but no bombs were falling, and the sound of planes was retreating. "I think we will be able to go soon. We just have to wait for the sirens to stop."

Lissy sat quietly in the darkness, not speaking. He returned and sat next to her on the other packing crate. He was uncomfortable and wouldn't look her in the eye. The silence enveloped them with only the rustling of vermin and wailing of sirens to accompany them. Eventually he spoke.

"You're a brave and inspiring woman, Lissy. You saved my life and have thrown yourself into the war effort. You carry on despite everything life has thrown at you. I don't know how you do it, but I do know I admire it." He paused and then looked at her. "I admire you. Maybe I shouldn't have said anything, but I can't deny my feelings. I know you're promised to someone else, and I'm just a boring policeman, with little to offer, but I can't stop the growing feelings I have for you."

Lissy turned to look at him, his face lit by the eerie yellow glow of torchlight. Kind, brave George. The man who looked after her when she learned her brother had died. If she hadn't ever met Richard, she knew that someone

A NIGHT OF THUNDER

like George would be the perfect man for her. But she was promised to Richard, even if he was missing.

"I apologise, Lissy. I've upset you."

"No. You haven't upset me, you never could. Oh George. If things were different, if I hadn't met Richard or got engaged to him, I'd happily consider everything you're saying, but..."

"But..."

"I don't even know if Richard is still alive. In my heart, I think he is, and until I hear different I just can't... I don't want to lose your friendship, though. You've been so kind to me. You saved my life tonight. You're important to me."

"I understand." George leaned forward and gently kissed her cheek. She placed her hand on his and leaned her head on his shoulder. "You're the only friend I have, George. I don't want to lose you. Can we still be friends?"

"We'll always be friends, Lissy. You're important to me, and if friendship's all I can have, then friendship I'll take."

"You're too nice for your own good, you know that, don't you?" Lissy smiled.

"You mean I'm a stupid love-struck doormat."

"No! I'd never call you that, and please don't talk about yourself that way. You're kind and thoughtful, and in some respects braver than any RAF pilot."

George simply nodded.

"Listen!" Lissy said.

"What? I don't hear anything."

"Exactly! The sirens have stopped!"

"Well in that case, Miss Cook, let me walk you home." He held out his arm for her and she linked hers through it.

"It would be my pleasure, Constable Perkins."

They left the safety of the railway arches, stepped out into the dark night and walked back towards her house. The night air was filled with the acrid smell of smoke and an orange glow was visible in nearby streets. As they turned into her street, Lissy was relieved to see her home was still standing. George bade her goodnight in the most gentlemanly way and she closed the front door making her way up to bed.

Laying back, she stared up at the darkened ceiling and closed her eyes, but sleep eluded her. Her mind replayed the conversation with George, and she found herself becoming more confused, as the realisation of her own burgeoning feelings for George Perkins finally hit home.

SEVENTEEN

Zakynthos, Greece, 1944

It had been a long, hard war and life on Zakynthos had become unbearable. As well as Greeks turning against their own and siding with the Nazis, many islanders had lost friends and family from hunger or at the hands of the enemy.

On the 12th September, things changed. Angelos tore into the house in a wave of excitement. He lifted Sophia high in the air, spinning her around and she giggled, enjoying her father's game.

"We are free again *koukla*! The war is over! We will have our island back again! *Mana*, come!" He placed Sophia on his hip and walked over to a shocked Pigi. He took hold of his mother's hand, and pulling her mother along with him, they ventured out into the bright sunshine-bathed streets of Exo Hora, which were already filled with people. Angelos hadn't seen this many people out on Zakynthos streets since before the war had begun. Every person in the village and surrounding areas had gathered to trade information, not caring who saw them.

Niko was sitting in a cart grinning. "The British are here! We are saved!" he shouted loudly. A loud cheer went up, and villagers shook hands and patted each other on the back.

"What?!" Pigi looked around her at the chaos. "What do you mean? What is happening?"

"Into the cart, mother. We are going for a ride!" Angelos and Niko sat and talked as they traversed the streets, whilst Pigi bounced Sophia on her lap. Filled with joyful excitement, they cut across country lanes, eventually finding themselves on the coast by Planos, where they took the road up to the high point of Bochali. They weren't the only islanders who had ventured out, and they joined the throng looking down over Zakynthos Town, watching as British boats sailed towards the island. The news was true! The allies were coming!

"Oh Angelos! My son! We are saved!"

"Yes *Mana*. We are saved. The war is over and we will be free again."

As the crowds grew, they all stared in awe. News of the gathering crowds had reached the Nazis, and they arrived, desperately trying to move everyone on. Brave locals refused to obey them. The enemy's time was at an end. They were no longer their captors; there was nothing to be afraid of.

Nazis still tried to order the Greeks and hit out with their weapons, but the crowds stood together and the Nazis were pushed back and shouted down. Knowing there was a bigger fight ahead, the enemy soldiers retreated, leaving the happy Zakynthians on the headland, heading back down into the town to regroup.

Angelos, Niko and his family watched as the allies landed in Zakynthos harbour and the air was filled with cheers and cries of relief. He knew it would take a while for things to get back to normal. He knew the Nazis wouldn't give in so easily and that arguments and negotiations lay ahead, but it was a special day for all of them. One Zakynthians would never forget.

"I wish Elena was here for this, *Mana*. She would have been so happy."

"I know, my son. She would. We finally have our beautiful island back and for that, we must be thankful. Elena's spirit remains here. Wherever you go, she is here. She walks among the olive groves. She is the waves that wash along the shore and the wind that whispers through the mountains. She watches over us during the worst of storms when there is a night of thunder. She is still in your heart, Angelos, and if Elena is in your heart, she is always with you, wherever you are, whatever you do."

"Thank you, *Mana*."

The crowd dispersed and Niko took them back to Exo Hora. As they arrived, the village was alive with sounds of celebration they hadn't heard in a long time. Neighbours and friends greeted each other with hugs and drank *Ouzo*, *Tsipouro* or *Zakynthian wine* that had been carefully hidden away for years.

Music played and there was dancing in the street. Pigi and Angelos watched the joyful sight as they joined the throng. It was good to see people happy again. It had been so long since they'd been able to live their lives this freely, and they revelled in the moment, wishing for it to last forever. The trio joined the villagers, grabbing a bottle of wine and glasses, sitting on a low stone wall.

"Father will be angry tonight," Niko said. "He is about to find his allies gone, and he will be alone on the island with very few friends. He made poor choices during the war. I hate carrying his name; it is an embarrassment!"

"Your father will be okay, Niko. Men like him always find the luck. You may have his name, but you are not him, you never will be. Everyone knows it. You are a good boy, Niko," Pigi said, pouring him a drink.

"This time I am not so sure. This time I think his luck may have run out. I think the trouble he has avoided for so long will finally catch him up."

"Time will tell, Niko. Time will tell."

"And what of you, Angelos? Will you restart the olive business now? Now the Nazis have lost the war, you can take back your family home. It is rightfully yours," Niko said.

Angelos looked at his friend. Of course! He'd forgotten all about the house and business. Nazis had lived in his old family home for so long he no longer thought of it as his. If the war was over, however, maybe he could reclaim what was rightfully his. He could give his mother a proper place to live. He could grow something for Sophia that could be passed down to her and her family in the future. The thought cheered him greatly. Angelos reached over and grabbed the half-empty bottle of Zakynthian wine and filled their glasses. Putting the bottle back on the stone wall, he lifted his glass.

"To the end of war. To freedom!" he shouted.

"To the end of war. To freedom!" Everyone around him echoed.

"To you, Elena. You may no longer be here, but we did it. We are finally free."

A NIGHT OF THUNDER

"You cannot do this to me! I am one of the island's most respected and well-known Greek families! We are in the Libro D'Oro!" Stelios Makris screamed as he was dragged from his home into the streets of Zakynthos Town by the resistance.

"You are a fascist pig, Makris. You have been responsible for the deaths of good people and the shame this island has carried all these years. Say goodbye to your son."

Niko Makris stepped forward and spat at his father's feet. "He is no father of mine. I do not know who this man is. Take him away." Niko turned his back on his father and heard his screams and yells as he was dragged along the street by Greek resistance.

Niko knew the war was over and that people would be punished for their wrongdoings, but he no longer cared. There were too many on the island who had treated others worse than dogs in the street, and they deserved what they got. His father was still screaming for help when the cart passed him heading inland. He'd no idea what his father's fate would be, neither did he care. Someone else would mete out the punishment, and it was better if Niko's hands were clean. It was time to put the war behind him, embrace peace and begin a new life.

∽

A day after the celebrations, Angelos awoke with a sore head, but he felt lighter in heart than he had for a long time. War wouldn't end overnight; there was still a German army presence on the island, and it would take time for Zakynthian life to return to normal.

They were still subjected to rules and curfews, but now they could see the light at the end of the tunnel. They could see full freedom in sight. The news from the rest of the world was that the war was almost over, and that soon, Europe would be at peace once more.

How long it would take everyone to rebuild their lives and towns, however, was a different matter. The war had ruined millions of lives, and the news of what had happened in some parts of Europe was too much to bear. The biggest news on Zakynthos was the death of Stelios Makris. He had been taken from his home by the Greek resistance and their punishment had been harsh and swift. The man's body now lay at the bottom of the cliffs at Keri with a bullet in the back of his head.

Angelos felt no emotion; the man deserved his fate. One day he would have to explain it to Sophia, and it was a day he dreaded. For now, though, it felt like good justice for Elena. And he was looking forward to life without war, even if that life would be devoid of some important people.

EIGHTEEN

Mainland Greece, 1944

Richard was awoken by a loud clatter of dishes. Rolling over in bed, he rubbed his eyes, momentarily unsure where he was. The familiarity of the cold mountainside hut was gone, replaced by the comfort of a house. The rough, thick, fur bedclothes he'd become used to had been replaced by cotton sheets and woollen blankets. An icon of a Greek saint hung on the wall and curtains covered the windows.

As his brain recovered the pieces of the resistance plan, he still wasn't entirely sure it had been the right thing to do. Thanasis had taken control, though, and Richard and Athena had been moved into Manos and Vivi's home. Thanasis insisted it would make them a family. It would make anyone who stumbled across them to be less likely to think of Richard as an outsider. Richard still had reservations. He didn't want the family to be at risk. He knew the penalty would be severe if the plan was uncovered.

The previous night, the Greek couple had fed him and allowed him to bathe in an old tub in front of a welcoming warm fireplace; the hot, soapy water had made him feel better. Whilst he enjoyed the bath, removing months of grime from his skin, Vivi and Roula had fed, washed and reclothed Athena.

Vivi had then stood over him as he hid his modesty. She washed his hair through, cutting matted chunks out and treating his remaining hair with olive oil for the lice that had plagued him.

"You and the child will need to do it again in two days. The oil will kill the lice quickly, but it is better to do it twice to be sure," Vivi said as she'd gathered his clothes and thrown them out the window to burn them on the fire, before finding fresh clothes for them both.

Now he'd awoken, clean, lice free and grateful to be in a new bed that was his own. The only thing they'd kept from their previous life in the hut was Elena's letter and locket, and Athena's bear, which had also been given a good bath. Richard's new bed was warm and comfortable. It was much safer than the wooden shack, too. It also meant Athena had a real home.

The hut had been no place for a young child. The world was still at war, though, and the danger still present. He was a long way from home, and he knew Athena was his responsibility. His life had become blurred, and he was no closer to getting back home to Lissy.

Anger simmered in Richard as he lay in bed and thought of his fiancée, the woman he'd loved and foolishly left behind. He'd been a stubborn man, full of bravado, desperate to fight for his country. There were so many men like him, and none of them had spared a thought for those they'd left at home. Their parents, siblings and other loved ones were all waiting for them. Some with little to no news. Some of those waiting at home had already lost their brave

A NIGHT OF THUNDER

husbands, fiancés and sons and would never spend another day with them, all wiped out for protecting their freedom.

Throwing back the bed covers, Richard pulled on his clothes. Looking in the small mirror, he didn't recognise the man staring back at him. His face was thin and pallid in colour, partly covered by a full, scruffy beard. His hair, long and unruly, now reached his shoulders. It wasn't the Richard he knew. Thanasis was right, though, it made him look more Greek and less English. He'd blend in well.

Downstairs in the kitchen, the quaint family scene stopped Richard short. Manos and Vivi sat at the large wooden table eating. Athena was on Roula's lap, and both were giggling. It was a happy family scene. Richard leaned against the door-jamb and watched, feeling like a stranger. It wasn't far from the truth, but this would change. Whether he liked it or not, they were his family, for now, even if it was for the short term.

Joining them, Richard nodded morning greetings to everyone. Heading to the back door, he opened it and pulled on a pair of boots, heading out into the weak morning sunshine. He took in the steep mountainside that ran upwards from the house and the land that surrounded it. It was a typical farm. Stone walls encircled the house, a gate leading to outbuildings was open, and he walked towards them, surveying this new place called *home*.

Farm equipment, hoes, rakes and scythes lay scattered about. A wooden cart and other detritus had been stowed in an open-ended barn. On the other side of the gate were smaller outbuildings, including a log store. The other was closed. Intrigued, he pulled open the door. Like the first barn, it was filled with more farming equipment. In the corner was a small stack of grain. He closed the door behind him and stood staring back up at the mountain. Breathing deeply, he took in the clear fresh air.

Spying an axe and a pile of logs, he walked over and lifted the long-handled blade. Placing a log on the old stump, he swung the axe over his head, bringing it down hard to connect with the log. With a crack, the log split and the pieces fell to the floor. Bending down, Richard threw them to one side before placing another log on the stump and repeating. The pile of split logs grew, and with every wood-cracking swing, the anger and frustration that had swirled in him dissipated. He continued to work, stopping every now and then to take the cut logs into the barn to stack them. As he lifted the axe to continue, Manos appeared next to him and handed Richard a cup of coffee.

"You are angry?"

"I was. Not anymore." Richard put the axe down to drink his coffee.

Manos motioned for them to sit on an old tree trunk that was waiting to be cut. "We know little about you, Richard. We know you are kind and honest, we see that in you. But we do not know why the Englishman found his way to the Greek mountains in wartime, and why you are now part of our family. The child is a puzzle too."

Richard sipped the coffee. It was strong, hot and welcome after the energy he'd used up. He spoke to Manos of his thwarted escape from Zakynthos and journey across the mainland.

"So, you are a man far from home and lost."

"Yes. I am grateful to you and your family, Manos, but I long to go home. My life and family are there, not here."

"And the child?"

"Athena?"

"Yes. She is not your child. Why do you have her?"

A NIGHT OF THUNDER

"It is complicated. I made a promise."

"You should have left her in Peloponnesus. Why keep her? Why bring her here? Many would say you are foolish and weak."

"Do *you* think me foolish and weak, Manos?"

"Maybe. Many men are. I do not know your reasons for your decision. Maybe if you tell me, I will understand."

"It is a long story, Manos."

"You think you will bore me? Greeks invented long stories. Tell me."

"I was a pilot. My plane was hit by Luftwaffe gunfire and I crash-landed on Zakynthos. There was a big dogfight in the sky; we were winning, but my plane was hit. I thought I could make it back to Malta, but my plane failed. I was too low to land safely. I had to parachute out or crash and die. I saw land and steered towards it, but the landing was wrong. I broke my leg. I had no idea where I was and I blacked out with pain. When I awoke, I was in a mountain cave being looked after by resistance." Richard took another sip of coffee.

"The woman who rescued me was called Elena. She and another man from the resistance looked after me. They got me well again, helped fix my leg. They organised an escape plan. I was supposed to go to Malta. But it went wrong. As I was escaping, Nazis arrived on the beach. Elena had been in love with an Italian officer. At least, I think they were in love. I know she trusted the Italian enough to think the two of them and her daughter, Athena, would escape Zakynthos in the same boat as me. It did not work out. She was betrayed on the beach." Richard stood and paced for a moment before turning to sit back down again.

"I think the Italian betrayed her, Manos. It all happened

so quickly. Athena was put in the boat with me. Elena told me I must look after the child and protect her. The boat left the beach; we were already at sea. Elena made sure we escaped before turning back to the beach. I sat there holding Athena, watching the Zakynthos coastline disappear into the darkness of the night, and I found myself adrift in the ocean with a fisherman and a child who was not mine. How could I possibly abandon Athena after that? All I can think about is how to get her back to her family. Yes, I could have left her in Peloponnesus, but they might have treated her cruelly, maybe even abandoned her. They could have put her on a boat back to Zakynthos and a mine could have killed her. Athena could have been left somewhere to die. She is so young, Manos. These circumstances and this war are not her fault. She is a child, and she never asked for this. No, she must stay with me. All this has run around my head every day and there is never a right answer. In the end I did what I thought was the right thing at the time. I promised her mother. I must keep that promise, even if it sounds strange to other people."

"You are a brave man who has been through a lot. This war has given us all a life we never asked for," Manos said. "You say you will look after Athena?"

"I will. I will look after her until the war is over and I can return her to her family on Zakynthos, where she rightfully belongs."

"It is an honourable thing you choose to do. But you will find it is an impossible task."

"The war will end, Manos."

"Yes, it will. And we will win. We must. But you might find there is no family to return Athena to. You might find a family who does not want her. Leaving her to die or be abandoned may have, in the end, been the best thing for her. Sometimes our lives do not follow the plan we want. Sometimes our destiny is already written; sometimes that destiny is harsh or sad, like her mother's. You do realise the mother is probably in a concentration camp or dead? Athena's destiny may have been to have a short life. Her destiny may have been not to live. Sometimes we can only do what life at the time allows us."

Manos stood, patted Richard on the shoulder and returned to the house. Richard watched Manos retreat. The Greek had been brutally honest. There was no way he could abandon Athena, though. He wasn't the sort of person to just leave her to fate. There was no way he'd have risked leaving the child to die. The haunted look in Elena's eyes had spurred him on. He had to do the best he could for the child. Athena deserved to live. Destiny could always be changed, and if Richard was the one to do it, then he damn well would.

~

Richard settled into his new life in the Greek mountains with Manos and his family, and Athena thrived. Her laughter rang through the small house as she enjoyed the simplest of things. Roula seemed to settle into the role of older, surrogate sister. Whatever Roula did, Athena copied her with great delight. Despite her tragic past, Athena now had a family of her own, and it was as though she and Richard had always lived with the family.

Greek mountain life was hard, an endless round of tending the scant animals Manos owned, chopping wood, looking after the land and mending stone walls. It became Richard's daily existence. It was essential hard work that occupied his body and mind. In return, he had a roof over his head, a bed to sleep in and food on the table. At the end of each day, he was exhausted and occasionally his leg, that had never quite set comfortably, pained him.

Their life was far removed from the ongoing war. Occasionally passing resistance knocked on the door late at night by the cover of darkness to give them news or much-needed items, but otherwise they were left alone, and the enemy stayed away. Only the occasional warplane overhead and distant sounds of munitions reminded them of the wider implications for their country.

Thanasis was still the thorn in Richard's side. The Greek might be head of the resistance, but Richard didn't like nor trust him. There was also something about the man that made Richard wary, and he was glad he'd heeded Roula's warning. He'd only had one conversation with Thanasis since moving to the house, and he wanted to keep it that way.

Thanasis had unexpectedly arrived at the house several weeks ago, filled with anger about the enemy who still held its grip on Greece. Thanasis had shared personal information with Richard about the recent loss of his wife and child whilst defending their home against the Nazis. Thanasis told Richard he'd been out fighting with the resistance. He'd returned home in the dead of night to find the shot and bloodied corpses of his family dumped in the street. His fellow partisans had helped him bury them as Thanasis had wept and raged for their loss.

Thanasis had told Richard he had nothing left in life except to fight against those who had taken everything from him. No one should've faced what Thanasis had, but his grief had turned to hatred and anger, which was a dangerous mix. Richard remembered what Thanasis had said about taking on Roula if he hadn't been married and the words sent a chill through him. Richard would be extremely careful around the Greek in future. The vein of hurt and fury that ran through men like Thanasis was dangerous to everyone who encountered him.

The loud crowing of a cockerel awoke Richard that morning. It was the same every morning. He turned over in bed and lay on his back, listening to the busy sounds coming from the house below. As the cockerel crowed again, he heard Athena giggle and Roula's voice as they ran out the back door. Every morning they went out together to check for eggs. They would hunt for them, find them and bring them back for breakfast.

Richard swung his legs over the edge of the bed, had a cursory wash and pulled on his clothes and boots. It would be another day of hard work on the land, eating what food they had and looking out for Athena. His life in Greece was simple and comfortable, despite the hardships. He wondered for a brief moment where Lissy was and what she was doing right now. It had been a while since he had thought about her and wondered why that was.

He was thousands of miles away from where he was meant to be, but it didn't feel wrong. It felt right, as if he was meant to be here. As each day passed, he felt more at home in the Greek mountains with this loving family who had taken him under his wing and treated him as one of their own. It was unexpected.

∼

Weaving their way along the path, Roula and Athena ran to the chicken coop. It was one of her favourite times of day. She loved coming out into the fresh air with the young child to search for eggs. She laughed as Athena carefully picked up the eggs one by one, counting them as she placed them in the basket. Roula sat on the low wall, watching as Athena chattered away to the poultry, stroking them when she got close enough.

Roula glanced up at the house. Her life was different with Richard and Athena here. Before their arrival, life on the mountain had been incredibly boring; she'd never had a loving relationship with her parents and there were no siblings to spend time with. Much of her childhood had been spent on her own. The mountain and its enticing wilderness and nature had become her friend.

The village was almost deserted now; young men had left to fight against the enemy or join the resistance. Girls of her age had married and moved to their husband's homes and all that remained was an enclave of older couples and frail grandparents. Roula had been left behind and felt trapped. There had been no one to fill the monotonous hours. She had been confined in a place the rest of the world had turned their backs on.

Then Richard and Athena had arrived, and they had changed her life. She had a purpose. He was a man she wanted to talk to and learn from. A man she dreamed about when she was alone in bed at night. A man she wanted to hold tightly and never let go.

Her love for Athena grew with every passing day. The young child was a whirlwind that made her smile. Roula hadn't had a brother or sister to share her life with. But now Roula realised how much she'd missed out on.

Athena brought joy to Roula's life every day through the simplest of things. They may still be living in the mountains, but now, Roula had two people to share her life with. People she could talk to, learn from and have fun with. She was grateful Richard and Athena had arrived.

Richard appeared at the back door and waved before disappearing back inside the house. Waving back, Roula's heart soared. There was one problem, though. Like every Greek girl, her life was already planned. She was promised to a Greek boy from the village. He was away fighting, and no one knew if he was alive or dead. Even if the boy was still alive, Roula no longer wanted him. Richard, the handsome Englishman, stirred a fire within her she couldn't contain, and it was Richard she wanted with all her heart.

Roula felt Athena's hand patting her leg. She stood and picked up the basket before taking hold of Athena's hand. They walked the short distance back to the house. In the kitchen, her father and Richard were sitting, talking. Her mother was busy at the sink.

"The chickens have been kind to us! We will eat a good breakfast today." With Roula's help, Athena lifted the basket onto the table, and Athena ran to Richard. He lifted her up and sat her on his lap. It was a perfect family scene that would fool many if they ever stumbled upon the farmhouse.

NINETEEN

Bristol, England, 1942

Constable George Perkins patrolled the park for the seventh time that day. It wasn't somewhere he normally patrolled, but black-market deals in the city were prevalent and conducted away from prying eyes in quiet parks, canals and riversides.

Hearing footsteps behind him, he turned and was pleasantly surprised to see Lissy running towards him. As she neared, he saw her distress.

"Lissy? Is everything okay?"

"George? What are you doing in the park? This isn't your beat."

"It's war. Everything is different. I just do as I'm told. The park is nice to walk around, though; it makes a change to bombed out streets."

"It's beautiful here." Lissy sat on a nearby bench and George joined her.

"How are you, Lissy?"

"I'm fine. Exhausted, but fine. It's been endless months

of war work. Life is so monotonous. Rationed food. Long, hard working hours. Sewing up old clothes to make them last. Mending broken items because it's almost impossible to buy new. Then there's the fear of air raids, losing my home or my life, never knowing if I'll survive. Bristol changes every day. It'll be a completely different city when the war ends; some of the city's oldest and most beautiful buildings have gone. Homes lost. Gaping holes of rubble in the streets, the owners dead, injured or homeless. Shops too, their glass fronts shattered and contents ruined. Not even our churches have escaped! St Peter's Church on Castle Green and Temple Church have been attacked and are now burned-out shells, their roofs and windows gone. Why? I don't understand any of it. Why George?"

Lissy leaned her head on George's shoulder and they fell silent. The dark shadows of night were creeping towards them, encasing them in a bubble of twilight. George wanted to comfort Lissy; her need seemed to be greater than anything else, but he was supposed to be working.

"How can I help..." he whispered.

Lissy sat up. "I don't know. Thank you for listening, though."

George leaned in, slowly closing the gap between them. "Are you sure there's nothing I can do?"

"I... I can't..." she whispered.

"You can, Lissy." He reached out and gently took hold of her hand, and she clung to him.

"It will change everything."

"I know. But haven't things already changed?"

He pulled her to him and wrapped his arms around her arms, and she didn't resist. "Tell me," he persisted.

"I want you, George. I shouldn't. I mustn't. And yet I do. I want you very much."

Sliding his arm up her back he ran his fingers through her hair and pulled her lips in to meet his. He felt her eagerness to be loved as she willingly responded. Their kiss deepened, and only broke apart when a rustling in a nearby tree disturbed them.

∼

Lissy soothed her aching muscles inside the old tin bath in front of the fireplace. The heat enveloped her body, relaxing every punished sinew, as she thought about recent events. Lissy and George's first kiss had been a month ago, and they'd secretly met up and kissed several times since. Lissy had fallen for George in a big way, and whilst she still thought about Richard and kept his photograph on her mantelpiece, the reality was he was missing and may never come home again. She was fed up of being alone, and lonely.

George was kind. He was here, right now, and she readily accepted his attention. The reality of the situation hit her one day whilst at work, drinking a glass of water during a break. She was in love with two very different men. It was a messy situation which was likely to end badly for all of them.

Lissy hated keeping secrets, but keep it she must. The shame and guilt had already begun to wash over her, but she had put herself in this situation and no one else. Anger and frustration occasionally bubbled up, too. If it wasn't for the war, Richard would never have left her. He would be by her side, and she wouldn't have met George. If it wasn't for the war, her heart wouldn't have been split between two men.

As the water cooled, Lissy got out of the tin bath. As she was drying herself, she was disturbed by a knock at the front door. Pulling on her dressing gown, she grabbed the lit candle and padded along the hallway.

"Good evening, miss." George grinned as he quietly slipped inside the house, closing the door behind him. "Have I interrupted you?"

"I was just bathing." She clasped the edge of her dressing gown tightly together, conscious of her nakedness underneath. "I wasn't expecting you."

"I've just finished my shift and was passing. The street was dark; I thought I'd surprise you."

"You have. I should change." Lissy went to pass him, but he caught her arm.

"Don't change on my account," he whispered.

His whisper sent a shiver through her, and she stopped. George lifted the candle and placed it on the hallway shelf and pulled her to him, and he kissed her deeply. His fingers found the opening of her dressing gown and parted it. Gently he caressed her naked breast with the back of his hand.

"Do you want me to stop, Lissy?"

No. She wanted more, but knew there would be no going back. Running her fingers through his hair, she kissed him. Pushing back from him, she took his hand. "I don't want you to stop. But not here."

Lissy lifted the candle and pulled him along, up the stairs and into her bedroom. The blackout drapes were up, and the yellow glow from the candle cast eerie shadows throughout the room. She placed it on the bedside table and turned back to George. He stepped up to her and undid her dressing gown belt, pushing the garment from her shoulders to the floor.

Lissy stood naked in front of him and allowed him to kiss her trembling skin as she unbuttoned his tunic. "It's unfair, you're wearing more clothes than me." She laughed nervously. Seeing the picture of Richard on the mantelpiece, a wave of guilt washed through her. Quickly, she pushed back from George, walked over and turned the photo over leaving it face down.

George watched her as he removed the remainder of his clothes with haste and then pulled her back to him and down onto the bed, their naked skin touching.

"We don't have to do this if you don't want to."

"I want to, George."

Slowly, they began to explore each other's bodies, enjoying the comforting closeness of each other. When they could stand it no longer, they became one. So connected were they that neither cared about the air raid siren that sounded or the rumbling of aircraft overhead. If they were to die tonight in a bombing raid, then both would rather die happy wrapped in each other's arms than in an air raid shelter or out on the street.

∼

The bed next to Lissy was empty. She'd no idea what time George left, but knew it would have been under the cover of darkness to avoid unneighbourly suspicion. Slipping from bed, she walked to the mantelpiece and lifted the photo of Richard.

"I'm sorry, Richard. I know I have betrayed you, but it's your fault too!" Waves of guilt washed through her and sobbing wracked her body as she held the photo to her chest. Once she'd ceased crying, Lissy washed, changed her clothes and padded downstairs to the kitchen. As she lit the stove to boil water for tea, she spied a note on the table.

My dearest Lissy,

I hope waking alone didn't upset you. I hated leaving without saying goodbye. Leaving your house in broad daylight would've caused trouble for both of us. Everyone knows neighbours in this street are prone to gossip, and you're not someone I would want to see them gossip about. As much as I love you, and I truly do love you Lissy, I don't want to be the person who ruins your reputation; you've been through enough already. I want to be the person who wakes up with you every day, but if this is all I can have for now then I will take it.

If we're ever to be what I hope we'll one day become, I want to do it the right way. I love you too much.

I'll see you soon.
My love to you always.
Your George.

He loved her. Her heart momentarily flew. The proud policeman, the man who had protected her and been in her life for nearly two years now, loved her. The kettle boiled with a loud whistle. She lifted it and poured the water onto the meagre tea leaves in the teapot. Opening the cupboard, she ate a lean breakfast whilst the tea brewed.

A knock at the front door disturbed her as she was pouring her tea, and she went to open the door.

"You're alright then." It was Mrs Hubert, a neighbour from two doors down. The nosiest neighbour on the street, who as usual was trying to peer into the house.

"Can I help you with something, Mrs Hubert?"

"You wasn't at the shelter. We was worried."

"No. I wasn't. I sheltered somewhere else."

"Is that right? You see, old Elsie says you was home. She ain't never wrong about these things."

"Elsie was wrong. I was out. I had to work yesterday. I sheltered on the way home. Now if you don't mind, I must get ready for work. Some of us have important war work to do to support our brave servicemen! We can't all stand around gossiping all day!"

Lissy slammed the door in the face of the shocked woman before returning to the kitchen. She shouldn't have lost her temper, but the old women and their idle talk were unbelievable. Locals couldn't walk down the road and drop so much as a farthing without news spreading that you had been mugged for a shilling.

Sitting back at the kitchen table, Lissy sipped her weak tea and read George's note again. He loved her, but he shouldn't. Lissy shouldn't love him either as she was promised to someone else, but she knew she loved the policeman too. They'd spent a wonderful evening together and everything had felt right. But it shouldn't have. What they'd done was wrong; she'd betrayed Richard, and she was already feeling the guilt.

Lissy lifted the box of matches and struck one, watching it catch and brighten. Touching the flame to the corner of George's note, she watched as it caught and travelled along the paper, eating up the words, deleting them forever. She blew the match out and dropped it into the ashtray as the edges of paper turned to blackened, crumbling dust. The remains of the note joined the spent match, and she watched as the last of the note curled and burned itself out.

A NIGHT OF THUNDER

All that was left was a small blackened reminder of what she'd found on the table that morning.

Lissy took the ashtray to the front room and threw the remains into the fireplace. The note was gone, but the words would remain etched on her heart forever, a reminder of the greatest mistake she'd made. Only she and George would ever know about it.

Lissy looked at the photo of Richard. What happened last night would never happen again. Her affair with George was short-lived and over. She wouldn't see the policeman again.

Lissy's promise over George wavered, however, and her love for him was too strong. Sitting on a bench in the park in the depths of night, she held George's hand. Lissy broke the strained silence. "Are you okay? You're very quiet tonight."

"I've seen so much during this war, Lissy. A bomb nearly killed me, but I was lucky and survived. So many others haven't been so lucky. It was such a lovely morning when I started my beat. The sky above me was clear and blue. I thought about the seaside. I thought of sitting on a beach with you, with the sea lapping at our feet as we ate ice cream. It was a lovely thought. Then it all changed. I heard a noise as I reached Broadweir. It was the sound that scares us all; a plane. I thought there was no way it could be the enemy. How could they? In broad daylight? They would never attack us then. How wrong I was, Lissy." He shook his head for a moment before continuing.

"It was a solitary plane, Lissy, but I never knew one plane could do so much damage. There were three double-decker buses waiting at their stops; people were just getting on board. All those people, off to work, going to see family or friends. Who knows, but each one of them was out living their life with a purpose. As the plane passed overhead, we heard it, the bomb... it was too late to do anything. There had been no sirens to warn anyone. The bomb hit. There was no warning, and the bomb fell and killed so many. I can still see it all, Lissy. The buses a mass of tangled metal full of fire, the road damaged by shrapnel, nearby buildings damaged from the blast. And the people. Oh Lissy, the people..." George buried his head in his hands and sobbed. Lissy put her arms around him and held him tightly, allowing him to cry. Eventually, he lifted his head and looked at her.

"A minute earlier and I would've been there, Lissy, underneath that bomb. A minute earlier and I would've died. That's twice I've survived now. Those other people didn't, though. There was no warning, and the fires were awful, burning too hot. We couldn't save them. We had to wait for the fire engines and ambulances. All we could do was help those in the road and on the pavement to check they were alright, to see who was still alive. So many died, Lissy. So many, and there was nothing I could do to save them. Nothing."

"You did everything you could, George. You helped the only way you could. You're incredibly brave, and you've been a great support to so many people in this city. Never forget it. I'm glad you didn't die. I would've been heartbroken. You were supposed to live, George. You're supposed to help people. It's in your blood; that's why you survived again. Don't ever feel guilty about surviving. You're a good person. The world needs more of you."

George smiled weakly. "I'm lucky to know you, Lissy Cook. I know things... our life... is not perfect. I do love you, though."

"I know. I promised myself we couldn't continue this between us. That I would walk away. I can't, though. I love you, George. Come, come home and eat something. You need looking after tonight."

"What about your neighbours?"

"I no longer care. Let them say and think what they want. You're what's important. Tonight, you're my priority."

Lissy took George's hand, pulled him to his feet and lead him out of the park and back to her home.

TWENTY

Zakynthos, Greece, 1944

The only sound on the track was the light clopping of hooves as the horse and cart wound its way through the country lanes. Angelos, Niko and Pantelis were heading to the old Sarkis house.

"It is so long since I have been here and yet everything looks the same," Angelos whispered as the cart passed through the gateway. His head filled with a waterfall of childhood memories. They ended with the death of his father as they passed the spot where it had happened. Finally stopping outside the house, the three men got out of the cart and looked up at the Sarkis home.

"I cannot believe I am finally back. I expect *Baba* to walk from the house and yell at me for something, but he will not. He will never be here again." Angelos took a step towards his old home. Niko and Pantelis followed and the three men cautiously stepped up to the front door. Angelos tried the handle. It was locked. Pounding heavily on the wooden door, they waited. The grinding of a key in the lock punctuated the air and the door swung open.

"Who are you? What do you want?" A nervous young Nazi demanded, pointing a gun at them.

"I am Angelos Sarkis. This is *my* house. *You* are trespassing, Nazi. I want you to leave. Now!"

"The house belongs to the Führer. It is not yours, peasant!"

Niko and Pantelis raised their shotguns, levelling them at the Nazi, and stepped forward. Outnumbered, the young soldier stepped back into the hallway, unsure what to do next.

"I will say it again, Nazi. The war is over. Your evil army are not welcome on our island, or in *this* house. This house is mine! Get out or my friends will shoot you the same way your bastard commandant shot my father!" Angelos bellowed.

The young Nazi bolted, running away down the drive.

"See how scared they are now! Cowards! You are a pathetic coward, Nazi!" Niko yelled after him.

"Come Niko, leave him. Let us check the rest of the house." Pantelis stepped forward, his gun still raised. With Niko at his side, the two men set about searching every room. Angelos stepped over the threshold. Finally, he was back. It had been so long since he was last there. So long since he was last in the house he'd grown up in, the place that had once been his home. A lot had changed since, and now he owned it. It was his, and he'd make the life he and his family so rightfully deserved.

Angelos took his time reacquainting himself with his home. It was full of Nazi propaganda, weapons and provisions. Much of the Sarkis family furniture and belongings was still in the house, although some of the more expensive items had disappeared, including paintings and ornaments.

No doubt they'd been shipped off to the mainland to be lost forever.

It didn't matter, though. They were mainly his father's things, and he was just glad to have the house back; it was all that mattered. Furniture could always be bought, and he'd never liked his father's taste in paintings and ornaments anyway.

"Thank you, St Stylianos." His prayers were slowly working. Angelos had ensured to visit the church as often as he could, to silently light a candle and speak the same words over and over. *"I light this candle in honour of the bravery of Elena Petrakis, courageous daughter of Zakynthos. May the war end and return my home to me. Let me find Athena, St Stylianos, and bring her back to the island so that we can be a family again."*

No one knew of his promise to the saint. Not even his mother; it was a secret he kept and would keep until he went to his grave.

Niko and Pantelis returned, interrupting his thoughts. The young Nazi had been the only enemy in the house. The three men set to work and removed everything that belonged to the Nazis from the house, except for food and essential items. Angelos told Niko to put any useable clothes and shoes on the cart and give them to those who were most in need. The Nazi propaganda was thrown out of the front door, piled up at the side of the house and burnt. The three men sat on the ground with a glass of *Tsipouro* and watched the enemy's belongings burn.

"You have your home back, Angelos," Niko said, throwing a spent cigarette on to the fire. "It must feel good."

"It does. Thank you for helping me. You are good friends. *Mana* will be happy to be back again, and Sophia will like growing up here. I know it will be hard for *Mana* after my father's death, but this has always been her home. It will be good for her to return to her home, to lay her ghosts to rest and move on with life."

"You are lucky the Nazis did not destroy it. Some families on the island have not been so fortunate and have lost everything. It is good you have your home, Angelos," Pantelis said.

"I hope we can all live happily now. There has been too much hurt for our island. To all those we lost in this terrible war," Niko said. The men raised their glasses in salute as the flames began to dim.

"You are here! Come in, come in!" Angelos beckoned to Pigi and his daughter. He'd spent his first night back in the house alone overnight whilst Pigi packed their belongings. It had been good but strange to be back; the feel of the rooms as he walked through them making plans; nighttime noises as the house settled and creaked. Noises he hadn't heard in so long. It was all so familiar, even after all this time.

Niko collected Pigi and Sophia, and brought them and their belongings to the house. As Pigi stepped across the threshold, she clasped her hands to her chest and burst into tears. Quietly, she walked from room to room, brushing her hand lightly over old familiar furniture and furnishings, muttering to herself. Angelos knew how much it meant for her to be back, and he left her to enjoy old memories.

"Sophia, come see your room. You will share with *Nonna*, and when you are older, you will have a big room to yourself!" Angelos carried his daughter upstairs, watching as her wide eyes took everything in.

"This is the house I grew up in. It is where *Nonna* grew up. We have many rooms, Sophia."

Angelos heard his mother come up behind him. "I have not seen you this happy in a long time, Angelos. It makes me happy too, my son."

"I am happy, *Mana*. I do not remember many good times here, but I am happy to be back. We are lucky. And you, *Mana*? It must be strange to come back here. Are you happy?"

"Yes, my son. There is sadness for those we have lost, but it is good to be back. I have missed this house. I never thought I would see it again. I thought the war would go on forever, and I would die before it ended and the house was ours again. I can now cherish my good memories. Whatever you thought of your *Baba*, there were good times."

"You are still alive, *Mana*. We will have a happy life here. Come, we have our olive groves back too. We may have something to harvest this year!"

Angelos and Pigi ventured outside to the ancient olive groves, carrying Sophia between them.

"The trees are alive, it is good to see! Look, *Mana*, this one is healthy, so is that one, and this one too!" Angelos shouted gleefully as he ran between large gnarled tree trunks. "Bastards..."

"What is it?"

"These trees, look. Bastard Nazis. The trunks are full of bullet holes. They used my trees for their target practice! Do they not know how important and sacred our olive trees are to us?"

"They were soldiers who invaded us, Angelos. They did not care about us. If they did not care about people, they do not care about trees. We have a lot of work ahead. Some trees are good, others will need our care. We will coppice them, make them well again. Some we might lose, but what we have is enough. You can build from here, Angelos."

"You are right, *Mana*. Those we cannot save can be cut down and used for firewood. Nothing on my land will go to waste. I am looking forward to getting started."

Angelos had found an old leather-bound notebook in his father's office. Pulling it from his pocket, he turned to a fresh new page and wrote the date. Walking through the grove, he made copious notes. The olive groves were his family's lifeblood, and he needed to get it back up and running as soon as possible.

As Angelos walked and made notes, Pigi and Sophia sat on the grass, leaning against a stone wall. Pigi talked to Sophia about the trees, flowers and olives whilst she giggled. Angelos smiled, catching sight of them.

It was good to be a proper family again. His life had been tough after losing Elena and Athena, and his heart ached for them both. Reminders of Elena lay everywhere, especially in the olive groves, but he'd finally turned a corner. He had family and friends, and most importantly, his daughter, Sophia. Now that the war was finally over, Angelos was going to live a good life, with purpose, and he wasn't going to waste another moment.

TWENTY-ONE

Mainland Greece, 1944

Time had become an ever-changing being. It trundled along, days merging into weeks, which merged into months. Seasons changed from harsh, cold winter to a beautiful warm spring, swiftly followed by a sweltering summer. Richard and Athena had continued to live with the family at the farm, and he now felt as though England was a distant memory.

Unexpectedly, Richard was settled and happy. He enjoyed his work on the farm, and ensured Athena was cared for as though he was her father. Slowly, he relaxed into Greek life, embracing it. Life in the mountains was hard work, but it was also rewarding. It was far removed from Bristol, and as the months passed, he thought less and less about Lissy and his home city.

War continued, but news, when it reached them, spoke of small shifts. Tiny waves of hope that swirled about them, indicating it could all end soon. As much as they wanted to cling to this glimmer of hope, none of them dared. Richard had been drawn into helping the Greek

A NIGHT OF THUNDER

resistance; if he couldn't fight the enemy from the skies, he would do it on the ground. When he was out with fellow partisans, the thrill was similar to being up in the air, searching for enemy aircraft. It was what he'd needed. A purpose.

For months, the resistance had slunk through mountain passes and forests in the dead of night to set in motion events that would ensure the Nazis suffered. He'd enjoyed the nighttime games of cat and mouse with an increasingly desperate enemy. They'd been successful too. He still didn't trust Thanasis, but Richard couldn't fault him for his tactics of mountainous fighting against a vicious enemy.

It was now Autumn, and Richard was dropping supplies at a hidden location in the mountains. The drop site was past the dense woodland and up a high mountain path. Early parts of the route had been out in the open, and it had been risky, but now he was at the woodland, he was sheltered, hidden from prying eyes.

He was hot and tired from the climb, and his long hair and beard that helped to hide his face and made him fit in with the locals was itching. During the climb, he'd slipped and fallen in a patch of undergrowth and the dirt had left its mark. He could no longer see the valley that stretched out below him.

As he finished hiding the goods, he heard the snapping of a tree branch underfoot. He squatted in place, shielding himself in the undergrowth, silent and still. It was probably an animal, but his senses were always heightened. Nazis were becoming braver now they were losing the war. Soldiers were venturing into areas they would never have gone before.

It was silent. After checking around, he left his hiding place using the cover of trees as protection. As he reached a rocky outcrop, he spotted a lone figure and ducked down. Roula.

"Dammit!" Scanning the area, he rushed forward, grabbed her by the arm and pulled her back to the outcrop.

"What the hell are you doing here?" he whispered. "There are Nazis everywhere. It is too dangerous for you here!"

"I was out walking. I wanted to come to the cave."

"Cave? What cave?"

"It is a secret. Only I know where it is. No one ever comes here."

Richard spun her to face him. He and the girl's parents had become concerned about her lately; she kept disappearing and none of them knew where. She lead a life of her own, doing what she wanted when she wanted, and it would get her into trouble if she wasn't careful.

"Show me this cave."

Roula turned and headed back into the trees, following a hard line of rock the other side of the outcrop. Richard followed, gun at the ready, keeping watch for the enemy.

They reached a mass of overgrown bushes and trees, and Roula disappeared behind them. After ensuring they hadn't been followed, Richard slunk in after her.

Unseen from the outside, a narrow fissure in the rockface led back into the mountainside, opening out into a small cave. Richard looked around him; it was sparse with just a couple of old crates and a scruffy woollen blanket.

"This is where you come?"

"Yes."

"What do you do up here on your own?"

"I escape."

"Escape?"

"Life. I escape from life. From all the madness. It is my sanctuary."

"You escape to a damp, dark cave because it is better than life?"

"Yes."

Roula took a box of matches from her pocket. Reaching behind the crates, she lifted an old hurricane lamp. She lit the wick, allowing the hiss and spit of flame to light the dim space. Roula took Richard's hand, walking them over to the far wall of the cave. Lifting the lamp, she smiled at Richard as he drew in a sharp breath. The walls were covered in drawings, all created in charcoal. They were depictions of people, life and war.

"I drew them all, Richard. This is why I escape here. Everything good or bad in my mind is drawn on the wall. It is how I cope with life. I am no artist, but this is what I must do. See."

Roula took her time and showed him the length of it. All her emotions, thoughts and worries laid bare on the rock. It was all there. Her home, family, Richard, Athena, her hanged friend, the Nazis fighting the resistance.

They were expressive and haunting images, cutting straight to the point of the horrid complexities of the war they were forced to endure. There were also simpler images too, like food, trees and animals.

"This is incredible, Roula. You are talented. Your entire life is here. Where did you get the charcoal?"

Roula grabbed his arm and pulled him over to the crate which held an old wicker basket. Richard laughed.

"Fire ashes. Clever. I wondered why you always insisted on cleaning out the fireplace when you hate helping your mother in the house."

Richard sat on a crate and looked around the cave, the

eerie yellow gloom of the lamp highlighting further images he hadn't yet seen. Roula was a girl untamed. She'd been like it when they first met, but he'd never expected this.

This was a new side to her. It was wild and expressive. It was also soft and slightly melancholy too, and he admired her greatly for it. It showed him another Roula, one he wanted to learn more about.

"Are you lonely, Roula?" he said, taking a cigarette from his pocket and lighting it. He offered her one, but she shook her head.

"No. Once I was lonely. I was all alone. Now I am not." Roula glanced sideways at him. "When you arrived on our mountain, Richard, my loneliness left me. You and Athena make my life happy. Before you both came here, my life was all about the monotony of war. It took everything from my life. The village is empty. My friend is dead, and I was lonely. I used to spend my time on the mountain, stalking the enemy, wishing to fight, wishing them harm. Maybe I was hoping they would just kill me and put me out of my misery. I do not know. Now it has changed. I still hate the enemy, and will always defend my family and my home, but now I have more. I have Athena. I have you."

"You are a brave woman, Roula. So brave. You must take care, though. The enemy are everywhere, and I do not want you to get hurt, and they will hurt you if they catch you. I cannot always be there to protect you. Please take care of yourself."

"You care about me, Richard?"

"Yes of course I care! Your parents have taken me in and shown me and Athena great kindness, as have you. I would be horrified if something happened to you, the same as if something happened to your parents."

"Do you miss your home in England?"

A NIGHT OF THUNDER

Richard stood and walked over to the drawings and studied them again; he had missed one. A family. Five people: Manos, Vivi, him and Roula holding hands, Athena by his side. Was that how she thought of them? Or was she just documenting the cover story the resistance had instilled in her?

"I left England a long time ago, Roula. Things were different back then. Life was still normal, and war had barely begun. Many thought the war would not last long and everyone would be back home again months later. They thought it would be easy and that we would all be celebrating, having chased the Nazis back to their own country with their tails between their legs. It did not happen. The war dragged on. Many died; many of us are not where we should be. Back in England, I had a fiancée called Lissy. We were in love once, before all of this began. We were going to be married when I returned from the war. Now time has marched on and many things have changed. I have no idea if Lissy is alive. I have no idea if she is still waiting for me or if she has found someone else."

Richard turned and looked at Roula for a moment.

"I was the same when I signed up, Roula. I thought war would be over in a couple of months. A year at most. I did not expect it to go on all these years. I did not expect to find myself thousands of miles from home, stranded in Greece. I did not expect to become protector of another woman's child. I still think of home, my parents and my friends and occasionally of Lissy. But it all seems so far away, sometimes like it was someone else's life and not mine."

Richard walked over and sat next to Roula.

"An old friend of mine in England once told me *'You make your life where you land on your feet'*. It seems my feet have landed in Greece, and I must make my life here. I hate the war, but I am lucky; I have a roof over my head, and I have food on my table. The views of the mountains and across the valley are special. This might not have been the life I would have chosen, but it has chosen me, and I am tired of fighting against it. We are still at war, and whilst war remains, this is my home."

"But are you happy Richard?"

"When I am with you, Roula, yes I am happy. There are times you infuriate me, like today when you follow me up here knowing it is dangerous. I worry about you, but yes, I am happy. I have a family, and it is something I always longed for. I do not miss my life in England. I thought I would, but my happiness here fulfils me and my life in England is no longer important."

"Do..." Roula began, "... do you..."

Richard smothered her mouth with his own, not even allowing the question to be uttered. Instead he confirmed her question by kissing her slowly and deeply. He no longer wanted to be with Lissy. He was happy here in Greece. Roula was his life now; she was the one he wanted. They savoured the close and loving connection with each other before breaking apart.

"I have grown to consider you as family even though we are not, Roula. Even closer than family. You are no sister to me. My feelings for you, Roula, are much more. You are good with Athena. She adores you. You are not her mother, but you make a good surrogate. I want to be with you if you want it and your parents will allow it?" He paused. "I know I had another life, one I was going to return to. My life there was all planned out, but plans change and sometimes what we thought was written for us changes too. Greece has woven its way into me. I like it here. I get pleasure and contentment from simplicity. It helps to rid the terror of war." He paused. "I love you, Roula. I love the brave woman who brought me food and a toy for Athena when we first arrived. You have more strength and courage than most men around this mountain. I love your courage, even if it does worry me. I love your desire to make things right. I love watching you with Athena, and I love how you look at me."

Roula flung her arms around him and held him tightly. "Never leave me, Richard."

"I will never leave you, Roula," he whispered. "I am part of your life and always will be. I love you Dimitroula Papadoulia. I will love you forever. Without you, I would be lost."

"And what about your Lissy?"

"When I met Lissy, we were young. It was a first rush of young love where we thought it would be the two of us forever, that we were meant for each other. The thing about Lissy is even though I did care for her, maybe even loved her in some small way, I know now I was never truly in love with her. We were more like friends, and I think it was just expectation that we got married. Since meeting you, I know I no longer love her. You have come into my life like a whirlwind, Roula. We are alike. We complement each other. When I see you from the bedroom window, I want to run outside and lift you up, spin you round and kiss you. When I look at you across the kitchen table when we are all eating, I want everyone else to disappear, so it is just the two of us. When I look at you now, sitting next to me, I just want to hold you in my arms. I want you and no one else, Roula. Be with me, be mine."

"I will Richard. I will be yours, always."

As Richard kissed her deeply, the hurricane lamp sputtered and flickered, the light dimming, and Roula's drawings enveloped them.

TWENTY-TWO

Bristol, England, 1943

Lissy stepped off the bus in the darkness and pulled her coat tightly around her. Winter was just around the corner and the nights were getting cold. She had worked another long shift at the factory and was growing increasingly tired of the monotony of war. Whilst she knew her work was important and greatly needed, the daily grind exhausted her. Today had been particularly gruelling. Her feet hurt, and she couldn't wait to get home and warm up.

As she rounded a corner not far from home, a man blocked her path. She tried to step around him, but he matched her moves, blocking her each time.

"Excuse me!" Lissy tried to push past him again, but he pushed her against the wall and reached to grab her bag. Thrusting it behind her, using her body weight to push it into the wall, Lissy used her free hand to try and push away the assailant, but he was forceful.

"Just gimme your money and you ain't gonna get hurt!"

"No! I won't!"

Full of rage, Lissy stamped hard on the man's foot with

the sharp heel of her shoe. Taking him by surprise, he stepped back in pain. Released from his grip, Lissy lunged at him with her full body weight, knocking him to the floor. Pulling off her shoes, she ran barefoot, her footwear dangling from her fingers. She kept on running as fast as she could towards her house, hoping she'd make it through the streets safely before the man followed and caught up to her.

Turning a corner, Lissy slammed straight into a firm body. She screamed and dropped her shoes. The person grabbed her arm, but she fought back.

"Get off me you brute! Get off me!"

"Lissy? Lissy, it's me."

Recognising the voice, she stopped fighting.

"Oh George, thank goodness it's you!" Behind her, running footsteps came closer; she immediately moved to stand behind George. Her assailant turned the corner, stopping short when he saw the policeman. He turned to run, but George was too quick for him.

"Stop right there!" George grabbed him, but the assailant wrestled from the policeman's grip and ran, disappearing into the darkness.

"Are you okay, Lissy, are you hurt?"

"No, I'm alright. I think he wanted my bag or some money, but I managed to get away." She rubbed one of her arms. Reaching down, she righted her shoes on the ground and slipped her cold feet into them. "Thank goodness I ran into you. I had no idea he was following me. I thought he'd given up."

"You must be careful out alone at night, Lissy. The war's created unsavoury characters. Lots of men and women are desperate. They're struggling, they don't have money or have lost everything. They prey on vulnerable people like yourself who are tired or alone, and they rob them for everything they have. You must take care."

"I'll be careful in future, but it's difficult when my shifts are long. I often finish late, and I must walk back from the bus stop, alone, in the darkness. What am I supposed to do, other than take my chances on the street with men like him lying in wait?"

"I could meet you, Lissy." He held his hand up to stop her from speaking. "I know the guilt of us spending two nights together has eaten you up. I know it's why you've been avoiding me. I won't apologise for what happened, though. I love you, and deep down you love me too. I want you to be safe. Let me help you."

Lissy looked up at him, kind, lovely George, who was always there for her when she needed him the most. The man who had declared his love for her only to be hurt so badly by her. She had chosen to take him to bed twice, and yet she had been the one to make him feel guilty and turn him away. Even after all that he still loved her and was offering to support her. She didn't deserve it. As much as she'd tried to distance herself from him, something always drew them back to each other.

"I appreciate your concern, but it wouldn't be appropriate. Thank you for helping me tonight, Constable Perkins."

Lissy started to walk away from him, but George clasped her hand as she went. He pulled her to him in the darkness, the shadows of the large brick wall hiding them. He spun her to the wall, and the coolness of the brick against her back seeped through her coat. She should have pushed him away, but she lost the will. She always felt safe in his arms, and she wanted that safety now.

"I miss you every hour of every day, Lissy Cook. I know this isn't normal for any of us. You had your life planned long before I came along. A life that may yet return, but I can't stop thinking about you. Whether you like it or not you've become part of me. You're in my heart. I want to be with you. Somewhere deep down inside I know you want to be with me too. For now, I promise to be the honourable policeman. I'll walk a shaken young lady, who had a terrible fright, to her front door so that she gets home safely. Tomorrow is a new day, though, and I'll come and see you when my uniform hangs in the wardrobe and I'm just plain George. We need to finish this conversation."

George released her and stepped back, indicating for her to walk. Lissy pushed away from the wall and shakily continued walking towards her house. George walked alongside her, a respectful gap between them. To anyone who saw them, they were simply a police constable looking after a young lady. Thudding hearts and occasional brushing fingertips in the darkness, however, told Lissy and George they were so much more.

∼

Daylight broke, wrapped in cold, thick fog. Wispy cold tentacles flowed along the streets, winding around lamp posts, licking windowpanes and doors, trying to enter. Lissy awoke and opened her eyes, reaching out for the body in the bed next to her. George. It had been three weeks since he'd rescued her from the assailant, and they'd seen each other almost every day after the promised conversation. George had been right. She loved him just as much as he loved her, and she wanted that love, no longer caring about the consequences.

Since the start of the war, Lissy's life had been chaos, but George Perkins brought calm. He gave her something to look forward to, a purpose that didn't involve the war. He made her feel good about herself, and above all else he loved her. George loved her with heart and soul, like no one else had ever loved her. Not even Richard had loved her that way.

Richard. A small flutter of love for Richard still existed, but it was nothing like the love she had for George. But Richard had abandoned her. Richard had chosen bravado and the war over her and their relationship. He'd left her to cope on her own. Now he was missing in action, dead for all she knew. Why should she put her life on hold for him any longer?

If by some miracle Richard returned, she'd face some very big decisions that would affect all of them. For now though, she didn't care. George was here and Richard wasn't.

Lissy threw back the bed covers and swung her legs over the side, the chilly air licking at her limbs. The fire had died down and she needed to top it up with logs.

"Where are you going? It's cold out there." George pulled her back into bed, throwing the blankets back over her.

"I was going to relight the fire. It's freezing."

They lay facing each other. Companionable in silence for a moment.

"I'll light the fire in a minute. I want to see you first. This is my favourite time of day. Waking up with you, Lissy, seeing your beautiful face, seeing your smile when you first see me. Knowing it's just us; it makes my heart soar."

"I... I've been wanting to tell you for so long, but I've been so afraid... I love you, George. I tried not to, but I do. I'm lying to us both if I ignore it. But I still don't know what to do."

"I love you too, but you already know it. I know you're finding it hard. I would too in your position. I'm well aware that Richard might turn up tomorrow, and you'd be forced to make difficult decisions about your life. I hope you would choose me, but life isn't straightforward. I know if Richard ever does come home, I'll probably lose you. For now, I'm content to love you here and now. It's all I can do. Tomorrow isn't guaranteed for any of us."

Lissy leaned in and kissed him, melting into his arms, their limbs wrapping around each other, warming each other before their day began.

TWENTY-THREE

Zakynthos, Greece, 1945

The slow rhythm of normality returned to the island after the war. Knowing their war was over, the Nazis retreated, and homes and businesses were slowly restored. Years of bitter war had brought hardship for many islanders. Rifts between war torn families and friends struggled to heal.

There was also a renewed purpose of starting again. Some islanders left, never to return. The Jewish residents who'd been heroically hidden across the island to prevent them being transported to concentration camps emerged from their places of safety alive, but lacking in food and possessions. They took the hardest brunt of all, facing the hard reality that the enemy had hated them so much they wanted them dead. A handful returned to what had once been their homes, but many Jewish islanders said goodbye to Zakynthos for pastures new.

Angelos had watched it all from his favourite Kafenion, when he wasn't putting life back into his home and olive grove. Sitting at his favourite table, he allowed his mind to tumble over. It landed on his daughter and father-in-law Stelios.

"You look sad, Angelos, my friend." Pentalis pulled out a chair and sat next to him.

"I was thinking of Sophia and Stelios. She still does not know her grandfather is dead, or why it happened. I want to tell her. It is too much of a burden. But how do I explain to Sophia that her grandfather betrayed us all and lost his life for it?"

"You cannot. Maybe you must bend the truth. Maybe you tell her Stelios has gone to the graveyard through ill health. There is time to tell her the truth when she is older."

"Will she not hate me, Pentalis, if I lie to her?"

"She is young, Angelos. She will not understand. She has not understood any of it. How can you explain to a child about war, about the good and evil in the world? How do you explain to a child that their own grandfather chose evil?"

"Do you know he pleaded for his life, Pentalis? I heard from the resistance. They took him to the same cliff where Elena was shot, and Stelios cried like a child, begging to live. He begged and lied saying he did not support the Nazis. He said he hated the Nazis. They did not believe him. He begged and cried for mercy, and they shot him, pushing him over to the foot of the cliffs. How do I explain that to a child?"

"You must do what is best. If she was my child, I would not tell her the horrific details. I would say he had been taken unwell which is why she was not able to see him. Take her to the Makris's burial plot in the graveyard so she has somewhere to visit when she is older. She does not need to know he is not there and lies with the fish."

"As always, Pentalis, you are the voice of all sense."

"Some of us must be. The war might be over, but the problems continue. You saw what happened in town only last week, Angelos. They took my remaining brother from his home and dragged him through the streets tied behind a cart. You saw how they crowded round and jeered at him. The man had no escape. The anger is still high."

"I remember that day. I know Kyriakos was an enemy; like Stelios he was a friend of the Nazis. He deserved the anger for betraying so many people. But punishment like that? I could not watch, Pantelis. I heard the cheers from Bochali as I left town. I stopped for a minute and the flag no longer flew above the castle. The poor soul had been strung up and swung from a noose on the flagpole, his punishment cruel and swift. He betrayed us with the Nazis, but he was given a harsh punishment by people who had once been friends and neighbours. What did killing him do? What did losing your brother do for your family? What has it done for any of us?"

Angelos and Pentalis fell quiet in their own thoughts. The actions and punishment faced by those who were now called traitors was a stark reminder of war wounds that ran deep. The scene at Bochali wasn't the island Angelos knew or remembered. This was not how his fellow Zakynthians should be acting. He understood the hatred; what happened to people like Elena sickened him too. He'd never forgive those who'd killed her, but dragging men through the streets, humiliating them and hanging them wasn't the answer.

"Do not worry, Angelos. You are a good father. I know you will do the right thing. Finish your coffee and get home to your mother and daughter. They need you."

Pentalis patted his friend on the shoulder and left the

A NIGHT OF THUNDER

Kafenion. Shortly after, Angelos returned home to a glum and anxious Pigi.

"*Mana*. What is wrong? You are upset. Is it Sophia?"

"Sophia is well. The radio has bad news from Athens. They were all out celebrating the end of this war. A political party held a rally. They were attacked by police. Our own Greek police fired at them. And the British! Pah! They stood by and let them! Those fools with guns killed twenty-eight people! Twenty-eight! Many more injured. Where will this end, Angelos?"

"*Mana*, do not worry. Athens is a long way from here. We will be okay."

"We said that before the war, Angelos, and look what happened. They took everything from us. They took years of our lives, they killed your *Baba* and stole our home. Many have died. Now the communists want to take over Greece! Communists!"

"I know you are upset, but we cannot do anything from here. Let us worry about problems *when* they arrive, not *if*. Sophia has already been through too much. She needs calm, not worry."

"You are right. I do not think I could ever go through what we have been through again, Angelos. It was too much."

"I know. These people are always fighting. They have been battling each other since 1943. It was a skirmish *Mana*. Just a skirmish. It will be okay. Look after Sophia. She is your life now."

Muted celebrations continued on the island despite Pigi's worries and Zakynthians felt life returning to some normality. Throughout the year, Angelos and Niko, assisted by Pantelis, worked hard in the olive groves, tending the trees and land, ensuring his business would grow and thrive.

"The trees are looking much better, Angelos. We have done a good job," Niko said, sitting on a stone wall. Angelos sat next to him and smiled, surveying his domain.

"They are, Niko. I could not have done this without you and Pantelis. You are good friends. The Sarkis groves will be the talk of Zakynthos once more!"

"They will! You are a good friend to us too, Angelos, especially after all that has happened." Niko had moved into the old, smaller Sarkis house Maria and Angelos had lived in after they first married. Niko was enjoying being away from the town and the mansion he'd grown up in with his father. A mansion that now lay abandoned.

"Elena would have loved to see the groves healthy again," Angelos said.

"Her *Trisagion* seems so long ago now. I hope her soul is at peace. There is no grave for her other than deep ocean. She has no family now; they were all murdered by Nazis so soon after her death. She should be remembered," Pantelis said, whittling a piece of olive wood with his pocketknife.

"I remember her always when I pray," Angelos said, flapping at a fly.

"You pray?"

"You sound surprised," Angelos said. "It was all I could do."

"Maybe those who are left should remember her again. A memorial to her bravery. I am proud to have fought alongside her in the resistance. She was braver than most," Niko said.

"Maybe," Angelos said. "I will think about it." He stood and went back to tending his olives. His two friends merely looked at each other, before heading back to work.

A NIGHT OF THUNDER

On the two-year anniversary of Elena's death, Angelos, Sophia, Pigi, Niko and Pantelis went to the Church of St George of Filikon and St Stylianos under Bochali Hill in Zakynthos Town. It was a place Angelos had visited often recently. Each time, he'd lit a candle to Elena's bravery. Now, two years later, they were at the church to remember Elena's life. A small group of friends to honour the bravery of a young woman so cruelly taken. Pigi cried as the priest gave prayer, but Angelos stayed strong.

Stepping out of the church, Pantelis said goodbye. Niko took Pigi and Sophia home and Angelos made his way to Keri. As he neared the cliff edge, memories flooded back, but he refused to let them overwhelm him. He sat on the edge of the cliff and took a small olive branch from his pocket.

"I could not find a poppy this time, Elena. But I know you would like to see the olive trees are doing well. I have prayed so much for Athena to come home, but still do not know where she is. I promise I will find her, even if it takes a lifetime. Farewell, my beautiful Elena. I will love you always, but this is the last time I will visit you. You will always be in my heart, but my future must be to look after my mother and Sophia. Rest well." Angelos threw the olive branch to the sea below and stood to watch for the glint on the horizon. When it came, he smiled, nodded and hurried home to his family.

TWENTY-FOUR

Mainland Greece, 1945

Richard was up on the mountain surrounded by stone, repairing a wall. It was hard manual work, but he enjoyed every minute of it. It was a world away from Bristol, his friends, his parents and Lissy, a place and people he knew he should be missing. But he didn't; he was too happy here in Greece.

Things had changed in the last year. He'd no idea when. One day he'd been a stranger, taken in by strangers and hidden from the enemy. Somehow, at some point, the lines had blurred, and he'd become family. Athena became a happy child, and his relationship with Roula also changed.

He'd tried many times to pinpoint the exact moment but was unsure. Deep down, however, he knew the day she took him to the cave and he saw all her incredible drawings had something to do with it. They'd become closer still afterwards. His life was here in Greece now; Bristol and everyone he'd ever known there were forgotten, resigned to the past.

Richard stopped work on the wall and sat on the pile of

stones. Below him lay the valley, the house, and beyond, an endless expanse of Greece. His thoughts went back to Roula as he lit a cigarette. After the first visit to the cave, he started exploring the mountain with her when time allowed. It was a wild, untamed place full of beauty, wildlife and many more hidden caves.

Roula knew every inch of the mountains that surrounded them. One day, they were forced to shelter under an outcrop when torrential rain came down and the sky flashed and rattled with a ground-shaking storm. Hugging each other tightly, the wait had become too much for them both and their relationship ascended to another level. One that neither could return from. As the storm had crashed above them, they'd taken refuge and become one, their bodies entwining, finally succumbing to each other. Richard had held her closely afterwards.

"We are drenched, and if your father ever finds out what has just happened, he is going to horsewhip me."

Roula had smiled up at him. "He will not. He likes you. If I am happy then he is happy."

"You know I love you, Roula. This was not just a chance for me to have sex with you and walk away. I do not know what it is about this place. About you. But I am happy here despite this horrific war. You make me happy. I feel like we truly are a family."

"You love me?"

"Yes. I love you," he whispered.

"I love you."

He kissed her.

"I love you, Roula." He held her.

"It is a lot of love." She paused for a moment. "Do you not love your Lissy anymore? Do you not want to go home anymore?"

"No. It has been too long. The world has changed. I have changed. I do not want the things I once wanted. I have a new life now. That life is you and Athena."

"I love you too, Richard."

"I still think your father will whip me!"

"No. I told you, he likes you. He will be glad someone wants his daughter. I know my parents do not like me running around the hills like some wild animal. What else did I have to do up here? No friends, no brothers or sisters. I have been so bored. Even the man I was supposed to marry is now dead. You have brought light to my life, and you make me happy. My father will be happy too. They both will."

After the storm had passed, Richard and Roula had run back to the house, hand in hand. They were still holding hands as they entered the kitchen. Roula explained everything to her parents, and they'd taken the news well. Manos's only caution was that Richard treat their daughter well.

Days later, the family had held a private ceremony with the local priest in the village church. Roula wore her mother's wedding gown and Richard borrowed smart clothes from Manos. With Manos and Vivi each holding one of Athena's hands, Richard and Roula had been joined together for life.

Richard was now a husband, and he couldn't be happier. His wife was a beautiful, feisty woman he couldn't wait to have children and grow old with. Every day they awoke together was pure pleasure, and he relished his new life in Greece. His one small doubt was that he should tell his parents where he was, and how life had taken an unexpected turn into something different and new, but things in Greece were still turbulent, and getting news to Bristol would be difficult, if not impossible. Enemies lurked everywhere, both Nazi and Greek, and Richard wouldn't risk anyone getting hold of a letter with information about him in it. It would've put him and the entire family at risk. It would have to wait until the war was over.

Bringing his attention back to the wall he was building, Richard's thoughts turned to other matters as he set another stone in place. The news had become more positive, with indications that the war may be close to ending. How ironic that he'd always been so desperate to get home after the war, but now it was close he wouldn't be going anywhere. The Greek political situation was worrying him, though. There were whispers of a communist uprising. He hoped they were unfounded. The last thing the country needed was more trouble.

Richard looked up from the wall to see his wife walking towards him. Wiping his hands on his trousers, he smiled.

"Is it lunchtime already?"

"Yes. I missed you." Roula placed the basket on a large stone, opened a blanket and spread it on the ground behind the piles of stones. "I thought we could eat."

"Good idea." He reached down and pulled the blanket further along behind the wall. "The view will be hidden if we sit there, though." He pointed to the blanket.

"I do not care about the view. I see it all the time."

"That is true. I lied. I do not want us to be disturbed, Roula. Do you?" Richard swiftly pulled his wife to the blanket, kissing her deeply, all thoughts of food forgotten. His stomach could wait.

The night was dark, and the family meal was disturbed by Thanasis's secret code knock. Manos stood and opened it, allowing the partisan inside. The family watched as the man slunk to the fireplace, pulled up a chair and lit a cigarette. Manos shut the door and sat back at the table.

"What do you want, Thanasis? We are eating."

"We have almost won this war. The Nazis are retreating. Every day we are closer to our freedom."

"This we know. What is it you want?"

"There is another enemy causing us trouble. Communists. They threaten the future of Greece. You and your family, you helped us through this time of war. I hope we will be friends when it ends. I hope you will choose to be on the right side for the future of Greece." Thanasis pulled on a cigarette before slowly exhaling a pall of smoke.

Manos nodded to Richard; he pushed his chair back and lifted Athena up, giving her a kiss goodnight. "Time for bed. Roula, take Athena upstairs."

Roula knew better than to argue, and she took the child from her husband. Vivi followed her daughter and the child from the room and closed the door, leaving the three men alone.

"You come to my home and threaten me in front of my family?" Manos stood, and Richard followed suit.

"Threaten? I do not remember any threats."

"You should leave, Thanasis. We thank you for everything you have done. We have played our part in this war, but we will do no more. We will not make more enemies!" Manos spat.

Thanasis stood and threw his spent cigarette into the fire grate. He walked over to Manos and placed a hand on his shoulder, gripping him hard enough to leave a bruise.

"Look after your family. Troubled times will come

again. Communists are not welcome in Greece. You should choose the right side. Anyone who supports the communists is an enemy of Greece and will be punished." Thanasis walked to the door, flung it open and stepped out into the darkness, disappearing into the night.

"Bastard!" Manos yelled as he slammed the door and firmly bolted it.

"Why was he warning us? Are you communist?" Richard said.

"He is a stupid fool who has let his power of resistance go to his head. He has no idea who he is dealing with! We are not communist, I have never been communist! He thinks he can treat us like this? He thinks he can treat the people of this mountain this way? He is badly mistaken! He will pay for his disrespect."

Richard took the *Tsipouro* bottle from the side and poured two short measures. He handed a glass to his father-in-law and swigged from the other. Both sat at the table contemplating a future that now seemed less certain and more perilous than when they'd awoken.

TWENTY-FIVE

Bristol, England, 1945

Spring had sprung, coating everything in a rich blanket of colour. Vibrant hues of yellow daffodils and primroses had followed swathes of white snowdrops. Apple trees were in early leaf and woodlands were bathed in a carpet of bluebells.

Lissy and George walked hand in hand through their favourite woods on the outskirts of the city. It was a rare day off for them both, and even though they'd tried to see each other as much as they could in the last year, they'd agreed to keep their relationship a secret. Hiding it from the rest of the world.

Lissy didn't want her neighbours, landlord or work colleagues to know. Gossip was rife enough as it was, and she didn't want Richard's parents to find out. Her relationship with Richard was still unresolved. He was still missing, and until Lissy had news, dead, or otherwise, she had to hide in shadows. Stepping out publicly with another man would be callous and brazen.

The woods had helped them to keep their secret well,

A NIGHT OF THUNDER

and it was always just the two of them, alone with the beauty of the changing seasons and accompanying wildlife. Today was no different. Birds chittered overhead, a woodpecker was busy hammering a tree and the wind whispered through the overhead branches.

As they wound their way through the vast carpet of blue flowers, they headed into the denser part of the woods. To where the branches touched above them, forming a canopy. Lissy shivered, pulling her scarf tighter around her neck.

"Are you cold?"

"No, just a little shiver. The wind isn't as cold as it was in the winter, but every now and then it catches me."

"At least we can get out. Get away from the city to explore somewhere beautiful. I've missed you, Lissy."

"I've missed you too."

George motioned to a fallen tree under a canopy of branches that were beginning to leaf. He laid his jacket on the log for Lissy and they sat.

"I wish we didn't have to hide, Lissy. I really wish we could be together every day and just be us."

"I know. I do too. I must do the right thing, though. Richard deserves more respect and so do his parents. If he suddenly came back and found us together... the hurt it would cause. They deserve more."

"I understand." George took her hands in his, turning her towards him.

"Do you really believe he will return? It's been so long now. Surely if he was alive, someone would've told you? Surely he'd have got word to you?"

"I don't know. You think he's dead? You do, don't you?"

"I don't want to upset you, Lissy, but so many men have gone missing and haven't come back. Their families don't know where their loved ones are and have been forced to move on with their lives. We are at war. It's not unusual. I know you feel guilty, and want a clean answer, but you may never get it, Lissy. Do you want to put your life, your entire future, on hold? It could be for years."

"No! I don't. But what more can I do? This war isn't yet over. How I wish it was, but until it ends, there's still the possibility Richard will return!"

"And what would you do if he did come back? If Richard walked up to your front door today and said he was back, what would you do?"

"You know what I'd do George!"

"No, I don't. Not really. You say you love me. You say you'd stay with me and tell him it's over, but would you really? You keep his picture in your front room. You hide it because you don't want to upset me, and yet I know it's there with the telegram still."

"I..." Lissy stood and walked across the path to gaze at the bluebells. Such bright beauty in a time of hardship and devastation. She turned to face George. "I know you love me, George. I know you want a life with me. I know that you are desperate to marry me so that we can grow old together. I love you and want all that too. The war has been tough, though. I was... am... still engaged to a man who is missing. He might be dead, but I don't know that; he might still be alive. Years have passed, and I'm not the same woman he left behind. I know he won't be the same Richard who left, if he does ever come home. I know we can't put back together what we had. And then there's you. My wonderful George. I love you as much as you love me. You make my heart soar. I want a life with you, so very much. But how can I deny my past? It's a past still unresolved, and it's tearing me apart!"

George stood and went to Lissy. He wrapped her in his arms and held her tightly. The woodland fell silent, punctuated only with heartbreak and the occasional sound of birdsong.

∼

Lissy ran down the stairs wrapping her dressing gown around her. She swung the front door open to a cacophony of noise and a street full of people. She stared in shock. She tapped a passing neighbour on the shoulder.

"What on earth is going on?"

"Oh, Lissy me dear, ain't you 'eard the news? It's over! The war! Hitler's done a runner! We won!"

Lissy flung the door shut, ran to the front room and switched on the wireless. The crackling voice of Winston Churchill filled the space, his speech stern and full of determination. "Hostilities will end officially at one minute after midnight tonight..." was all Lissy heard as the rest of the prime minister's speech faded into the background. She ran up the stairs to change into her clothes. The war was over! They were free again!

After she changed her clothes, Lissy ran back downstairs, slipped on her shoes, flicked off the wireless and left the house to join a throng of neighbours who were celebrating. There was singing; two young boys were handing out bottles of brown beer from a wooden crate; and women stood in groups hugging each other. The joy was infectious and overwhelming.

Lissy wound her way through the crowd and allowed herself to be swept along by the wonderful scenes.

"Careful now, miss," a voice said as she was jostled

forward. "It may be a celebration, but watch yourself. There are still unscrupulous people about."

"George? It's you! Did you hear? The war has ended!"

"I heard."

"You don't seem happy."

George led her away from the bustling crowd and into an alleyway. The noise dimmed and shadows of the neighbouring buildings blocked out the brightness of the spring sunshine. "Of course I'm happy to see the end of the war. Things haven't changed, though. Our problem still isn't resolved."

"Right now, I don't care. Today is all that matters. Kiss me, George."

"I'm on duty. I can't."

"Damn people's thoughts and feelings. We've just heard the war is over; they're too busy celebrating. Kiss me." She reached up and removed his helmet. "Kiss me... Constable Perkins."

George pushed her up against the wall, moving them further into the shadows, and did as he was told. Neither could say how long they stayed there, but as the celebrations swirled through the streets, Lissy and George held each other tight, revelling in the moment.

TWENTY-SIX

Zakynthos, Greece, 1948

Sophia Sarkis was growing up fast and had become a very clever, walking, talking, five year old. Angelos was proud of her. Every day was a joy, and he was glad to have her in his life. Over time, her happiness and love had filled the cracks of the loss he felt about Athena.

Sophia marvelled at everything life put in front of her. The war had barely affected her; she'd been too young to understand it. Now they were a loving family on their own land again. His olive trees flourished with care and attention from himself, Niko and Pentalis, and he was reaping the rewards.

If only the rest of Greece was the same.

Pigi had been right, and Greece had suffered a vile civil war. The Greek government had fought against the communists, and whilst everyone had hoped the war would stay on the mainland, the troubles eventually wound their way to every corner of Greece. Being plunged back into another war so soon had shocked everyone. This time it was Greek against Greek; both sides were stubborn, and so the fighting continued.

Angelos stayed home and away from politics and fighting. Even his trips to the Kafenion had stopped. The only time he left the property was for business or to attend church, but even church was less frequent. His need to avoid getting caught up in trouble to protect Sophia was greater than his need to light a candle for his missing child.

News of disagreements and fallouts between those who had once been neighbours and friends circulated the island again. Rumours spread of attacks on good men who were killed and thrown into wells, or over cliffs. Angelos couldn't believe history was repeating itself so soon, or that his fellow countrymen could be so stupid.

Even Niko agreed the fight was unnecessary, as he and Angelos sat under the stars one night drinking Zakynthian wine. Pigi was in the house putting Sophia to bed. Niko pulled up a chair next to Angelos and poured himself a glass.

"They killed another man today, Angelos. Christos from the next village."

"Christos! What did he do?" Angelos slammed his hand on the table making the bottle and glasses shake.

"He walked past the communists. They demanded to know why he walked on their road. He ignored them and refused to stop. They shot him in the back."

"When will this madness stop? Was the big war not enough? Did the Italians and Germans not divide us enough? Now this!"

"We live in a bad world, Angelos. Christos was a stubborn fool, but he did not have to die that way. Even I do not agree with this, Angelos. I will not fight. I will keep my head low and do my work here. I hope it is over soon."

"I hope so too. We should pull together and support each other, not fight like dogs in the street and for what? Because pig-headed Greeks do not like the opinion of someone else? Where will it end?"

"I do not know Angelos. I do not know…"

∼

Zakynthians faced the instability of fighting for another year, until the autumn of 1949. After three years of conflict, the communists retreated into Albania.

"It is over!" Pantelis ran down the driveway of the Sarkis house shouting. He had been absent from the olive groves for months, scared of travelling too far from home.

"What is over?" Angelos was sitting at the outside table with his family and Niko. He poured some coffee and passed it to his mother.

"The civil war. It is over! The radio said the communists have run to Albania!"

Angelos laughed, beckoning for Pantelis to join them. "May Albania enjoy their company and keep them there for many years! Sit, Pantelis, and have coffee. It has been too long since we have seen you and this is good news to celebrate!"

"Now is time to look forward. There has been enough war to last us a lifetime! Let us hope that is it now," Pantelis said, taking a slug of his coffee.

"Yes. I hope so! I do not want my daughter growing up in such a world." Angelos smiled as Sophia ran towards him. She had been playing at the back of the house, running around the trees and searching for insects in the grass. It was her favourite thing to do. Nature was in her blood, and she adored all plants, animals and insects no matter how large or small.

"Uncle Niko! Pantelis!" She ran up and greeted them with a big smile. "Flowers for you *Baba*!" She dropped a clutch of grass and battered petals in her father's lap. She ran towards the trees, gathered more and returned to the table, throwing the contents onto Niko's lap. "For you too, Uncle Niko!"

Pantelis wasn't left out and received handfuls of grass and flowers a minute later. The men took the gifts as though they were the most expensive Bougainvillea, trying not to laugh.

"Why thank you, young Sophia. The flowers are beautiful. Did you grow them yourself?" Niko carefully lifted the tangle of grass and wildflowers from his lap and put them on the table.

"No! My *Baba* did!"

"And *Baba* would like some left in his groves! No more flower picking; you remove more grass from my grove than a hungry goat!"

"Do you not like my flowers, *Baba*?"

Angelos lifted his daughter on to his lap, and she snuggled into him, not caring her gift was now being crushed. "My beautiful Sophia, your gift of flowers is always lovely. It shows how much you love me. And when I say thank you, it shows how much I love you, too. But do you not think the flowers are more beautiful when they have the roots in the ground, with the sun on their heads?"

Sophia looked at the groves for a minute before hugging Angelos and kissing him on the cheek. Scrambling down from his lap, Sophia smiled. "Okay, I will leave the flowers and stop picking them. Instead, I will go and find a lizard and you can keep it for a pet!"

"Sophia! No! Leave the lizards alone!" Angelos bellowed, but it was too late. His little daughter had already run towards the olive groves.

"That child!"

Pantelis and Niko laughed as they watched Sophia intently scouring the grass for any unsuspecting lizards.

～

The Church of St George of Filikon and St Stylianos in Bochali was silent and gloomy as Angelos removed his hat and stepped inside. He allowed the calmness of the building to wash over him. Two candles flickered, a sign that others like him had been to the church recently to honour their prayers to the saint. He was now alone, though.

Angelos lifted a new candle and lit it, placing it in a holder next to the already lit ones. He closed his eyes and spoke aloud, his voice reverberating in the old building.

"I light this candle in honour of the bravery of Elena Petrakis, brave daughter of Zakynthos. Let me find my daughter, Athena, St Stylianos, and bring her back to her home."

He allowed the echo of his voiced prayer to finally dissipate, leaving him in complete silence. He watched for a moment as the flame flickered before turning and walking out of the church. He put his hat back on his head and stood looking down over the main town. The island seemed alive, and it was good to see people out and about, embracing post-war life. The island was starting to feel more like Zakynthos again.

Angelos walked down the hill to Solomos Square and along the harbour, nodding in acknowledgment each time he passed someone. He was enjoying walking, being able to traverse the island without worrying about being in the wrong place at the wrong time or being stopped, fearing punishment.

An arm waved to him from across the road, and he walked over to say hello to Pantelis.

"You are far from the olive groves today, my friend, what brings you to town?"

"Business, my friend. Always business!"

"Sit, I have five minutes. Fotini will bring us a coffee." Pantelis disappeared for a moment, shouting through the open doorway of the café and guest house he ran with his family. Taking a seat, Pantelis stretched.

"It is not often I get to sit. We have a nice view, eh?" Pantelis said as his sister, Fotini, appeared, placing two coffees on the table.

"It is nice you come to see us, Angelos. We do not see enough of you. How is Sophia?" Fotini asked.

"She is good. Growing every day and more mischievous!"

"Yes, I heard about the lizard! I cannot believe she managed to catch one; they are fast!" Fotini laughed.

"She was lucky. The lizard was stupid. She fooled it into a trap. The creature is safely back in the olive groves where it belongs! I think I need to watch her as she gets older! I do not know what she will do from one minute to the next. My poor *Mana*. Sophia runs the circles around her every day, and *Mana* is getting older now and it is too much for her."

"Well, if I can ever help... of course you will have to ask my brother, but as you are one of his closest friends, he will of course say yes!" Fotini smiled. "I will leave you men to talk. It is good to see you though, Angelos. You must visit us more often."

Fotini disappeared into the café and the two men sat, drank their coffee and watched as life in peacetime Zakynthos Town continued around them, as it had always meant to.

TWENTY-SEVEN

Mainland Greece, 1948

"Where are you going?" Roula demanded.

"I must help your father. There is work we must do in the mountains. Trees need to be felled for logs and the old hut needs fixing. Stay with your mother and look after Athena."

"I want to help you, Richard."

"I know you do my brave, beautiful wife, but your mother and Athena need you here."

Having washed and changed, Richard kissed his wife and left her cuddling Athena in bed. He trod downstairs to get breakfast before the hard day of labour started. He loved his life here in Greece and never wanted it to end. As he trudged up the mountain, the warning Thanasis had given to the family resurfaced, making him feel uneasy. Manos had told him not to worry, it was just Greek bluster. It was what Thanasis did. But Richard wasn't so sure. He was worried, and had a wife and child to look after. Richard didn't trust Thanasis, and he would protect his family against the man whatever it took. Stopping, he turned back to look down the valley; it wouldn't be long and he'd be back with them.

∽

Roula threw back the covers and sulked her way downstairs. She wanted to be on the mountains with Richard, not stuck in the kitchen with her mother. At least she had Athena. She was a beautiful child, and one day soon, she and Richard would give Athena a brother or sister.

"You are late up. Come, sit and eat. Then you will look after Athena and I will get some supplies."

Roula sat and ate. Through mouthfuls of food, she smiled at Athena in her chair, and spoke to her mother. "Could I get the supplies? I have not been out in ages."

"No, it is better if I do it. This civil war, it causes too many problems. I do not want to see you come across trouble."

"I will be careful. I am younger than you, so if I need to run I will be much quicker."

"If you promise you will stay safe, my daughter, with none of your foolishness. The enemy are everywhere."

"I will." Roula stood and flung her arms around her mother. "I love you, mother. I am bored stuck at home. It is true I am a wife now, and have responsibilities to my husband and child, but you need my help too."

"Fine. You can fetch the supplies, but you go where I tell you and then come home. You do not go wandering. And you stay away from Thanasis. He has an evil head this week."

"Thank you! I will."

An hour later, Roula walked along the dusty track to the next farm to collect the items on her mother's list. The haze of a dust cloud ahead, accompanied by the rumbling ground, alerted her to an approaching vehicle. Deftly, Roula snuck through a gap in the stone wall. As she crouched down, the wicker basket slid from her arm and rolled back through the gap into the road. The vehicle was close now, and it was too late to grab it, so she stayed where she was. Hopefully it would go unnoticed, and the vehicle would drive over the top, and she could sneak back out to rescue it once they'd passed.

Fate wasn't on her side, however, and the vehicle drew to a stop. Peeking through the gap, she saw Thanasis, and her heart dropped. The one person her mother had told her to avoid.

The Greek stepped down from the vehicle and lifted the basket, smirking. "What is this? A peasant's basket. Come out, wherever you are, or we will shoot you from your hiding place for being a spy!"

Roula shuddered; she refused to face the man. He couldn't be trusted. Slowly, she slid back into the long grass, hoping he'd get bored and move on.

"Out now! Or we will come and find you," the man bellowed.

Roula sat silent and still.

"The scared peasant disobeys us men. They want to play games. If that is what you want, then you can be our prey. We will be your hunters, and you will be our scared little prey. Run prey!"

Roula's limbs trembled with fear and her throat was dry. She looked about her. Despite the long grass along the wall, the trees and other vegetation were sparse on this part of the road. There was nowhere she could go without being spotted. She made a run for it anyway, heading towards a copse of trees in the distance. Her feet pounded the ground, matching the loud thudding of her heart in her chest. The pounding was joined by shouts and further running of feet behind her.

They were chasing her. Hunting her, like a rabbit was hunted by dogs.

In the copse, she threw herself to the ground and rolled under an old decaying tree trunk, hoping in vain it would cover her. Her breathing was ragged and her skin drenched in sweat, and just as she thought she'd escaped them, a rough hand grabbed her ankle and pulled her from her hiding place and along the ground. She didn't know the man holding her, but she kicked out with her free foot anyway.

"Let me go, you pig!"

The man released her foot and she scurried backwards, her back hitting a tree stump. Thanasis stepped forward and stared down at her. "It is little Roula, the whore wife of an Englishman. Tell me, little Roula. What does he have that we do not?"

"Manners! You are filthy pigs!"

Thanasis laughed. "Why are you here?"

"None of your business!"

"It is my business. Now tell me!"

"I am getting supplies for my mother."

"You lie to me, little Dimitroula Papadoulia. Your mother would never let you out of her sight. I ask again. What are you doing out here?"

"I told you. Getting supplies! I dropped my basket."

Thanasis grabbed hold of her hair and glared at her. His hot, stale breath brushed her face, and she turned away from him. "I know you are a spy. You mountain peasants are all the same. You will pay for lying to me. I will punish you. Hold her down."

Roula fought hard as two men held her to the dusty ground. She knew what was coming and fought them like an angry cat, but they were too strong for her. Thanasis unbuttoned his trousers, kneeled over her and took her roughly where she lay.

She screamed for help.

She screamed for mercy.

She screamed for Richard to save her, but her desperate pleas went unheard.

When Thanasis had finished, his cowardly friends took their turn. Time passed slowly as she endured the vile punishment. Earth slid under her nails as she dug her fingers into the ground. Stones stabbed into her back, scraping and cutting her skin through her dress under the unwanted weight of the men.

By the time they'd finished with her, she was exhausted, bruised and beaten. Her clothes were ripped, and her face wet with tears. She was dragged to her feet, but didn't have the energy to stand. As she listlessly leaned against a tree, Thanasis's foul breath permeated her nose again as he whispered, "Now it is time for you to run again."

Glancing down, she saw the gun. It wasn't over.

Her body ached and screamed with exhaustion. She pushed herself to her feet and wobbled unsteadily, before digging deep and running from the copse. Stumbling out into the sunshine, Roula headed for the road. Her battered body slowed her down, and she could hear them behind her, but she knew she must run. It was the only way she would survive.

Thudding footsteps grew closer as she reached the gap in the stone wall again. She ran out onto the dusty track, narrowly avoiding the static vehicle. A gunshot rang out and pain seared her back. Her legs crumpled, dropping her to the ground.

As sticky blood marked her skin, life began to ebb from her. Rough arms took hold of her, and she was pushed against a tree. A rough rope scraped her bare skin as a noose was slung around her neck. Roula finally blacked out as the men pulled hard on the rope, lifting her off her feet, breaking her neck. Laughing, Thanasis and his men drove off, leaving Roula's lifeless body swinging at the edge of the road in the gentle breeze.

∽

Richard heard his mother-in-law's wailing before he reached the house. Raw sounds of pain and anguish. He knew instantly something was wrong and rushed into the kitchen.

"She is dead! She is dead… She is dead!"

"Sit, Vivi. What has happened?"

All she could do was point, and he followed her finger. The sight made him collapse. Roula. His beautiful wife's battered and bruised body had already been cleaned, and been respectfully covered in a sheet. Only her face was visible. She was dead. Taking her in his arms, he cried, bathing her in tears of love as though trying to heal her, but she remained dead.

His grief was punctuated by his father-in-law who wailed at the sight of his daughter, and the two men held each other tightly sharing their grief and loss.

It wasn't long before the house filled with friends, who offered their support, and Roula was carried up the mountain to be buried. It was all so quick, but Richard knew it was Greek tradition.

As they began to leave the burial site to return to the house, Thanasis arrived. Swaggering up the mountain, a hush fell, and he walked over to Manos and Richard, wedging himself between them.

"It is a shame, but you were warned about the consequences. Your family has paid the highest price, Manos. Let that be a lesson to you."

"Say that again, you bastard!" Richard spat.

"You are better off without her," Thanasis taunted.

Richard flew at Thanasis, punching him, catching the man off guard. Reaching down, Richard slid the gun from Thanasis's holster and turned it on him.

"Tell me again, you bastard. Tell everyone what you just told me!"

As people stared in horror at the unfolding drama, Thanasis laughed as he stood and dusted his clothes down., rubbing his jaw. "He is filled with grief and does not know what he says. Ignore him."

"You are correct. He *is* grief stricken, Thanasis, and I heard what you said. *You* killed my daughter. You dare to call her vile names in front of her father and mother. In front of her husband! You bastard!" Manos raged.

"I put her out of her misery. Her shame would have killed her if I had not. She was soiled, Richard; a stupid mountain girl who let me and my men take her far too easily."

Thanasis spat at Richard's feet and walked away, his vicious laughter wrapping itself around them. Richard didn't hesitate and did the unspeakable. He lifted the gun and slew Thanasis where he was standing. Thanasis was dead before he hit the ground.

A NIGHT OF THUNDER

Richard sat on a boulder next to his wife's grave, looking out across the valley. It was a fitting resting place for the girl who loved the mountains the way she had. From afar, Richard watched as Manos explained the injustice Thanasis had dished out to Roula and the family. Thanasis's men slunk away, fearful of reprisals, and Vivi was inconsolable. Men from the village gathered, lifted Thanasis's traitorous body and threw it into a ravine to rot for eternity.

It was then Richard knew it was over. His life in Greece was at an end. Everything he'd built here was lost; his beautiful wife, dead. It was time to return to Bristol and start afresh. It was the only way he would ever banish the memories of Roula's death and his own actions of cold-blooded murder he'd be forced to live with until the day he died.

TWENTY-EIGHT

Bristol, England, 1948

Life had settled into an easy post-war rhythm. The factory had returned to normal work and Lissy had moved back to the office to take up an administration role. Her relationship with George had blossomed, and receiving no news from Richard, they slowly began to step out in public. Neither had been brave enough to tell Richard's parents yet, though.

Lissy was looking forward to curling up on the rug in front of the fire with George – a welcome end to a long tiring day of shuffling paper and making cups of tea – when the secretary came to find her.

Out of breath and flustered, the secretary spoke quickly. "You've a message from a Mr and Mrs Hobbs."

The room tilted and nausea rose in Lissy's stomach. Sitting on a nearby chair, she gripped it tightly, her coat and bag falling to the floor.

"What did they say?" Lissy whispered.

"They've asked you go and see them as soon as you get this message. It's urgent. They've phoned three times."

A NIGHT OF THUNDER

"Thank you. Was there anything else?"

"No, just that. Are you okay, Lissy?"

"Yes, I'm fine. Just tired. Thank you for finding me."

"Look after yourself." The secretary turned leaving Lissy alone. She took a deep breath, stood, picked up her belongings, and headed to the bus stop. She boarded the first bus that arrived, knowing she'd have to change buses in the centre to get to Clifton. She stared out of the window, watching as the post-war streets passed by in a blur. Her mind whirred with the endless possibilities of why the Hobbs family wanted to see her. After changing buses, she alighted in Clifton, walking the rest of the way. Nerves bounced around in her stomach and her skin was clammy.

As she reached the house, she almost turned and ran away, but she forced herself to face the news, whatever it was. Knocking on the front door, Lissy waited patiently. Mrs Hobbs opened the door and smiled at her.

"You got our message. You'd better come in, dear."

Lissy walked into the familiar house, following Mrs Hobbs into their front room. An unrecognisable man was sitting by the fireplace in a wingback chair. Mr Hobbs sat opposite him. As she entered, they stopped talking, and all eyes were on her.

"Richard?" The word was barely a whisper.

The man rose and walked towards her. He was thinner than the man she once loved and remembered. His face was etched with age and she noticed a slight limp in one of his legs.

"Yes, darling Lissy. It's me."

Lissy stepped towards him and lightly touched his cheek with her index finger. He was real. Stepping back, she stared at him.

"Where have you been? What happened? It's been too long."

Mrs Hobbs indicated to the sofa and Lissy sat. Richard sat back in the wingback chair next to his father.

"It's hard to talk about it. In 1942 I was shot down over Greece. I crash-landed on an island called Zakynthos and broke my leg. I was lucky to be rescued by the resistance. They looked after me. The resistance helped me recover and worked out a plan to get me home." He paused. "The plan went wrong, and I never came home. Until now."

"Oh Richard. Did they... the camps... did they..?" Lissy was finding it hard to speak.

"No, I never ended up in the camps. I was one of the lucky ones. I ended up on the Greek mainland hidden away with other resistance. They protected me. I became one of them. It was for my safety. In the end, I continued fighting and joined the resistance in their war against the Nazis."

"The war ended years ago. Why has it taken so long for you to get home? I don't understand. Surely you could've been home sooner?"

"*Papa*! Hungry. Need food!"

Lissy's attention was brought sharply to the small child who'd run to Richard and climbed onto his lap, speaking in broken English. Richard responded to the child in Greek, then in English.

"You've already eaten, Athena. You can have more later. Sit quietly while we talk. It's important."

Mrs Hobbs walked over to Richard and lifted Athena from his lap. "I'll take her upstairs and you can continue talking."

Lissy looked on in confusion as Mrs Hobbs and Athena left the room.

"Who was that?"

"Her name's Athena."

The words left her uneasy. "You're going to have to explain it to me, Richard. I'm struggling to understand. You've been fighting with Greek resistance. The war was over years ago and you never came back when hostilities ended. Suddenly you're here, and have a child with you? Where have you been? Who have you been with and who is the child?"

"You must understand the war changed so many things for so many people, Lissy..."

"Don't bloody condescend me, Richard! I might not have flown planes, but I did my bit for the war too. I witnessed my own horrors! Who's the child and *why* is she with you? Why did she call you *papa*?"

"Athena is the child of the woman who rescued me on Zakynthos. I made a promise to take care of the girl after her mother was captured by Nazis. Athena stayed with me and lived with us on the Greek mainland. She's like my own daughter now. Deep down I know she must be returned to her own family. It's something I promised to do, but I couldn't leave her behind on the Greek mainland when I came home. It was too dangerous. It's been a difficult situation."

"She's not yours?"

"No, she's not mine."

"And who's *us*?"

"Sorry?"

"You said *she lived with us on the Greek mainland*. Who's us?" Lissy demanded.

Richard breathed out and closed his eyes momentarily. "A lot happened during the war, Lissy. Things people will never understand. *Us* was a family I lived with, some resistance fighters." He paused knowing what he said next would change everything. "One of them was my wife."

Dizziness washed over Lissy. She forced herself to stay conscious, digging her fingernails into her palms, as the bottom fell out of her world. All the time she'd been so guilty about betraying Richard's memory with George. The guilt had eaten her up. Now Richard was back, and not only had he met another woman and fallen in love, but he'd married her!

Lissy leapt across the room and pummelled Richard with her fists. "You selfish bastard! You bastard! A wife! You have another wife! I was supposed to be your wife! Me! But you left me. No, you abandoned me! You abandoned me to go and fly your precious plane! Your stupid plane and grandeur of war was more important than I was! Now you return as though nothing's happened, and I find out that not only did you desert me, you *chose* to stay in a country that isn't yours, you chose to fight for that country and not me! You forgot about me and chose to marry someone else! You selfish bastard!"

"Enough! I won't have language like that in my home, especially not from a young lady. We've all had a shock today, but this isn't appropriate behaviour, Lissy!" Mr Hobbs dragged Lissy off Richard and held onto her.

"What is happening, *papa*? Why is everyone angry?" Mrs Hobbs ran into the room after Athena.

"I don't understand what she's saying; her English is poor. She wouldn't stay upstairs. It's you she wants, Richard. Only you. What's going on?"

Lissy glared at the child and Richard. She shook Mr Hobbs free and ran from the house, slamming the front door behind her. Lissy didn't stop running until she reached the bus stop.

A NIGHT OF THUNDER

Lissy paced her front room waiting for George. Her anger had continued to simmer ever since leaving the Hobbs's house. She was being incredibly hypocritical. She hadn't been so angelic when it came to close relationships. But Lissy had thought Richard was dead. Almost everyone declared missing in action never returned. Lissy choosing to be with George was her way of getting closure, of moving on. As the years had passed, she'd never expected Richard to return.

But he had, large as life and married. This was what hurt the most. Richard had known she'd be waiting for him. He could've contacted her any time but he hadn't. Instead, he'd chosen another life. He'd met someone else and married.

Lissy stopped pacing for a moment. If Richard was married, where was the woman, and why had he come home? And what about the child? A child he said wasn't his. Was he telling the truth or just trying to spare her feelings? Was the child actually his?

Lissy's mind whirled trying to make sense of everything, but the more she thought about it, the more confused and upset she became. By the time George arrived, Lissy was frantic. She'd drunk three glasses of brandy and almost paced a hole in the front room carpet.

"Lissy! I'm sorry for being late. I picked up something for tea." George appeared in the doorway, smiling, holding two packs of fish and chips. He scowled, placed the packs on the side table and took her hands in his.

"What's happened?"

"He's back," Lissy whispered. "Richard. He's at his parents' house."

"Oh... When?"

"I'm not sure. A message came to go to his parents' house. I expected the worst, George. I thought this was it and they'd finally found his body and I could get closure, and I could move on... we could move on."

"And?"

"He was alive all this time, George. He wasn't just alive. He was living in Greece with another family. Married to another woman. The bastard! Even worse, he's come home with a young child who calls him *papa*!"

"A child?" George gently steered Lissy to the armchairs and they sat.

"Yes. He told me she's the daughter of some resistance woman who rescued him. But what if the child is his? Why would she call him *papa* if she wasn't his?"

"It's odd." George blew out a long breath. "What did you say to him?"

"I got angry. I hit him a couple of times. I yelled at him and stormed out. I've no idea what to do now."

"Do you want him back?"

"No! Yes... no! God, I've no idea, George. I expected him to be dead. I'd come to terms with him being dead and never coming back. I was moving on with my life, but how can I now?"

George stood. "Let me put the food in the kitchen and we'll talk properly." As he left the room, a knock sounded at the front door. George shouted that he'd answer it. Moments later, her worlds collided as George and Richard both walked into the front room.

"Lissy. I thought I should come to see you. Things were left badly, and I should explain properly." Richard glared at George. "I didn't know you would have company."

"A bit late don't you think? You could have come back

years ago. Why now?" George glared back, before turning to Lissy. "You don't have to talk to him if you don't want to."

"Who are you, sir? I don't remember meeting you in our circle of friends before I left the country to go and fight in the war."

"I'm Constable Perkins. The man who's been supporting Lissy since *you* disappeared."

"Are you sleeping with him?" Richard asked bluntly.

"If she is, it's none of your business!" George countered.

"As she's still my fiancée, it *is* my business." Richard pushed at George, who squared up to him, poking Richard in the chest.

"If you were so worried about your fiancée, Mr Hobbs, you wouldn't have stayed away. You left Lissy to worry about you for all these years and believe you were dead! Neither would you have married someone else!"

"Stop! Both of you, just stop it!" Lissy screamed.

Richard stepped towards her and lightly rested his hand on her arm. "I'm truly sorry, Lissy. I haven't handled things well. I could have been easier on you at my parents' house. It must have been a huge shock. But I had to come and see you. You stormed out without giving me a chance to explain everything, and I do want to explain it all to you. Please, just give me an hour of your time. If you're still angry by the time the hour is up, you can throw me out."

Lissy turned away from both men and stared at a painting on the wall, allowing the image of a woodland in spring to calm her. Did she want to talk to him? Did she want to hear all the gory details? More so, did she want to have to explain her own actions? Neither had been a saint over the years; they were both guilty of betraying the other. She needed to know, though. Whatever had happened, and whatever she chose to do next, she needed all the answers. It was the only way any of them would be able to move on.

"I'll give you one hour, Richard." She turned and put her hand up to George. "Please give us some space, Constable Perkins. Mr Hobbs and I have things we need to discuss."

Without speaking, George walked out of the house, slamming the door hard behind him. The silence was deafening, and it was Lissy who sat down and spoke first.

"Please sit. Where's the child?"

Richard sat in the chair on the opposite side of the fireplace.

"Athena is with my parents. I thought it best to speak to you alone."

"Thank you."

The uncomfortable silence appeared again for a moment. Finally, it was Richard who spoke.

"I never meant to hurt you, Lissy. I won't lie, though, I'm glad I went to fight. I enjoyed being in the squadron and flying planes. It was exhilarating. Swooping and diving through the skies, fighting the enemy. With every flight, I was fighting for my country. I was proud knowing that every enemy plane I engaged in battle with was one less plane that would make it to England. Up in the sky, I felt like I was keeping you and my parents safe. Then everything changed. In 1942, one of the bastards hit me, they got me. Like so many other pilots, I thought my time was up and I'd end up as fish food or die in a fireball. Somehow, I was lucky. I didn't die. I parachuted out and despite a hard landing, I felt the earth under my feet. It was pitch black, I had no idea where I was and from the pain in my leg, I knew I'd busted my leg."

He paused, rubbing his lower limb. Lissy remained

silent, allowing him to continue. She needed to hear every word, however difficult it may be.

"Anyway, I was lucky. The Greek resistance found me. They took me to a secret hiding place in the mountains: a cold, damp cave, where I stayed for over a year. A man called Dionysios and a young woman called Elena looked after me. I eventually learned I was on a small Greek island called Zakynthos. Elena and I became friends. She was my saviour in a bleak time. She tended to my wounds, brought me food and water and talked to me. Elena kept me alive and sane. In 1943, Elena and Dionysios arranged to smuggle me off the island. A boat was to collect me and take me onwards to Malta, where I could get home to England, to *you*. But it all went wrong. Sorry, can I get some water?"

"Yes." Lissy went to the kitchen to fetch a jug of water and two glasses. Placing them on the table with shaking hands, she sat and watched as Richard poured himself a glass and drank. Her mind was screaming with a thousand more questions, but she needed to let him talk. The time for questions would be later.

"Where was I? It all went horribly wrong, Lissy. In the depth of night, we went to a beach and waited for the boat. To get information for the resistance, Elena had been forced to start a relationship with an Italian soldier. She'd tell me how she felt about it, and she had hated it. Elena also told me about her life on the island. She had trusted the Italian, I think might have even fallen in love with him a little, but the Italian betrayed us to the Nazis. The boat arrived in the darkness as planned, but the Italian turned up on the beach, followed by Nazis. I got in the boat, desperate to get away. Dionysios was shot, and Elena did everything she could to get me out of there. She saved me. I've no idea what happened to her, but she saved me, and in return I saved her child. Athena is *her* child, Lissy. Elena had planned for her and Athena to escape too. Athena did, but Elena never did. By then, the boat was out in the sea, heading away from the island. The last I saw was Elena being dragged away by the Nazis. I've no idea if she lived or died."

Lissy paled. War in Bristol had been horrendous, but this was something else. Everyone had learned just how despicable the Nazis had been during the Nuremberg Trials. She went to speak, but Richard stopped her.

"It was rough for us afterwards, Lissy. I found myself adrift at sea in the pitch of night with a young child I'd been asked to save. A deed I'd promised to do in the heat of the moment. The rest of the rescue plan failed. Athena and I ended up on the Greek mainland where we were met by more Greek resistance. We were hidden away in the darkness, transported through lanes and roads at night to keep us safe. Eventually, we ended up in the mountains somewhere in Greece you wouldn't even be able to find on a map. There, Athena and I were taken in by a family. Manos, his wife, Vivi, and their daughter, Roula. They protected me and Athena, Lissy. Just like Elena, they put their lives on the line for us. There, my life changed. I became one of them, a resistance fighter. I fought the war the only way I could, all the while protecting a young child that wasn't mine, but one that in the heat of the moment I'd promised to care for. The Second World War ended, and Greece ended up in a horrific civil war. It was bitter and bloody. People who had been friends and fought alongside each other in the Second World War suddenly became enemies. I won't say anymore because it hurts too much, but Roula died. She was murdered by a member of the Greek resistance; a man we'd fought alongside." He buried his head in his hands for a moment. A small sob escaped him. "I'd settled in Greece,

Lissy. Despite the horrors of war, I'd started a new life. I'd fallen in love with the country. I'd found a woman I loved with all my heart. A woman who made even the hardships of life worth living. She was my everything. She was ripped away from me. Her murderer cruelly took everything from me. Her murderer turned me into a murderer, too. After losing my wife and killing *him*, I had no choice but to come home to England."

He paused to drink some more water. Lifting the jug with shaking hands, he poured himself another glass. He put the jug back on the tray and fell forward in his chair, heaving great sobs. Lissy dropped to the floor next to him and enveloped him in her arms. She'd never have believed it if she hadn't heard it from him. Her Richard. So brave, so hurt, so exhausted by such dramatic and traumatic events.

"I'm sorry Lissy. I know I've put you through hell. I should have told you where I was. I was a foolish coward."

"It's alright. You're here now." She paused. "Roula, she was the one you married?"

"Yes. How did you know?"

"Your face, Richard. Your face lit up at the mention of her name. I could see the love you had for her. I'm sorry she died."

"Really?"

"Really. Whilst I'm angry and upset, and will admit this will take a long time to come to terms with, I don't hate you, and somewhere deep down inside, I still love you."

"You do?"

"Yes. I've seen how war changes things. It's left all of us different people. As with you, my war was difficult. Nowhere near as traumatic as yours. I'd never pretend that. But it was hard nonetheless."

"And Constable Perkins?"

Lissy knew she must be as honest with Richard as he'd been with her. "Yes. He and I are together. You were missing. I didn't know if you were alive or dead. As the war ended and the years passed, hope faded. I was lonely and hurt. I needed someone and George was that person."

"Are you married?"

"Oh no, nothing like that."

"So, there's hope for us yet, Lissy Cook?"

"I don't know, Richard. So much has happened, and I must think hard about what I want. I do have to consider George in all of this. He's a good man; I love him and he deserves to be treated respectfully."

"I understand." Richard stood and straightened his trousers. "I'll leave you to think. I'm staying at my parents' house. When you've decided either way, let me know. I may have loved another and married her, and will always love her, but there is still a place for you in my life, Lissy."

Richard left the house and Lissy sat alone in her front room with a head full of jumbling thoughts and questions. Deep down, however, she knew what she must do.

Almost as if he'd been watching, there was another knock at the front door. Lissy let George in. She smiled, beckoning for him to go into the front room. She stood by the fireplace instead of sitting, holding onto the mantelpiece for strength.

"Are you okay?"

"I am, George. I've something I need to say; please let me speak. Richard's arrival back in Bristol has been turbulent for all of us. I'm sorry George, but we must break it off. I do love you, but my love for Richard was there first, and I was engaged to him; technically I still am. He has returned and I must fulfil my agreement to marry him. I don't want to upset you, but it's my decision."

"You're making a huge mistake, Lissy. You don't love him! If you truly did, you would never have shared my bed. You would never have told me you love me. He married another woman! He has returned with another woman's child! Would he have even come back if his wife hadn't died?"

"It isn't up for discussion, George. I've made my decision."

"Fine. But don't come running to me when it all goes wrong." George stormed from the house, slamming the front door for the second time that day.

TWENTY-NINE

Zakynthos, Greece, 1950

"Come here. Look at me!" Pigi beckoned to her granddaughter who was doing a good impression of someone who had been dragged through the olive groves upside down. "I put you in a good dress and look at you! You will need a wash and another clean dress if you do not sit still and behave!"

Sophia poked her tongue out at Pigi and ran around the large front room of the Sarkis house, climbing over the furniture, doing forward rolls onto the carpet.

"Stop!" Pigi threw up her hands and muttered a string of Greek words unsuitable for young ears.

"Sophia Sarkis! Behave for *Nonna!*" Angelos bellowed as he entered the room. Dressed in smart clothes and wearing a new hat, he smiled at his mother. He hadn't seen her looking this relaxed and happy in a long time. Kissing her on the cheek, he clapped his hands. "Are we ready? We will go!"

The family headed south to Zakynthos Town to meet up with Niko, Pantelis and his sister, Fotini, to watch the

A NIGHT OF THUNDER

carnival celebrations. On the harbour, the group of friends joined the already growing throng of people waiting for the passing parade.

"Can I hold your hand?" Sophia asked Fotini.

"If *Baba* says it is okay, then yes you can."

"*Baba*, may I hold Fotini's hand?"

"Yes, but you must do everything Fotini tells you. You behave and let go for nothing," Angelos said.

"Yes, *Baba*." Excitedly, Sophia took hold of Fotini's hand, gripping it tightly. She skipped alongside her as they walked.

"It is good to see her happy with other people," Pigi said, waving to an old village friend. "Fotini is a good girl. I cannot believe she is almost twenty-five! I had always hoped she would find a good man."

"Sometimes the sins of families remain long after the bad deeds have passed. My Brother Damiano was a good soul; we lost him too early. Kyriakos, *pah!* That man put a dark stain on us and our family name. Everyone knew him, knew his noble name that is centuries old. He betrayed all of us with Nazi association. It has scarred us. Some still do not trust us; they think we are the same when we are not. Fotini has paid a big price. No man wants her." Pantelis shrugged and shook his head.

"It is a shame I am not younger, or I would have offered!" Niko laughed.

"You are a dear friend, Niko. But you are not a man for my sister!"

"She is still young, Pantelis. Maybe one day a man will love her. Keep hope." Angelos patted Pantelis on the shoulder supportively.

"Look! Look! They are coming!" Sophia had stopped and was clapping her hands together in excitement. Fotini stood behind the girl with her hands on her shoulders. The group stopped where they were and huddled together, watching the long train of people parade past them. Some wore costumes of the ancient Venetians; others wore everyday clothing. Each passing group represented something special or traditional about Zakynthos. The crowds cheered and clapped the parade, and enjoyed being out on the streets celebrating. The tradition was so important to Zakynthians, and they'd missed it during the war.

As the last group paraded past, Angelos, his family and friends heard music and followed the sound. Dancing had begun in Solomos Square. True celebrations had now begun, and the family and friends joined in with great abandon.

As the lilting sounds of *bouzouki*, *lute* and *toumbi* wove their way around the square, Niko bowed to Fotini and swept her off her feet before she had the chance to say no; and Pantelis lead Pigi into the square to join the traditional dance. Not wanting to be left out, Angelos took his daughter's hands in his, beaming proudly as he taught her the intricate moves.

It was hours later when Angelos, Pigi and Sophia said goodbye to their friends and returned to the Sarkis home, tired but happy.

"I have not danced like that in years. Oh, how I have missed it!" Pigi declared.

"It has been a wonderful day. Sophia enjoyed it too, and something has finally tired her out," Angelos said as he carried his sleeping daughter up the stairs and laid her on her bed. Pigi gently removed Sophia's shoes and drew a blanket over her. Closing the door, they went downstairs and sat outside.

"It is good to see you happy, Angelos. I do not think I have seen you like this since..."

"It is okay, *Mana*. You can say it. You can say her name. *Elena*."

"I saw you both dance at the Agia Mavra Festival in 1939. You had no idea I had been searching for you. I saw you both from a distance. You looked so happy together. I wish I had supported you both more. I liked Elena."

"You did?"

"Oh Angelos. My son. Many saw me as a timid, frightened woman before the war and during it. It is true. To some extent I was frightened. My life was never what I would have chosen for myself. There are Greek traditions that mean we do not always get what we want. You yourself saw it. Stelios and your father made a stupid marriage between you and Maria for their own reasons. I did not agree, but there was nothing I could do. They were all about money, their grand houses and their status in life. Neither man knew what love was or even cared about it."

"*Mana* I..."

"I have not finished, son. Let me speak. I have so much to say, and if I do not say it now, I will never do so. My father was like yours and Stelios. My father decided my purpose in life when I was born. My only purpose was to be the glue that joined two families of status together. Your father neither loved nor cared about me. He did care about his status in Zakynthos society, though. My father's name, like Stelios's, was in the Libro D'Oro. Watered down nobles from centuries ago who still think they rule the island even though they do not. The point of this is to say I am sorry, my son. I have not been the best mother I could have been." Pigi held up her hand as Angelos tried to interrupt her again. "Your father was as cruel to me, Angelos, as he was to you. I should have stood up to him, but I was too feeble. If I had, he would have turned his anger on me. It would have been worse for you, too. Oh, but how I wish I had stood up to him. If I had, maybe your life would have been better. Maybe Elena would have been your wife and not Maria. Maybe Athena would still be here and maybe Elena would not have died." Pigi buried her head in her hands, sobbing. "Oh, Angelos, my boy. I am so sorry. It is all my fault."

Gently taking his mother's hands in his, Angelos knelt at his mother's feet. She lifted her head, her face wet from shed tears. "You never did anything wrong, *Mana*. Never! It was all him. *He* did this to both of us. *He* is to blame for everything. You are to blame for nothing! I love you. I see how you are with Sophia. The true *you* has come to us from under its shell, and it is good to see. Do not blame yourself for the past. It was not your fault, *Mana*. It was all him."

Pigi smiled, placed a hand on her son's cheek and then stood. "Thank you for listening. I love you too, son. Good night. Sleep well."

"Sleep well too." Angelos watched his mother walk into the house. His mother had liked Elena and would have supported their marriage. Oh, how different life would have been. After a day of laughter and celebration, the sadness wrapped itself around Angelos as he sat in silence, stared up at the stars and allowed the tears to silently fall.

THIRTY

Bristol, England, 1950

After ending her relationship with George Perkins in 1948, Lissy had gone to meet Richard on the Downs. It had been a meeting of nerves and uncertainty for them both, but they'd walked through the expansive greenery and talked for hours.

"This isn't easy for me, Richard. It's going to take time. There will be a part of me that will never fully get over what's happened. War made fools of us all. It forced us into situations we'd never have endured in peacetime. I've told George it's over, and you and I are going to try again. It will not be like it was before, though, and trust won't come quickly."

"I'm happy that you're giving me a second chance, Lissy. I think you, me and Athena will make a good family. It's all I ever wanted with you."

"About Athena. She can live with us for now, but it's on my terms. I know she's been through a lot, Richard, but we matter too. I won't take second place to another woman's child."

"I understand. You're my life now, Lissy. We'll be a proper family."

"We'll see. Athena isn't yours and at some point, we'll have to discuss her long term future."

"Of course. It will all be okay, Lissy."

The conversation on the Downs had taken place two years ago and much had happened since. In spite of her reservations, Lissy and Richard had married within a month to start their new life together as soon as possible. It was a small ceremony, held in the company of the few people who needed to attend.

Once married, they'd moved into a new home of their own near to Richard's parents. It had a small garden and nice neighbours. Lissy had no hesitation leaving her old, rented home behind. It held so many reminders of the war. Things she'd rather forget. It also meant she was able to leave George behind too, and not risk seeing him on his beat.

Eventually, Richard and Lissy adopted Athena, allowing her to become part of their family. It hadn't been easy, and Lissy still had concerns about the child and her own Greek family. Eventually, however, Athena had become Athena Hobbs, the adopted daughter of Richard and Lissy Hobbs.

The first year was a good one for the small family. They enjoyed their life together and settled into their new home. After struggling to find his feet, Richard's father found his son a job working in insurance. It wasn't as exciting as flying planes, but it paid well and kept a roof over their heads.

After working so hard during the war, things changed for Lissy, too. Her job was now mother and homemaker, looking after the house, cleaning, cooking meals and ensuring Athena was well cared for.

A NIGHT OF THUNDER

Richard found a place at a local school for Athena, and she settled in reasonably well, but was quiet, and often withdrawn. At such a young age, she'd been through a lot, and they knew it would take her time to settle in.

1952 brought changes for the family. Lissy and Richard had settled into a comfortable pairing. Neither was madly in love with the other, but they respected and cared for each other. Both older, having been through a lot, they were settled and no longer in the early stages of young love. Both had fallen in love with another during turbulent times, but the love Richard and Lissy had originally experienced before the war had disappeared.

Richard missed Roula, the true love of his life. Each year, on the anniversary of her death, he'd sought his own company somewhere quiet where he could grieve and remember the strong Greek woman who still held his heart.

Lissy missed George. She'd tried not to, trying her best to settle into life with Richard and Athena. She wasn't happy, though, and realised early on that George was the man she loved and should've stayed with. She'd no choice now, though. She and Richard were married, and she was a mother. She was forced to accept the life she'd chosen.

Now twelve years old, Athena had started to come out of her shell and show her true personality. Full of tenacity and courage, Athena knew her own mind and wasn't afraid to share it. She adored Richard and spent as much time with him as she could, always asking questions, her enquiring mind constantly pushing boundaries. Her relationship with Lissy, however, was strained and showing signs of problems.

Lissy tried her best to install discipline, but Athena refused to listen to her. When seeking support from Richard, Lissy found herself on the outside as Richard caved in, allowing Athena to do the very thing Lissy had just denied the child. This put strain on Lissy and Richard's relationship.

This problem became more apparent one Sunday when the family, armed with a blanket and wicker picnic basket, had set out in Richard's car for a day out. The sun shone and the day was hot. They'd driven out of the city to the countryside. They pulled up next to a small river surrounded by trees.

Athena jumped out of the vehicle and cartwheeled across the grass, laughing.

"She's enjoying herself already," Richard said, lifting the blanket and picnic basket from the car boot.

"She's been full of energy this week. It will do her good," Lissy said. They walked to a flat piece of grass, close to the river, shaded overhead by large tree boughs. Lissy laid the blanket on the ground and sat on it as Richard put the picnic basket in the shade. They sat in silence, watching Athena as she picked daisies, ran around and sang to herself. She ran up to them.

"Can I go in the river please?" Athena begged. "I want to look for fish!"

"After lunch. We're going to eat soon," Lissy said. "Come sit on the blanket."

Turning her back to Lissy, Athena tugged at Richard's arm. "Please. Can I go in the river and look for fish?"

"Come on, let's go." Richard stood, took Athena's hand and they ran to the river's edge. Turning back for a moment, he smiled and waved at Lissy, before taking off his shoes and wading into the water. Athena copied him and squealed in delight as she stepped into the cool water.

Lissy watched them, trying not to be angry. Once again, Richard had overruled her decision. All Athena had to do was look at him and he said yes. It was frustrating. At times like this she might as well not even have bothered coming. Sighing to herself and trying not to get upset, Lissy opened the lid of the picnic basket and took out the tea flask. Pouring herself a cup, she drank, enjoying the taste of a proper cup of tea. Closing her eyes, Lissy enjoyed the heat of the sun, the sound of the birds and rippling sounds of the water as it passed by. Woven through it all was the sound of Athena and Richard laughing together. Momentarily, she opened her eyes to see Athena climbing a tree.

"Oh, for goodness sake. I give up!" Lissy said before closing her eyes again and laying back on the blanket to enjoy the sun.

"Lissy? Is it you?"

The voice stirred her, and her eyes flew open. "George?" She scrambled to her feet, and there he was, out of uniform and looking more handsome than before. Constable George Perkins. Her George.

"Hello, Lissy. It's been a long time. How are you?"

"I'm okay, thank you." She glanced nervously towards the river. Athena was still up the tree and Richard was watching the child. "How are you, George? What are you doing here?"

"I'm well. I like to get out of the city and this is one of my favourite places to go walking. I've never seen you here before."

"No. It's our first visit."

George glanced across at the river. "You're still with *him* then."

"Please don't, George. Not here. Athena is with us. I don't want any trouble. The past is the past and we've all moved on."

"You might have moved on, Lissy, but I haven't. You're

still in my thoughts; you're my everything, the only woman I ever loved. The only woman I'll ever love. I can't move on."

"Please don't drag everything up again, George. Richard and I are married. We adopted Athena. We're a family now."

"You don't look like much of one. All I see is a happy father and his daughter, with a bored stranger waiting for them."

"I thought it was you. What do *you* want?" Richard strode up to them and pushed George away from Lissy.

"I saw Lissy sitting alone and came over to say hello."

"You've said hello. Now you can go!"

"*Papa* look! No hands!"

Lissy, Richard and George turned to see Athena walking along a high tree branch as though it was a tightrope. Her hands were high in the air. Suddenly, she slipped on the bark and tumbled off, landing below with a loud splash. "*Papa!*"

Athena's scream brought them to their senses and they ran over to the river. Athena was sitting in the soft silty riverbed, water flowing around her as she cried. Richard waded in and crouched next to her.

"Is she alright?" Lissy asked with concern.

"How should I know?" Richard snapped, before turning to soothe his daughter. "What were you thinking, Athena? You could have really hurt yourself."

Lissy kicked off her shoes and stepped into the river. "Here, let me."

She crouched the other side of Athena and smiled. "I was a nurse once, Athena; well for a short while anyway. I learned to help people just like you who get into scrapes and injure themselves. Let's see how you are." Lissy looked at Richard, communicating she needed some space, and was grateful to him when he went and sat on the riverbank. George stood watching from a distance.

Lissy checked Athena over, and other than a couple of scratches and bruises, she'd miraculously escaped any serious injuries. "You're fine, but I think that's enough tree climbing for today. You need some food. Come on, let's sit on the blanket and dry out."

Lissy took hold of Athena's hand and helped her out of the water. They walked up the bank and over to the blanket where they sat. Lissy dried Athena down with a spare towel and began to hand out the food.

Richard walked over to George.

"Is the child okay?" the policeman asked.

"Yes. *Athena* is fine. Not that it's any of your business."

"Good. It looked like a nasty fall."

"It wasn't. The branch was low and overhanging the water. Now you're satisfied everything's okay *Mr Policeman*, you can leave. You're not welcome."

"It's a public park, *Mr Hobbs*."

"Public or not, *you're* not welcome. Now leave my family alone. Leave Lissy alone; she's mine not yours."

George turned and began to walk away. He stopped and looked back at the family on the blanket. "I'll be waiting for you, Lissy. However long it takes. I *will* wait for you."

Lissy closed her eyes as George's words hit her. In a perfect world, she'd run into George's arms right now and leave Richard and Athena to be a family on their own. She couldn't go back, though. She mustn't go back. The only option she had was to go forwards with her family. The future was what mattered, and the future was sitting on the blanket as the past walked away, slipping from her hands.

THIRTY-ONE

Zakynthos, Greece, 1952

Zakynthian sunshine was always at its harshest and brightest in the summer months. It was also the time Angelos and Niko worked hardest in the olive groves. This year it was unbearably hot. They had a lot of work to do, but even Angelos was feeling the effects. Lazily, Niko sat on the grass under the shade of a tree and drank from a glass bottle.

"I have not known it to be this hot in ages, Angelos. Even the canopy of trees do not give relief. I can do no more!"

"I am the same." Angelos sat next to his friend, wiping beads of sweat from his forehead. "I want to forget about the olives and take Sophia to the beach to enjoy the coolness of the sea before sleeping. Maybe we should work in the night, by the light of the moon!"

Niko laughed. "No, we cannot do that. I am too fond of my sleep; I cannot sleep in the day. You are right about the beach. It is a nice idea. Come Angelos, these trees can wait. Let us go to the beach. Sophia would love it."

Angelos stood and pulled his friend to his feet. "The

beach it is!" They cleared their tools away and walked back to the Sarkis house.

"*Baba! Baba!*" Sophia ran to Angelos and threw herself into his arms. He lifted her, swinging her around and making her giggle.

"Angelos. You are back early. Is there a problem?" Pigi said, wiping her hands on her apron.

"All is okay, *Mana*. It is too hot for me and Niko to work, so we will all go to the beach. It is time we enjoyed life and our beautiful island more, and Sophia can enjoy the sea."

Pigi smiled and nodded, taking hold of Sophia's hand. "Come and get ready. *Baba* is taking us to the beach!"

It wasn't long before Angelos and Pigi were sitting under the shade of a tree, enjoying the welcome respite of sea breeze. They watched Niko and Sophia enjoying themselves in the sea; Niko splashing his young niece with water, making her squeal in delight. Each time the sea water drenched her, she tried to get Niko back, but he was too quick, disappearing under the surface and swimming around her to pop up unseen by her side or behind her.

"It is good to see her happy after everything that has happened, Angelos. You are doing a good job raising her."

"It is not just me, *Mana*. You have helped me to carry the load. I could not have done it without help from you or Niko."

"We are family, Angelos. It is what family do."

Sophia and Niko ran out of the sea up the beach to join them, plonking themselves down under the tree. Pigi passed them all something to eat and drink, and they tucked in. Angelos smiled at his happy little family. They were unconventional, especially for Greece, but they had been forced into a different way of life after the war. What had once been tradition had changed for many, and whilst that tradition was still important, and they'd always *be* traditionally Greek, family took on a new meaning. Angelos would always ensure the Greek way of life came first as much as possible.

As they were enjoying the cool breeze and the sound of the waves, Sophia spoke.

"Why do I have no mother, *Baba*? Some boys in the village whisper horrible things when I go to get eggs for *Nonna*. The boys say my *Mana* was evil, and men killed her for being evil..."

Angelos, Niko and Pigi dropped their food to their plates and all looked at each other. This wasn't a conversation Angelos wanted or expected to have with his daughter at such a young age. "Come, sit next to me, Sophia."

Sophia did as she was asked.

"There was a big argument between many countries who were all fighting with each other. Greece ended up in the argument too, even though we didn't want to," Angelos began.

"I know, *Baba*. They told us about the war at school."

"That is right. The argument was called a war. We were all part of the war – the big argument – here on our island. Bad people came, and they were in charge and told us what we were allowed to do and things we were not allowed to do." Angelos took a deep breath, his eyes flicking up to his mother and Niko, before ploughing on. "Your *Mana*, Maria, was a brave woman. She fought for what was right, Sophia, and she argued with the bad men, but they did not like it. She died, Sophia. She was a brave woman, though, and you must ignore what people say about her and remember her as your *Mana*. Your *Mana* who loved you very much."

"Okay, *Baba*." Sophia stood. "Thank you. I have finished, and I am going to look for shells now."

"Okay. Just not too far from us," Angelos said, giving his daughter a brief hug.

Sophia skipped away from them, down the beach, occasionally stopping to bend, choose a find and slide it into her pocket.

"Oh, Angelos. Do you think it was right to tell her that?"

"What else could I say *Mana*? How can I tell her that her mother hated me? How can I tell Sophia that her mother was a Nazi sympathiser who cared more for the Nazis than for her own family? How can I tell Sophia all that? She is only nine years old and would never understand it. It is better she believes the spiteful young boys are just that: spiteful liars who got it wrong."

"You have done the right thing, Angelos," Niko said. "The war is the past. It is over. What good is there to drag up something Sophia would never understand? There is plenty of time in the future, when she is older, if you want to share the truth. So much happened to us during that time. It is not anything a young child needs to know of."

"Thank you, Niko. *Mana*? Do you agree?"

Pigi looked at Sophia, then her son. "Niko makes a good argument. I will trust your judgement, Angelos."

"Thank you. I hope we do not have to speak of it again." Angelos stood. "I am going to see how many shells she has collected; we may need to choose carefully and leave some behind or the beach will be empty!"

Angelos set off along the beach leaving Niko and Pigi to talk. He hated lying to his daughter. It was not something he ever wanted to do. But how could he tell her everything that had happened? Where would it stop? There was so much she didn't know, and how could a child of her age even begin to understand it when he barely understood it himself?

No, it was time to forget about the past and all the hateful things that had happened. They had to look to the future. He still had a family; that was what was important and nothing could risk that now.

THIRTY-TWO

Bristol, England, 1952

Lissy Hobbs was at her wits end. The boredom of being a housewife had reached its peak. She was frustrated and fed up with parenting a petulant child who wasn't her own, and Lissy longed for a different, more exciting life. Since the day at the river, when Athena had fallen out of the tree, the child had continued to push the boundaries and sometimes beyond them. Richard never told Athena off or explained what the consequences of her actions could be. When Lissy stepped in and tried, Athena ignored her. The relationship between Lissy and her adopted daughter was fractured, and with each passing day, becoming impossible to fix.

The spring school holidays had arrived. Instead of spending time together as a family, Richard had announced he would be working away for the next week. Lissy was furious. She was forced to spend the time alone with Athena and she was dreading it. After stripping the bedding, folding the towels and cleaning the kitchen, Lissy removed her apron.

She walked into the front room where Richard was

sitting with his feet up reading the paper and smoking a pipe, the scent of tobacco permeating the room. Athena sat on the floor playing with a doll she should've grown out of by now. Lissy watched the serene scene for a moment feeling far removed. She didn't belong with them. She never would.

"Richard, I've had a great idea." Lissy sat in the armchair opposite him. "Your parents haven't seen Athena for ages, and I know they love to spend time with each other. Maybe Athena would like to spend the week at her grandparents' house instead of being stuck here at home with me doing housework."

Athena's eyes lit up as Richard lowered the newspaper.

"Oh *Papa*! I would love that! It would be like a holiday, just for me! Please say yes, please!"

"I'll have to ask your grandparents, but if it's alright with them, then I see no reason why not. Won't you be lonely here alone, though, Lissy?"

"Yes, a little, gosh the house will be so quiet with both of you gone, but I think this will be good for Athena. I'll have plenty to keep me occupied here, and now that the weather is getting nicer, I can potter in the garden too."

"That's settled then. If your grandparents say it's alright, you can spend the holidays with them."

The following day, Lissy awoke late to a blissfully empty, quiet house. She turned onto her back and lay looking up at the ceiling. She had the whole house to herself for the next week. There would be no one else to look after, and she couldn't wait. Richard had left early, dropping his daughter at his parents' house on the way to work. He would collect her on the way home, in a week's time.

Lissy couldn't wait for some time alone without being at the beck and call of everyone else. After catching up on the minimal housework, Lissy went into Bristol city centre on the bus. Walking around the city, she marvelled at the changes that had occurred since the end of the war. The rubble had been cleared, and most of the old, ruined buildings were gone. New buildings were going up fast and the city felt alive again. People no longer worried about being bombed, and even though rationing was still in place, the future was finally filled with hope.

On a whim, Lissy left the centre to visit her old street. Taking the bus, she alighted at her old bus stop and walked the short distance to her old neighbourhood. The street looked the same as it had when she'd left. She hadn't realised until now how small the houses looked from the outside.

Walking along the street, she allowed the memories to swirl around her. Growing up with her parents, the early days with Richard, the loss of her brother. Lissy stopped outside her old house. The street was quiet, but she knew there would be net curtains slowly moving to catch a glimpse of the stranger who was in their street. Turning to look at the houses opposite, she raised her hand and waved, seeing a net curtain drop back into place.

Lissy walked to the nearby park she used to visit.

Being here in her old neighbourhood, walking through the park, stirred many more memories she'd buried and forgotten. The war, the air raids, packing parachutes. Sitting on a park bench, Lissy thought back to when she had sat there with George.

Her mind wandered to her current situation: her life with Richard and Athena. It was testing her, trying her patience. Athena wasn't the quiet and shy child she'd been when she arrived. She had turned into a demanding twelve-year-old who very much knew her own mind, and refused to behave. Athena continually wrapped Richard around her finger to get what she wanted. Whatever Lissy said was ignored. Most days it was as though Lissy didn't exist.

Lissy had always wanted to have children with Richard. A child who belonged to another woman had never been the plan, though, and certainly not a child who caused so much trouble.

Lissy pondered her decision to get back together with Richard. Had she made a mistake? Had they rushed into rekindling their relationship because both were grieving their losses in a time of war, hoping their shared past would heal the hurt they'd both experienced?

Deep down, Lissy knew going back had been the wrong choice to make. Her and Richard had both changed so much during the war. They'd become different people, and there was no putting back together the early relationship they'd had. Too much had changed.

Sitting alone in the park, Lissy realised she should've stayed with George and allowed Richard to move on and live his life without her. Then she would have been free to continue her relationship with George. The problem was, she hadn't, and now she and Richard were married. To complicate matters, they'd adopted Athena. As much as she longed to walk away and tell Richard it was over, there were other people involved. A child.

"Lissy?"

As though she'd conjured him just by thinking of him, George Perkins stood before her.

"Where did you spring from, Constable?"

"I walk through the park every day; it's still on my beat." George motioned to the bench. "May I sit?"

"Yes. Of course." Lissy moved along to give him some space.

"No Richard or his daughter today?"

"No. Richard is away working. Athena is staying with his parents for the week."

"So, what are you doing here? This park is a long way from your new life," George asked.

"I was in a reflective mood and wanted to visit the old street. The city is starting to look different after all the changes since the war."

"Well, to us it's all pretty much the same. Nothing much changes round here. The same gossips still gossip. The same criminals still rob the unsuspecting, and I still walk the same beat. Most of the people you left behind still live in the street. We're all the same. You're the only one who changed, and you did it by leaving us."

George's words hit home as though he'd slapped her.

"I..." She turned to face him, her eyes wet with tears. "Everything is such a mess, George. My relationship with Richard isn't the same as it was when we were younger. The child's a nightmare; she doesn't listen to me. It's as though I don't exist. Athena is Richard's world, and she is his. In all honesty, if I walked out the house one day and never went back, they probably wouldn't even notice. I'm just the person who cooks, cleans and looks after the house. I hate it and wish I'd never gone back to him."

"I'm sorry you're unhappy with your life, Lissy. I will admit that I'm angry you chose *him* over me, but I'd never want you to be unhappy. I need to know though, Lissy, why did you choose him? I know you once loved him, and his going missing was a huge wrench. But you and I had something. We loved each other. I thought we'd get married and settle down after the war, but you ripped it all away and you chose him. He abandoned you; he married another woman and then came home with another woman's child in tow.

Even after all that, you chose him over me. I don't understand why."

"Oh, George. My darling George. I don't fully understand it all either. I don't know why I chose him. I suppose I felt a sense of duty to him. When he left for war, I had promised to marry him; then he came home and we were still engaged, and I felt it was my duty to marry him. But I..."

"You...?"

"Oh, George do I need to spell it out?"

"Yes, Lissy, you do."

"I made a mistake, a terrible one. I love you, George! I never loved Richard like I loved you... love you. You're the man I truly love. My body, heart and soul. Everything about you, George. What I thought was love with Richard doesn't come close to what I thought was love until I met you. I love you, George Perkins, always have done and always will do."

George took her hands in his. She glanced around, but they were alone. Even holding his hands made her feel complete. Happy.

"I want to be with you George, but it's impossible. Richard and I are married, and we adopted Athena. I can't be with you in the way you want me to be."

"Then I'll share you," George whispered, moving closer to her.

Lissy let go of his hands and stood, walking away from the bench, heading for the cover of trees. Surrounded by the shadows of overhanging branches, she leaned against a tall oak. She needed space to think. George still wanted her despite being married to Richard, and mother to Athena. He said he'd be happy to share her. Lissy's mind whirled.

George stepped into the shadows. "I'm sorry. I scared you. I compromised you."

"Not scared, confused maybe, but you could never scare me. I'm a married woman. I'm a mother, albeit adopted. But I don't love my husband. I love another man. I love you, George. I want you as much as you want me, but how can I? Now you say you want to share me? What does that even mean?"

"This..." George pulled her to him under the sweeping cover of tall trees, away from public view. Hidden amongst the greenery, George lowered his lips to hers and sought her out. Lissy closed her eyes, her body taking over and ignoring the sanity of her brain. His kiss deepened; it became more urgent and she revelled in it. She knew it was wrong and that she was on the road to self-destruction, but she'd missed this. She'd missed *him*.

George broke away from her and stepped back. "I should continue my beat. It was nice to see you again, Mrs Hobbs. You know where to find me when you've made your decision about what you want in life." George began to walk away, but she was fast. Lissy grabbed his arm and swung him around, pulling him back towards her. Her lips met his and they lost themselves in each other.

~

Lissy washed the kitchen counters, singing to herself. Richard and Athena would be home in one day, and she should've been dreading it. Instead, she was soaring with her head in the clouds. After kissing George in the park, she'd returned home. After pacing the house for an hour like a cooped-up animal, she'd headed to George's house. Nervously, she'd waited for him, and she'd entered the familiar property with him as he arrived home. Inside, Lissy sat on the sofa, but she hadn't remained on the comfortable seat for long. It was obvious what would happen between them.

George was the man she wanted. Richard was the man she was stuck with. Lissy and George spent hours naked in George's bed, reacquainting themselves with each other, making up for lost time.

"We must be careful, George. I must think about what I'm going to do about Richard. You must let me deal with it my way and not rush me," Lissy said, dressing herself several hours later.

"I promise. I'm just glad to have you back in my life, Lissy."

"I'm happy to have you back in mine, too. I'll see you soon."

Lissy had left George's house, returning to her marital home, feeling happy, but uncertain. She couldn't leave Richard without telling him why, and he'd be furious. She didn't want to hurt Athena either, as much as the pair didn't get on. As she sat on the bus, realisation hit her; she'd started something that wouldn't end well and would inevitably hurt a lot of people.

Lissy had no choice, though. It was time to be honest with herself. She loved George with all her heart. George was the man she wanted to be with. George was the man she wanted to spend her life with and grow old with. Not Richard. Richard didn't feature in her life. Neither did Athena.

Since the night of their reacquaintance, Lissy had spent every evening with George. She refused to stay overnight in case her neighbours noticed she hadn't come home. Tonight would be her last evening with George until she could find a suitable excuse, and she wanted to make the most of it. The thought of lying naked in his arms as he caressed her skin banished all thoughts of her daily existence as Mrs Hobbs.

It was perfect, even if it was for the shortest of time.

∽

"Can we please? Please can we go! I want to go!" Athena jumped up and down clapping her hands.

"Athena! For goodness sake, sit down and eat. We will talk about it later," Lissy said, slamming her knife and fork down on the dining room table.

"I was talking to my *papa*, not you!" Athena went to Richard and put her arms around Richard's neck, glaring at Lissy. "Please can I go *papa*?"

Richard gently placed his knife and fork on his plate. "If you apologise to Lissy for being rude, then I'll think about it."

Athena groaned. Looking at Lissy, she rolled her eyes and mumbled, "Fine. Sorry," as she ran from the room.

"Athena! Come back here and eat your supper!" Lissy yelled after her. But it was too late, Athena was already pounding up the stairs to her room.

"So once again, Athena gets her own way. You need to learn to stand up to her, Richard. The way she treats me isn't right. It's not fair!" Richard started to talk, but Lissy held up her hand to stop him, "And this... you need to speak to her!"

Lissy threw a diary across the table at him.

"What is it?"

"Open it. See for yourself. Try ten pages in. It'll give you a good idea of why I'm so bloody angry right now."

Richard opened the diary, flicked through the pages and began to read out loud. *"I'm so happy! A whole week away from that house and away from that bitch Lissy."* Richard stopped reading and looked up.

"I already know what it says, don't spare my blushes, husband. Do carry on reading," Lissy spat.

"I don't know what papa sees in her. I wish papa had never married her. She's miserable, ugly and not deserving of MY papa. He's mine and no one else's! He could do better than that horrible bitch... I wish we still lived in Greece with Roula. I don't remember much about Roula, but I know she loved me, and papa, and we were a happy family. Papa tells me all the time how happy we were and how much he loved her. I hate this new family; I hate that bitch Lissy. She's not my mother, she never will be!"

"It's probably just pre-teenage angst. They all get it, Lissy. Better she writes it down than says it to you."

"Better she writes it down? You think that's okay? She shouldn't say it at all, Richard! I'm her adoptive mother. She may not like me sometimes, but this is unacceptable. You need to speak to her about it."

"Oh, come on, Lissy. You always get like this about her. Your jealousy is ridiculous. Athena is a child. You've nothing to be jealous about!"

"Jealous! I'm not bloody jealous! She's a spoilt brat who takes advantage, wraps you around her little finger and treats me like shit. You let her do whatever she wants, with no consequences. You *always* choose her over me. Whatever I tell her to do or not to do, you say something different. My decision as a parent never counts! That's not jealousy, Richard, it's bad parenting!"

"You're being ridiculous, Lissy. You've no idea what we went through over there. I might allow Athena a little more freedom than she should have, but she deserves it. Her life has been hellish, disruptive and uncertain. She needs to feel that she's important."

"I understand her life has been traumatic, but the war was a long time ago and her behaviour is unacceptable. She's become insolent lately. She needs to understand boundaries, Richard. *We* are her parents and she's the child. You need to support me as much as I support you. We're a family, or at least we're supposed to be, but you both make it so bloody hard for me to feel like I'm part of it anymore. It's always the two of you together. I feel like I'm always on the outside. There are days I don't feel like I belong here anymore."

Richard stood and went over to Lissy. He pulled her to her feet, taking her in his arms. "I'm truly sorry. I didn't know you felt this way. I'll try and do better. I'll also speak to Athena about this diary she's writing."

"Thank you, Richard." Lissy hugged him back, thankful he had finally listened to her. Neither husband nor wife noticed as a furious Athena sneaked into the dining room, swiped the diary from the table and slunk back upstairs like an angry cat on the prowl.

THIRTY-THREE

Zakynthos, Greece, 1953

Stretching, Richard walked to the railing that ran the length of the boat to prevent passengers falling into the sea below. The sky overhead was clear, bright and blue, a hot but beautiful summer's day. As the boat pushed forward, slicing through the Ionian waters, it brought him closer to his final destination.

Zakynthos Town and its rambling buildings were clearly visible now. The ancient castle sat high on the acropolis keeping watch over land and sea as the harbour patiently waited for them to arrive.

He never thought he'd be here again.

When Richard had left Zakynthos ten years ago, things had been very different. The world had been at war. Athena had been a young child, and he hadn't known if he'd ever see Lissy again. Then he'd met Roula, fallen in love and married her. His perfect Greek life – and how he'd loved Roula. It was the only time he'd ever been truly happy.

Then Roula had been cruelly taken from him. He'd

committed murder and had been forced to return to England. To Lissy. Things had changed whilst he'd been away, though. Lissy wasn't the same person, and she'd fallen in love with someone else too. Richard had been jealous, and pulled her round to his way of thinking, wanting to blot out all the hurt of losing Roula. He didn't love Lissy, but he didn't want to be alone either.

In the end, Lissy had come back to him. He knew she wasn't wholly happy, and he repaid her with Athena, a child that wasn't hers. He knew the pair disliked each other and could never be friends, let alone mother and daughter, and yet he'd forced them both into it. He'd made a mess of everything.

This trip to Zakynthos was important. He loved Athena as though she *was* his own daughter. She wasn't, though, and it was time to fix things. He needed to find Athena's family. It was long overdue and something he should've done a long time ago. Athena wasn't his daughter; she'd never been his daughter, and his selfish actions had kept Athena from living the life she was supposed to live in Greece.

He had kept his promise to Elena, looked after the child and provided for her, but she didn't belong in England. Athena's increasingly foul, erratic behaviour and caustic diary entries about Lissy proved she was unhappy and needed to be among her own kind. She belonged in Greece, on the island she was born on.

Greece was Athena's home, not Bristol.

Several weeks ago, Richard had sat Lissy down and explained it all. He needed to return to Greece to find Athena's family. Lissy hadn't been happy about him making the trip, though.

"Why now? Why go on your own and leave me here

alone with Athena? If it's so important, why don't you just take her with you? At least she'll be out from under my feet! I can't stay here in this house on my own with her. She refuses to listen to me or do anything I say," Lissy had raged. It was all they seemed to do recently. Argue. And the subject was always Athena. Richard had tried his best to sort things out at home, but Athena knew just how to get her own way in every situation. As much as Richard tried his best, Lissy had been pushed out even more until Athena got her own way and became the centre of his world.

"I must do this alone, Lissy. It's not going to be an easy trip as it is. Imagine if I took her to Greece only to find that there *is* no family left? Why upset her and get her hopes up? Maybe a break will do both of you good and you'll finally be able to resolve your differences."

"Fine. Do whatever you want. You always do anyway!"

That had been the end of the argument. Once again, Richard was in the wrong for trying to do the right thing. He explained to Athena he was off on a work trip for several weeks, but would be back as soon as he could. Athena had begged to go to Richard's parents' house, but Richard refused. In the end, Lissy remained in stony silence and Athena became clingy, begging him not to leave. He remembered Athena's face upon leaving the house, knowing that neither female would be happy in each other's company whilst he was gone. All he could do was hug them both and promise to see them soon.

The journey to Greece had been an arduous one, filled with reminders of his return to England years earlier. It tested his strength of character, but the journey was necessary. It was about Athena and no one else, and he compartmentalised the hurt of Roula and his time in Greece.

This trip was about the thirteen-year-old child. The

child who sat at his feet and giggled. The child who loved making daisy chains, watching ducks at the pond or searching for pebbles in the river. She was all that mattered now. Even though Athena wasn't his blood, she was still his child, and he wanted to do the best for her, whatever the cost, even if that meant losing her. That was how much he loved her.

Turning his attention back to the approaching harbour, Richard had forgotten how much hotter the Greek sun was than in England. Summer was now in full swing. June and July had melded into one and a typically hot and bright August had arrived. Despite the intensity of the heat, it was a welcome relief from the inclement and unpredictable English weather he'd left behind.

The boat began to slow as it neared the harbour. He drank in the view. Zakynthos. Although unexpected, it was good to be back.

After disembarking, Richard walked along the harbour to find *The Repara*, a guest house he'd booked into. After checking in and leaving his suitcase, Richard went down to the café and sat there enjoying a welcome thick cup of Greek coffee. The taste immediately brought him back to his time living in Greece. It seemed like another lifetime, almost unreal. It had been real, though, and how he missed it. Finishing his coffee, Richard headed back inside to get some rest before setting out to locate Athena's family.

∼

The following day, Richard stood on a cliff top overlooking the vast ocean that clung to the island's shores. The horrors and memories of war had come flooding back in the night and remained with him as he travelled west in a borrowed car using limited island directions from the garage owner.

He had awoken, drenched in sweat, wrapped in a sheet, having dreamt about being shot down. He remembered opening the parachute and doing his best to tease it in the limited wind, to what he hoped was land. He had needed to avoid landing in the sea. If he landed in water and didn't release the parachute quickly enough, it would've soaked up the water and he would've drowned.

So he had worked the parachute and headed for the faint outline of land he'd estimated to be somewhere in Greece, hoping that wherever he landed would be in the presence of an ally.

He remembered getting caught by a sudden gust of wind as he came in to land and knew he'd mistimed it. The crunch of his leg snapping made him lightheaded, swiftly leading to unconsciousness. The next thing he remembered was staring into the face of an angel. A beautiful Greek angel who had rescued him and nursed him back to health.

That angel had been Elena. She'd saved his life, and she was the reason he was here now. He hoped she was still alive. He wanted to tell her that Athena was okay, and to arrange for Athena to come home. Richard didn't know how he was going to do it, but he was determined to.

His knowledge of the island was limited. During the war he'd been hidden away in a damp cave in the mountains. He'd only left the cave on the night he went to the cove to be rescued.

The vantage point of the cave had given Richard views across the island during daylight hours. He remembered the dark, green undulating hills surrounding his hiding place and the views that had swept down to a vast plain, occasionally punctuated by homes, farms and ancient monasteries.

A NIGHT OF THUNDER

He'd also seen tall cypress trees, olive groves and the rising hills of Bochali and Skopos in the distance. Beyond that had lain the sea that on bright summer days had merged with brilliant blue skies.

All of it had been a tantalising glimpse of Zakynthos, but he'd never been part of it. He'd been a carefully kept island secret, only known by two people: Elena and Dionysios. They'd kept him safe and undiscovered, until his miraculous escape.

If *he'd* never been discovered in the war, a decade earlier, how did Richard ever hope to find Elena now? She had been a resistance fighter, and many had used fake names. He also had no idea where she lived. She had told him some information about her family, the Italian soldier, Pietro, and her first love, Angelos, the father of Athena. Other than that, Elena's life had been a mystery. His Greek was rusty too, but he hadn't forgotten all of it, and knew he could use it to speak to the locals. All he could do was his best. He owed it to Athena.

Turning away from the beautiful view, Richard returned to the car and started the temperamental engine. Having already visited Keri village, he drove further into the mountains. Many people he met were reluctant to talk about the war and he'd come away frustrated, with no answers.

Driving up into the mountains with the sea to his left and the vast mountain plains to his right, the car juddered violently. A deep rumbling, whooshing sound met his ears. The car slid to a halt. Thankfully it was still upright and hadn't crashed, but Richard was no longer facing the road ahead. Instead, the car was sideways , with the front wheels on the grass edge, giving him a precarious but perfect view out across the sea, as the earthquake continued around him.

He braced himself in the driving seat, unsure whether it was safer to stay in the vehicle or get out, and prayed that the jolting didn't send him tumbling down the grass and over the distant cliff, into the sea, below.

Richard had felt random tremors during the war, both in Zakynthos and on the mainland. They'd been barely recognisable though; occasional mild movements of the ground, minor shudders for a few seconds, before normality had returned. This was different. This was solid. The movement was heightened and lasted much longer, making everything shake and rattle. It was a new experience that completely unnerved him.

The sound that came with it was new too, and unlike anything he'd ever experienced. Intermittent booming, creaking and groaning noises from deep within the mountains. It made him want to get off the road and hide somewhere safe, but he was frozen in the car seat. His palms sweaty, his heart thudding in his chest, an ever-growing frightened passenger of the unfolding event.

The earthquake stopped, and the mountain road settled. It was an eerie feeling and not the first minor tremor Richard had felt since his arrival. The locals had warned him the island was restless, and their warning had become clear, with the large jolt he'd just experienced.

Restarting the car, Richard reversed back onto the road and continued his journey, enjoying the drive through the beautiful mountains. The only evidence of the recent earthquake was an occasional snapped tree which now lay along the edge of the road. Richard drank in every inch of the island. He'd spent such a long time on Zakynthos and seen so little of it, and he couldn't wait to discover more.

The drive took him deeper into the Vrachonias mountains through some stunning scenery, and he occasionally stopped to take in the views across the island to the main town in the east. He passed through the villages of Kiliomenos and Agios Leon, where he stopped to ask about Elena, but no one could help him. There was another unnerving tremor in Agios Leon, but the villagers had seemed unconcerned.

"Earthquakes, we do not worry. It is part of Zakynthos life," one local had said to him.

"It looks like some of the buildings have been damaged," Richard said, pointing to one.

"Old building. Small damage. We do not worry. The broken trees, we clear and use for firewood," the man said, shrugging.

It was sad to see the old, damaged buildings, and the superficial recent damage in the villages. Richard offered to help clear up, but the locals had thanked him, saying his help was not necessary.

Richard had mulled it over as he continued his journey. The villagers reminded him of Elena and Dionysios. Stoic and determined. In the short time he'd spent on Zakynthos, he'd come to realise what strong, resilient people the islanders were.

He couldn't wait to find Elena and tell her Athena was okay. She must have missed her daughter so much, and couldn't begin to imagine what her life had been like without her. He just hoped she hadn't suffered too much at the hands of Nazis. He'd seen and heard what they'd done to Greeks during the war, and it didn't bear thinking about.

The main road wound its way through a group of houses that was the small village of Exo Hora. Parking the car at the side of the road, in front of a church, he marvelled at a huge olive tree, the largest he'd ever seen. Under the tree sat a man lost in his own world.

Stepping from the car, Richard looked up at the church. Wherever he went on the island there was a church, bell tower or religious icon, and he admired the Greek people for being proud of what was important to them.

Richard meandered up the road, but there was little more than a handful of houses set back from the main thoroughfare. Unlike the previous two villages, no one was out in the streets, except for the man sitting under the tree. It was as though time had stood still. It even seemed untouched by recent earthquakes.

Richard turned around and headed back to the car, stopping to look at the olive trees hugging the side of the road. The huge one fascinated him. It must have been hundreds of years old, maybe older. The man sitting underneath looked up at him and nodded. Richard nodded back, wishing him a good afternoon in Greek. The man stood, walked over to him and spoke slowly in Greek.

"You are tourist?"

"*Naí*. Yes." Richard responded, understanding the Greek clearly.

"Come, sit." The man indicated an empty chair next to his under the olive tree.

Richard accepted the invitation. "You are expecting a friend today?

"No. I put the chair there when I visit. But it is always empty. It always will be."

The hurt and grief flashed in the Greek man's eyes and Richard wondered what his story was. A man had never looked so bereft.

"I am sorry."

"You have questions for me? No one ever comes to this little village. It is too far away from the town and harbour.

A NIGHT OF THUNDER

You are a man who searches for something you have lost. Or maybe I am wrong. What is it you need help with?"

"I am searching for a woman."

The Greek man laughed. It was the first time Richard had seen even a glimmer of brightness in his expression, but as quickly as it had appeared it was gone again. "It is Greece. We all need a woman. Women are what makes our lives, our homes and our souls complete. Without a woman, we are lost. We are nothing."

"It's one specific woman I am looking for. She is special. She is important. I need to talk to her. I have something that belongs to her. I have been driving around the island trying to find her."

"That is a lot of hard work for a woman. We have many Greek women who would like a man like you. You could choose any of them. Why is it you need this particular woman?"

Richard sighed. "I met her a long time ago. We helped each other in a time of need. I need to make things right with her."

"I understand. Tell me of this woman. I will see if I can help my new friend."

"Her name is Elena. I do not know her last name, just that she lives here on Zakynthos. She was a very brave woman in the war."

The Greek man stood and walked out into the road, looking towards the olive groves. Richard sat uncomfortably as the seconds ticked by, stretching into minutes. He continued to watch the man, who stood stock still with his back to him. Richard stood and walked over to stand next to him.

The Greek man turned and Richard saw tears in his eyes and anguish on his face.

"I am sorry, my friend. I do not want to be rude. I am Greek and I have much pride. You spoke of a name that is well known on Zakynthos. Many, however, do not wish to speak of it. We choose to leave the past to the past."

"Why?"

"You must understand, we do not like to talk about the war. The war hurt our island and the people who live here. The enemy hated us and forced us to live under the thumb. Many Greeks fought for *this* island. Many died for it, too. Elena, the woman you speak of, was a hero, but she paid a heavy price for it." The man paused. Richard could see he was struggling to find the words he needed. "They killed her, my friend. Elena died for this island and its people. There are people who still mourn even now, but they do it quietly."

Richard stumbled backwards. Elena was dead? Athena was an orphan? This was the worst possible news. He'd desperately hoped he'd find her, to reunite mother and daughter. "She... Elena died? How?" he whispered.

"Elena was resistance. She helped hide people, keep them safe. The Nazis were angry; they took her. She was tortured. They took her to the cliffs and shot her. Her body now lies on the seabed at Keri cliffs. Her Italian lover too. He died the same way. The war was a bad time for all of us, but Elena, she paid with her life."

Richard walked back to the tree and sat down. His head in his hands, he allowed the tears to escape. He didn't care if anyone saw him crying, it was something he needed to do. He cried for Athena, and the mother she'd never know. Elena was the woman he owed his life to. The woman who saved him, kept him company and helped him escape. It was because of people like him Elena had died. It wasn't the news he expected, but now he knew the answer.

Elena was dead and it changed everything.

The Greek man disturbed Richard from his thoughts as he sat next to him. Richard lifted his head and wiped his eyes.

"I am sorry. It was a shock."

The Greek man shrugged. "On the outside, we are all tough men, but we are also born with hearts. Sometimes our sleeve is a good place to wear them. It makes us human."

Richard nodded. "What about Elena's family? They must have been through an awful time losing her like that."

The Greek man shook his head. "All dead. Nazis made sure none of them survived. They killed them all."

"I cannot believe it. Everyone who knew her is gone?" Richard paused, then tentatively began, "What about her child? Didn't Elena have a child? The father of her child. What happened to him? Is he dead too?"

The Greek man considered him through narrowed eyes for a moment. "The child I do not know. The father, he is still alive, but he is a bitter, lonely, sad man. He tries not to show it, and pretends to his family that he has healed and moved on with his life, but the war took everything from him. He hides his scars and tries to live each day."

"Do you know where I can find him? I would like to talk to him."

"He does not like visitors. Especially people he does not know."

"Please, it is so important I speak to him."

"No! It is not a time to drag up the past. Leave alone what you cannot heal."

"Okay." Richard didn't want to push the man further.

Birdsong filled the empty silence between the two men, until the Greek man spoke once more. "What is so important you needed to speak to Elena?"

"It was about her daughter. I did not mean to fool you. I just needed answers. Her daughter is alive and well."

"Elena's daughter, she is alive?" the man repeated.

"Yes."

"It is a shock. After so many years, it is a shock. She is happy? She is well looked after?"

"Yes, and she has a good home. Her adoptive parents always wanted to return her to her mother if it was possible. It is why I am here; I am trying to find her family. Even though the child doesn't know about Zakynthos and her upbringing, Greece is where she belongs."

The Greek man looked at Richard. "She does not know about this island and her Zakynthian family? You have not told her?"

"No, I have not told her." Richard sighed. "The girl thinks I am her father and that my dead Greek wife is her mother. It is how it has always been. The girl needs to know about her real family. I need to tell her. I wanted to bring her here and reunite her with her mother, with her family. How can I do that now when they are all dead, except for a father who refuses to talk to anyone?"

"You are a good man, my friend. Sometimes life makes plans for us that we cannot change. You tell me she is alive and she is safe? Then she is one of the lucky ones. She survived the horrors of war and has a home with people who may not be blood, but love her like they would their own. There is nothing more you can do. There is nothing here for her on Zakynthos. Let her live a good life."

"Nothing?"

"No. Nothing. Sometimes we do not get to live the way we want, but Elena would be happy to know her daughter is safe and loved. It is all that matters."

"And her real father?"

"*Pah!* Her real father was a stupid fool in love. He has no claim over her even if he wanted it. He can give her nothing. Why take the child from a life where she is happy? I will tell him you were looking for him. I will also tell him she is safe and well. If he wants to find his child, he will."

Richard nodded. In some respects he knew that the man was right, but he felt empty. It felt wrong. He'd come to Zakynthos to find Elena and tell her about Athena, but all he'd received was bad news. It wasn't the outcome he'd expected or wanted.

"Thank you for your time. I am sorry the war affected your island so badly and so many good people were lost." Richard stood and held out his hand. The Greek man stood and shook it.

"It has been good to talk to someone. My visits here are often quiet. It has been an interesting day: an earthquake and a visitor. A busy day for the sleepy mountain village."

"Goodbye. And thank you."

"Goodbye," the Greek man responded.

Richard walked to the car, climbed in and started the engine. Before pulling away, he grabbed a pencil and piece of paper and wrote on it. Pulling the car out into the road, heading back the way he'd come, he slowed as he passed the Greek man. Richard wound the window down, waved the piece of paper at him and stopped the car.

"This is the date and time of the ferry I am leaving on. Tell Athena's father if he wants to contact me about his daughter, to come and see me. I am staying at *The Repara* in Zakynthos Town."

The Greek man walked over and took the piece of paper and nodded. "I will tell him."

"Thank you."

With that, Richard took his foot off the brake pedal and started his journey back towards Agios Leon.

THIRTY-FOUR

Bristol, *England, 1953*

"I hate you! You're not my mother and never will be. God knows what *papa* sees in you. You're a pathetic, horrible woman. I want my *papa*. I want to be with *papa* and Roula, not here in shitty England with *you*. Roula was my mother, not you!" Athena screamed. "You're nothing to me. Nothing! I wish you'd leave us!"

As Athena ran to the door, Lissy stepped in front of it and slammed it shut, trapping them both inside the kitchen. The table, full of baking ingredients, was a mess. Flour had spilled onto the floor and butter was smeared across the wooden surface. A cracked bowl lay on the floor. The hatred between Lissy and Athena swirled around the room, its hateful tendrils licking everything. As it wrapped around them, the tense atmosphere increased. Like two stags preparing to attack each other.

"You won't speak to me like that, Athena!"

"I'll speak to you any way I want. You're not my mother! You're just some miserable bitch who married my *papa*."

The stinging slap that met Athena's face rang out in the room, momentarily making her stumble back into the wall.

"You hit me! You bitch. *Papa* would never hit me! I hate you!"

"You're right, I did hit you, and I'll do it again if you don't stop being a petulant little madam and using such foul language. Now sit down!"

"No. I won't!"

"Sit down, now, or so help me god I'll knock you into the middle of next week and throw you out into the street afterwards." Lissy had been pushed over the edge, but she'd reached the end of her tether with the child. Since Richard had left her alone with the unruly Athena, things had spiralled out of control. In Richard's absence, their days had been filled with daily arguments and screaming matches. Whatever Lissy did was wrong, and Athena continually spat back with hateful words.

"Where's *papa*! I want *papa*!" Athena slid to the floor with her back to the wall and buried her head in her arms sobbing. Lissy did what only a mother could. She sat next to Athena and took the girl in her arms and allowed her to cry. "I want my *papa*. Where is he? He was going away for a week, and it's been a month. Why has he left me? Doesn't he love me anymore?"

"Oh Athena. Of course your father loves you. His job is busy. They've given him more work than normal and he's had to go away for longer this time. He'll be back soon, though. I promise." Lissy gently parted the girl's arms to lift her head. Pulling a handkerchief from her pocket, Lissy began to wipe away the tears. "I know you miss him. I know how close you are, but we can still have fun together, can't we? And when he comes back home, think of all the wonderful things he'll be able to buy for us with all the extra money he's earned. How nice will that be?"

Athena shrugged. "Maybe."

"Now come on. Up you get. It's time to wash and dress for your day out with your grandparents. You love seeing them, and they're taking you to the zoo today. Imagine what you'll see! Don't let our argument spoil it."

Athena stood and nodded. Lissy took her hand and walked Athena upstairs to help her get ready.

Half an hour later, Athena was ready and waiting for her grandparents to arrive, excited about seeing all the animals at the zoo. As they bundled her into their waiting car, Lissy ensured a smile was plastered to her face as she waved them off. As the car turned the corner, she went back inside and cleaned down the still messy table. Once everything was stored away and the surfaces were clean again, Lissy removed her apron and hung it over a chair. An hour later, Lissy knocked on George's front door.

"I thought you weren't coming." He let her into the narrow hallway and shut the front door to the outside world, leaving the two of them together in the pale light.

"We argued again. She called me names. I think she's been writing in that diary again. I've looked for it, but despite turning the house upside down, I still can't find where she's hidden it. Oh George, I was so angry I slapped her face and threatened to throw her out. I feel awful. I'm a terrible mother."

"You aren't. You're a person who's put up with a lot. You've put everyone else first and yourself last. It's not your fault Richard has demons to slay. It's not your fault he's gone gallivanting halfway across the world. The war ended years ago; whatever happened during it should've stayed there. He should be here for you and Athena now, not out there searching for ghosts, as much as it pains me to say so."

"And you?"

"Ah, well, I'm the only man who truly loves you and dreams that one day all this madness will be over, and we'll finally be together. Properly. Just the two of us. Until then, I'm forced to share you, in small bite-size pieces."

"I'm sorry, George. I've been such a fool."

"No, you did what you thought was right. You put others first instead of thinking of yourself."

"But I hurt you."

"We've been through this before. Shush now. We only have a couple of hours and I don't want to spend our limited time together raking over the past. I want to look to the future and the possibilities it holds for us. For you and me. Come…" George gently took her hand and led her up the stairs to his bedroom. He kicked the door closed behind them, shutting out the rest of the world.

THIRTY-FIVE

Zakynthos, Greece, 1953

The earthquake that morning had spooked everyone. It had brought a sense of foreboding that had wrapped around the island, hugging it tightly. Then his *friend* had appeared in the battered old car. Angelos should have known it was a sign.

As he sat back under his favourite olive tree, and the car disappeared from sight, Angelos relived the meeting. He'd recognised Richard the moment he saw him. Yes, the man was older, and wasn't so thin, but the Englishman's face was one he'd never forget.

Still in shock, Angelos thought about what Richard had told him. His daughter Athena was alive. St Stylianos had answered his prayer. Well, partially answered it. Angelos should've been over the moon. For years he'd prayed for news of his daughter, and a messenger had finally come to confirm that she was still alive.

What a fool he was, though! He'd been given a chance to get Athena back, and like a stupid fool, shocked and confused, he'd let it go. The piece of paper Richard had given to him was still clutched in his hand. Maybe there was still time? Maybe he could go to Zakynthos Town and seek out the man.

In turmoil, Angelos didn't know what to do for the best. Athena was his daughter by blood, but he'd never truly been her father. She wouldn't know who he was, and he'd be nothing more than a stranger. What if she was happy in her new home, with her new parents? What if she came to Zakynthos and hated it? Hated him? He would never forgive himself for making her unhappy.

Worse still. What if Athena looked like her mother? The thought of staring at a mirror image of Elena for the rest of his days filled him with dread.

Angelos had always wanted this moment, but now he faced it, it scared him. His mind tumbled with a thousand thoughts, and the fear and hurt of Elena's loss came flooding back. He didn't want to upset everything again. He didn't want to make Sophia feel like she didn't matter. She was his daughter too.

Angelos had been reassured from what little Richard had said, that Athena was well, and taken care of. There was no need for Angelos to get involved. The past was best left in the past. He couldn't put himself through all that hurt again.

Just knowing Athena was alive was enough. Looking at the piece of paper, he saw the words, the connection to his daughter. He wouldn't use it, but neither would he destroy it. Instead, he quietly slipped it into his pocket and continued to contemplate life from his chair under the ancient olive tree.

Richard drove back through the mountains, down onto the plains and across to Zakynthos Town. He'd no idea what to do now. His plan was in ruins, Elena and her family were dead, and there was no reason to stay.

As Richard arrived in Zakynthos Town, the day was coming to a close and it wouldn't be long before the sun set. He dropped the car off at the garage, thanking them, before heading to the port to enquire about earlier transport off the island. He was relieved to hear that the next available boat would dock the next day.

Heading back to *The Repara,* Richard found a local taverna. There were only a handful of locals inside, but the much-needed food was good and service quick. Staring across the street, he watched the occasional car drive along the harbour. People strolled along the large stone pavement, enjoying the evening. He wondered if Lissy would like it here. Lissy. He'd no idea what he was going to do when he got home. Despite her anger at his leaving, Lissy had pinned her hopes on him finding Elena and her family. Lissy hated Athena and wanted the girl returned to her home country. It was now impossible. Athena would have to stay with them and Lissy would be furious.

The waitress appeared next to his table and smiled. She was beautiful, with striking Greek features, not dissimilar to Roula.

He smiled up at her. "Thank you. It was a good meal," he said in Greek.

"You would like anything else before I go?"

"No, thank you. You are leaving?"

"Yes. I have no more work; another waitress will work tonight."

"I do not want anything else. I am going back to my

room at *The Repara* to sleep. It's been a long day of driving and I leave tomorrow on the afternoon boat."

"I understand." The waitress leaned forward and lifted his plate, her long, dark hair brushing his shoulder.

"I can think of fun things to do, that is better than sleeping. If that pleases you. We have a beautiful town." Richard caught the glint in her eye laced with the underlying implication.

His mouth engaged before his brain, all thoughts of England, his home and his unhappy wife left behind him. He was in a different world, a world that connected him to the past, to another time, when things were so very different. Moments later, he'd left the taverna and was walking along the harbour with the beautiful Greek waitress, Fotini.

As the sun began to set, Fotini showed him the sights of Zakynthos Town and he took it all in. As they ran through a back street, laughing, she pulled him close into a doorway under a large hanging basket of Bougainvillea.

"Kiss me."

"I need to tell you something, Fotini."

"Yes?"

"Are you..." he was embarrassed by his question and didn't want to offend her.

"Am I...?" She looked at his uncomfortable expression and then laughed. "Ah... You wonder if I am a poor Greek girl who longs for the company of a handsome English man, or if I am a, how do you call them, prostitute?"

Richard felt the heat flush his face. "I apologise. I am married. I just..."

Fotini placed a finger to his lips. "I am not a woman of the night. I am merely a poor waitress who is bored of working day in and day out, and dealing with Greek men who would want me only for a washerwoman and baby machine. In you, I see a man I want to spend time with, even if it is only for one night."

Richard smiled. It had been a stupid question, but he knew from his time in the forces that many pretty women in foreign countries had slept with men like him to earn extra money. He neither had the money nor wanted the complication.

He did want Fotini though, as much as he shouldn't, he did. He needed her to erase the heartbreak of late. All the emotions of the day had hit him. He'd lost so much and didn't know what he was going to do. He knew that Lissy no longer wanted him, and he needed to feel wanted, even if it was by a stranger.

Pushing Fotini back into the shadows, he found her mouth and kissed her hard. She didn't disappoint and responded, wrapping her arms around him holding him tightly. Finally, they broke apart and he took her hand, weaving back through the town's streets to *The Repara*.

Upon arrival, he spoke to the receptionist, keeping their attention so that Fotini could sneak upstairs unseen. Moments later, he joined her, letting them both into his room. The night had darkened, and the room was filled with shadows, only punctuated by the light of the moon.

Richard pulled Fotini to him and kissed her again. Undoing her clothing, he pulled her to the bed. Naked in each other's arms, they revelled in pleasuring each other.

Lissy was forgotten, and suddenly Fotini's name was lost too. All he could think of was Roula, the woman he'd loved with all his heart, who'd been so cruelly taken from him. It was Roula's name he cried out with a mix of pain and pleasure, not that of his wife or the woman in his bed.

"Who is Roula? Is she your wife?" Fotini asked as she

propped her head on her hand and pulled the sheet over her.

"That was ungentlemanly of me. I apologise."

"You love who you love." Fotini shrugged. "Who is she?"

"Someone I met a long time ago. A woman I fell in love with and married, but she died."

"I am sorry. Do you want to tell me?"

"Tell you?"

"It seems whatever happened with this Roula, it weighs heavily on your heart. I will listen if you want to tell me."

"It is difficult. A long story, Fotini. Sad, heartbreaking even. I am in another marriage now that I should not have agreed to. It was a bad decision, and my life is a mess."

"Life is not always easy. Let me help you," Fotini whispered, as she kissed his neck. "Let me help you my Englishman..."

"How?"

"By making you forget..."

He didn't have to ask again as Fotini pulled her to him and he lost himself in her arms.

THIRTY-SIX

Zakynthos, Greece, 1953

Richard was alone when he awoke the following morning, with only an empty space in the bed next to him where Fotini had lain. The room was bright, sunlight flooding through the window, and only memories tinged with guilt of their night together remained.

Fotini had used him, but he'd used her too. Thoughts of Lissy stirred his brain, but he forced them away. He knew their marriage was over; it had been for a long time, and it was time to make some big decisions. Lissy could have her policeman. Richard wasn't blind, or stupid, he knew Lissy was sleeping with the man again. All that mattered now was honouring his promise to Elena and looking after Athena.

Turning onto his back, his mind returned him to the caves in the Zakynthos mountains over a decade ago. A memory that had lain buried.

It had been a bright day and he'd sat in the dank cave looking out across the landscape, waiting for the resistance to arrive with food supplies. As the night had drawn in, no one had come, and he'd hunkered down to sleep. It was then he'd heard it. A crack. A snapped branch, stepped on either by animal or human. Remaining still, Richard had cradled the gun in his hand, hoping not to have to use it. Moments later, he'd felt a presence and knew someone was in the cave.

"Richard, it is me," a low voice whispered.

He had breathed a sigh of relief and sat up, leaning against the wall of the cave. "Elena? It is late."

"Yes. I did not mean to scare you. There are Nazis nearby and I could not make a sound. I could not let you know it was me in case they heard me."

"It is okay. Come sit."

"I cannot. I have to get back."

"Please, Elena. I have been lonely today. I have nothing to do. I need to talk to someone for a while or I will go crazy."

"What do you want to talk about?" Elena sat next to him and leaned back against the cave wall.

"You."

"Me? Why?"

"Why do you do this, Elena?"

"Why not?"

"You are putting yourself and your daughter at risk."

"It is for my daughter that I do this!"

Richard laughed.

"Why are you laughing?"

"You are so defiant sometimes, Elena."

"I am Greek. It is how we speak."

"I know. I am not laughing at you. I find it endearing. It is what I like about you the most."

"It is?"

"Yes. Why do you sleep with the Italian? Do you love him?"

"You ask a lot of questions. Maybe you are a spy!"

"You know I am not a spy. I am bored."

"Fine. I did not choose it. The resistance said I had to do it to make him trust me. We need the enemy to talk; we need information."

"You willingly do it, just for information?"

"Yes. But I am not proud. Sometimes, when I am with him, I forget we are at war. He is nice and treats me well. But then he puts on his uniform and he is a horrible soldier. A man who has invaded my country."

"And what about the father of your child?"

"Angelos? I have not spoken with him for so long now. He chose his life when he abandoned me and our child for his wife."

"Poor Elena."

"Do not feel sorry for me!"

Richard laughed again. "I would never, dear Elena. But you must see that your life is a Greek tragedy. So many characters. So much love, so many men... who will you love next?"

"I love no one."

"I do not believe that. You must love someone."

"The only person I love is my daughter. I love no one else."

"Not even the Italian?"

"I do not think so." The cave had fallen silent, and Richard had heard a snuffle. "Are you crying, Elena?"

"No!" But the crack in her voice gave her away. "I hate my life, Richard. I loved Angelos. I loved him so much, but he married another woman. A woman he does not love. We still love each other and we tried to be with each other, but we cannot. I like Pietro. If this was not war, if he was not the enemy, maybe I could grow to love him. But how do I know he will not kill me or my family if the Nazis tell him to? I am proud of my country, and I choose to fight for it every day until the enemy are gone, even if it takes me my whole life."

"But...?"

"But, my life is messy. No one truly loves me. I am alone..."

∽

As Richard returned to *The Repara* in 1953, he smiled at the memory of that night with Elena. Wartime secrets were plentiful, and that night was his biggest. He'd never spoken about it to anyone, never even admitted it to himself and never would.

His mind turned to Roula. His beautiful wife; she had been the love of his life. He would've done anything to grow old in the mountains of Greece with her and had more children, to have been a proper family with her and Athena.

It had been torn from him, though, and he still grieved for her each day. Other women in his life, like Lissy, Elena and Fotini, had been a mere distraction or a mistake. It's why his marriage with Lissy had failed; she never measured up and never would. Had he always been this way? Or had war brought out hidden dark depths of himself?

Climbing from bed to stop the dark thoughts creeping in, Richard washed away the grime of sleep and changed his clothes. Leaving the guest house, he walked the streets of Zakynthos Town. The previous day's earthquake had damaged several buildings, but it hadn't fazed the locals.

Many were continuing as normal and had already begun to clear up as if it was just an everyday occurrence. Richard had time to waste until he could get the boat later that afternoon, so he'd decided to explore the town, relax in a taverna – if any were open – and maybe even visit the castle that looked over the town from its towering acropolis.

Richard walked along the main harbour towards the large church and bell tower that was almost a replica of the one in St. Mark's Square in Venice. It was a pleasant walk despite the signs of earthquake damage that were everywhere. The sun was shining, and for the first time he felt relaxed.

Richard liked Zakynthos. It was a nice island. Maybe he could leave Lissy, allow her to move on with the policeman. He could then bring Athena back home to Zakynthos and live on the island with her? He could start afresh, maybe find a nice Greek girl like Fotini, make a home, a future. Then Richard could tell Athena all about her mother, and how brave she had been.

It was a nice dream, and one he'd keep in the back of his mind. In Greece, it felt like anything was possible.

As he neared the church, Richard stopped for a drink before heading to explore the damaged back streets. The town was growing busy, and despite the slight uneasy air and the damage, he enjoyed watching Greek life carry on around him.

Halfway down the main back street, everything changed. It was as though a switch had been flicked. The air became intense, and all Richard felt was growing unease.

The ground began to vibrate, roll and shake, and like the previous day a great rumbling and jolting swept through Zakynthos Town. Stronger than the previous day, the earthquake struck violently with a vicious bang. Greeks wailed and screamed; people ran from buildings that were already crumbling around them like dry earth. Dust rose into the sky and flames erupted.

Richard had never experienced anything like it and he had no idea what to do. Whichever direction he turned, things were grim. It was an impossible situation, which was becoming more deadly by the second.

A loud explosion shook the street, and a large fire broke out. A throng of frightened people ran towards him, and he followed them, hoping and trusting that they knew where they were going.

As he ran, the street became covered in ever-increasing rubble and Richard struggled to stay on his feet. He tripped and slipped, finding it impossible to stand, and another jolt threw him to the ground. The fires around him increased and buildings continued to disintegrate.

With a final, hefty jolt, the earthquake ceased, but it wasn't over.

As Richard scrambled to his knees, he realised too late that his life would end there in that moment as the remains of a large building above him finally gave way, crumbled and fell.

As the masonry landed on Richard, it crushed the life from him. The final and only thoughts in his mind were Roula and Athena, and what might have been if they'd only been given the chance.

THIRTY-SEVEN

Bristol, England, 1953

Greek Island Hit By Earthquake! screamed the newspaper headline that caught Lissy's eye in the corner shop. She picked up a copy, scanned the details and sank to the floor. Zakynthos. Her worst fears became realisation. Zakynthos in Greece. The place Richard had travelled to and not yet come home from.

He'd been away for over a month now, leaving her alone with an increasingly unhappy Athena. Richard had said it was to try and find Athena's family, to put things right. Now, Zakynthos had been hit by a natural disaster, and the island and its people were suffering terribly.

Lissy stood, paid for the newspaper and fled from the shop, heading for home. Slamming the front door, she sat at the kitchen table and read the paper with shaking hands.

Ionian Islands Hit By Devastating Earthquake!

The true extent of the damage to the Ionian islands, off the coast of mainland Greece, is unknown, but limited news is the severity of the earthquakes, which were followed by hundreds of aftershocks, has displaced hundreds of people and may have killed and injured many more. As the world waits for more news, our thoughts are with the badly affected islands of Kefalonia and Zakynthos, which are said to have faced the very worst of the wrath of mother nature.

As Lissy continued to read, the report confirmed that the British Navy were already on their way to the island, but the situation was grave. The image on the front of the newspaper told her all she needed to know. A devastated town, with ruinous buildings, and smoke rising to the air.

She hoped Richard had already left and was on his way home, or that he'd been able to take cover and escape the worst of it. Laying the newspaper flat on the table, Lissy pondered living through an earthquake. They'd become used to the bombs of war, but ground-shaking earthquakes were alien to her. Lissy was transported back to the war, and the day she learned Richard had been shot down over Greece. It had been one of the worst days of her life and she'd waited years for news. Long, painful years that had changed her life and had only been eased by her relationship with George.

Lissy couldn't do this a second time. Whilst she cared for Richard and would never wish him harm, she couldn't wait years this time; she needed an answer and quickly. She needed to talk to him, to tell him their marriage was over, and she wanted to be with George.

She wasn't heartless, but it was the right thing to do for them all. Deep down, Lissy suspected that Richard felt the same about her. The love she'd felt for Richard before he went to war was no longer the burning passion it once was. She also knew deep down that Richard cared more for Athena than he did for their marriage, and time had run out for them.

Athena.

A NIGHT OF THUNDER

Until Richard came home, Lissy would have to continue looking after the girl. It wasn't that Lissy hated the child; hate was too strong a word. She just had no feelings for her at all. The child was a mere inconvenience. Lissy wished she could like her, but loving a child, who was temperamental at best, and didn't belong in their lives, wasn't easy.

Lissy was well aware that whenever Richard looked at Athena he was transported elsewhere, to another life, another place and time where Lissy didn't belong. It made her incredibly jealous.

Lissy stood and made herself a drink. Picking up the newspaper again, she scanned the page and hoped Richard was okay so they could all move on. Flinging the newspaper back onto the table, she began to clean the kitchen. She had to carry on as normal until news of Richard came through. Now was the time to stay strong. At least Athena was at girl guide camp. It would give Lissy a few days to gather her thoughts and wait for news.

Once the kitchen was clean, Lissy spurred into action and contacted the authorities to explain the situation – her husband had gone to Zakynthos and may be caught up in the aftermath of the earthquake. They'd promised to update her as soon as they could. All she could do was bide her time and wait.

Hiding the newspaper in a stack of old newspapers, Lissy changed her clothes and left home for George's house. Knocking on his front door, he greeted her with a smile. She fell into his arms, allowing him to envelop her as the door closed behind her.

"Are you okay?" He pulled back at her frowning.

"Have you seen the newspaper?"

"No, I've been working and I've only just got home. I

was about to brew a tea, light my pipe and read it. Is there something I should know?"

Lissy walked into the small front room and picked up the newspaper from the table next to George's favourite armchair. Unfolding it, she held the page for him to see. Seconds felt like hours as he scanned it. George took the newspaper from her and threw it onto his chair.

"He'll be fine. You know Richard. He's always fine." George walked to the mantelpiece, lifted his pipe and stuffed the barrel with fresh tobacco. Striking a match, he held it to the barrel and puffed on the pipe. The fragrant leaves caught, burning orange, expelling its pungent smell.

"He might not be, George. It's like the war all over again. The not knowing. The waiting. I can't do this; he can't do this to me again!"

"Then don't." George turned to face her.

"What do you mean?"

"I mean don't wait. Don't worry. You don't want to be with him anyway. If you did, you wouldn't be here. You wouldn't come running to me every time there's a problem, and you wouldn't still be sharing my bed as well as his."

"I…"

"You… what?" George faced her down. "Maybe now's the time to decide once and for all, Lissy. Find some blasted courage and do what *you* want in life instead of trying to please everyone else."

"What about Athena?"

George laughed and sat in his armchair, puffing on his pipe. "Athena. Oh, come on, Lissy, you hate the damn girl. She's been the problem ever since Richard came home. If Athena disappeared tomorrow, you'd be delighted. She's been the wedge between you and Richard, the cuckoo that invaded your life, and you hate her for it."

"I don't hate her. I just don't get on with her. She has a temperament I can't control. I don't understand her. She's unlike any child I've ever met. She's bloody obstinate, bordering on rude and her temper is appalling. When she gets angry with me, she talks in Greek. Her and Richard have their own little conversations in Greek. They push me out, knowing full well I can't understand a bloody word they're saying! Only Richard can control her or truly understand her. They have an unbreakable bond, and it's one I'm not party to. There's a difference. As much as I try, I've no control over her, and Richard lets her get away with whatever she wants."

"You wish she'd never come here; you wish she didn't exist."

"No, George I never said that!"

George put his pipe in the glass ashtray next to his chair and stood. He put his arms around Lissy and drew her close. "Don't lie to me. Lie to *him*, but never to me. You wish Athena had never come here; you wish she didn't exist don't you?"

Lissy breathed in the familiar tobacco and closed her eyes. "Yes," she whispered. "I wish Athena had never come here. I never asked to be her mother. I wish she wasn't part of our lives."

"Tell me, despite everything you've been through, you also wish Richard had never come home, don't you?"

Lissy felt the tears fall. "Please don't." She could barely speak.

"If you can't be honest with me, Lissy, you can't be honest with anyone."

Lissy sobbed and lifted her head to look at him. "You're right. I wish he'd never come home. I wish he'd stayed in Greece. I wish he'd never brought Athena back with him. I don't love him. I don't want to be with him. I want you, George. Just you. I want to leave him but I don't know if I can. Richard and I are married. He and I are legal guardians of Athena. That's my life. I wish it wasn't, and If I could leave him tomorrow, I would. It's such a mess, I don't know what to do, George. Please help me."

"I love you, Lissy. I want you. I know you're unhappy. The only person who can make the next step is you."

George kissed her on the head, sat back down, opened the newspaper and continued to read. Lissy sat at his feet, rested her head on his knee and allowed her brain to tumble over, trying to make sense of the terrible mess of her life.

THIRTY-EIGHT

Zakynthos, Greece, 1953

The views across the island never failed to make Angelos smile, and the views from his grove were particularly stunning. It was something that brought him great pleasure. He was enjoying his time alone in the groves. Sophia was at the house with his mother, and he'd come out to check the trees and ponder over memories of happier times spent under the branches.

The trees were thriving, and it looked like it would be another successful olive harvest this year. Life had settled into an easy rhythm, a constant of time spent with family, drinking in the Kafenion with his friends and watching his daughter grow.

Island life had become uncertain in recent days, though. The arrival of Richard the Englishman had surprised him. It was someone he'd never expected to see again, and yet there he'd been, standing in front of Angelos, as though no time had passed at all. Whilst he'd told Richard what had happened, he hadn't been wholly truthful. Angelos could've told Richard who he was, and they could've grieved together, but Angelos hadn't let that happen. His decision had plagued him ever since.

After all this time of hoping and wanting for news of his daughter, he'd found out Athena was alive. He should've told Richard he was her father, but something had stopped him. The Englishman had been well dressed, respectable. Angelos had a meagre life. He was an olive farmer with little to his name. What could he have offered Athena? Nothing when compared to the Englishman.

Angelos had carried his secret back home and hadn't told anyone about the meeting. Even though it broke his heart, and he was desperate to see her again, Angelos knew Athena would have a good life, want for little. She was alive and well and would have everything she needed and wanted. Angelos couldn't offer her that. Maybe one day, when she had grown up, Athena would come back to him of her own accord and they would be reunited.

It was time to stop wallowing in problems of his own making. Angelos stood, stretched and began to check the olive trees. Walking the avenue of twisted, gnarled trees, Angelos methodically checked them, relieved to see that the hardy trees were okay. Recent earthquakes had shaken much of the island and could've damaged them. He needed to make sure no dangerous branches were about to fall, and the fruit was fine.

As he neared the end of the line, a low rumbling beneath his feet unsteadied him. The rumbling grew louder, and the trees waved their heaving branches in an erratic motion. Angelos ran to the open field next to the grove, ensuring he was away from the trees. The last thing he needed was for something to fall on him.

Looking out across the island, he gripped a stone boundary wall with one hand as the island bucked and tossed with the intensity of the earthquake. More violent than previous earthquakes, Angelos was thrown to his feet, the wind being knocked out of him as he landed. The stone wall that had initially supported him now broke apart and fell, stones sliding and falling to the ground.

Angelos rolled away from the disintegrating wall and curled up in a ball, covering his head, waiting for the violent shaking to pass. His heart thudded in his chest, and he prayed over and over that his daughter and mother were safe. The shaking was too brutal for him to be able to stand, let alone run. He was forced to wait until the earthquake ended.

The earthquake thudded to a stop, and dust from the hot August earth slowly swirled back to settle on the ground. It was the most powerful earthquake Angelos had ever experienced. The stone wall had collapsed, and nearby olive trees had limbs hanging from them like broken arms. Angelos stood and wiped dust and grass from his clothes.

Across the island, between the two crests of Skopos and Bochali, the air was filled with a smoky haze and small explosions could be heard. It looked like Zakynthos Town had suffered badly.

Running back through the grove, Angelos jumped over stones and fallen branches to get back to the house he'd grown up in. The house the Nazis had stolen from his family. The place he, Pigi and Sophia now called home. Reaching the driveway, Angelos skidded to a stop. His beloved home was surrounded by swirling dust, the roof had fallen and part of the side wall had collapsed, strewing rubble everywhere.

"Sophia! *Mana!*" he cried in despair. "Sophia! *Mana!*"

With tears in his eyes, Angelos ran the rest of the driveway, his lungs and muscles aching and screaming in pain.

But he kept running. As his hand grasped the door handle, a disturbing creaking and groaning sound came from the building. As though it was remembering the hurt and despair it had faced during the war. As though it could no longer carry on. It gave an ear-splitting crack and groan and the remaining side wall collapsed.

A hand pulled Angelos backwards and he fell to the ground, covered by the protective arms of his daughter.

"*Baba*. I am okay. We are okay," she yelled through the sound of thudding debris.

Angelos sat up; his daughter was by his side and his mother was behind them, crying and wringing her hands.

Scrabbling to their feet, the family put distance between themselves and the Sarkis house and were forced to watch as walls fell in on each other, floorboards and beams snapped, and their furniture and belongings were crushed under the weight of masonry. The Sarkis home was gone, a shell of its former self. It had survived Nazi occupation, but in just a few minutes, an earthquake had reduced it to a pile of rubble.

After everything he'd been through, Angelos had thought life couldn't hurt him anymore, but it seemed it still could, and with such vengeance too. A cruel twist of fate had seen nature snatch his home from him a second time and there would be no getting it back this time. His home was in ruins and too badly damaged to repair. After hundreds of years of standing on the site, keeping a roof over the heads of generations of Sarkis family members, they were now forced to start again.

"Come *Baba*. Let us get away from here. There is nothing we can do now." Sophia tugged at his arm, trying to get her father to move.

Angelos shook his head. "Give me a minute. I just need

to sit here for a minute." Angelos watched Sophia walk over to his mother and embrace her. Putting his head in his hands, he cried, great tears dropping to the dusty ground staining it dark brown. They were alive – small mercies for that – it could've been much worse. They could've died, but they hadn't. They faced an uncertain future, and it would take some time for them to rebuild their lives, but at least they were all alive. A miracle indeed.

THIRTY-NINE

Bristol, England, 1953

Lissy was about to put tea on the table when there was a knock at the front door.

"Wait for me to start eating please, Athena. I'll be a moment." Lissy removed her apron and walked into the hallway, closing the kitchen door behind her. Checking her reflection in the mirror, she patted her hair before opening the door.

"Good afternoon, Mrs Hobbs. I'm Constable Perry. We are here about your husband, Mr Richard Hobbs. May we please come in?"

Lissy caught her breath. It was like the war all over again, but this time it was blue uniforms instead of brown. She nodded, widening the door for the man to enter. Surprised, she saw George with Constable Jenkins. He merely nodded.

Lissy closed the door and showed the two men into the front room. Whatever this was about, she didn't want Athena to hear. Lissy would tell the girl in her own time. Lissy offered them a seat on the sofa and they took it. Lissy sat in Richard's armchair, anxiously waiting for them to speak.

It was Constable Jenkins that broke the silence. "Mrs Hobbs. I'm very sorry to inform you that your husband is dead. He was a victim of the Greek earthquake. Rescuers found his body in the street when they were digging through the rubble several days after the earthquake. They're currently transporting him home from Zakynthos for you. We're sorry for your loss, Mrs Hobbs."

Lissy saw stars and sat back in the chair closing her eyes. A faint smell of Richard wrapped itself around her. He would never sit in this chair again. A lone tear slid from under her eyelid. She swiped it away with the back of her hand.

"What's going on? Why are the police here?"

Lissy's eyes flew open. Athena stood in the doorway, her arms defensively crossed over her chest. How much had the child heard?

Constable Jenkins stood and went over to Athena. Comfortingly, he placed his arm around her shoulder. "I'm here with news about your father, miss."

Lissy sprang to her feet. "He's not her bloody father! He never was!"

"He *was* my *papa*! He's more of a *papa* than you were ever a mother!" Athena screamed back. "What's happened to him? I demand to know! You must tell me!"

"Constable Jenkins, please wait outside for me. I know the family well. Let me speak with them," George said, motioning his colleague to the door.

"If you're sure."

"Yes, quite sure." George saw his colleague out and then turned to Athena. "Athena..." he began, but the child cut him off.

"I don't want to hear it from you, copper. I want her to tell me what's going on." She jabbed her finger in Lissy's direction.

"Richard's dead. He's never coming home." Lissy pushed past the girl and stormed up the stairs. Athena sank to the floor, opened her mouth and screamed, a deep guttural sound of heartbreak. It enveloped the room, licking the walls, pervading everything.

George reached down to comfort her, but she pushed him away. Her face was already stained with tears, her eyes flashed with anger and the emotion was just too raw. "I hate you. Leave me alone." Athena flung herself to the floor and sobbed, grief eating her up, expelling every emotion.

Quietly, George stepped away, closing the door. He ran upstairs and stopped outside of the bedroom. Lissy was sitting on the end of the bed, staring straight ahead.

"I see Athena is taking things as calmly as she always does. She always acts out making things worse than they need to be."

"She's still a child, Lissy. A child who's just been told her father is dead. Under the circumstances, I think she's allowed a little leeway, don't you? You're just as much at fault, you could have been compassionate, but instead you were stubborn and butted heads with her again. I've left her to cry it out of her system. You should probably do the same," George said.

"I'm sorry. It was unforgivable. I wasn't thinking. It's just such a shock." Lissy looked at him for the first time. "So, what happens now?"

George spoke to her from the hallway, not daring to cross the threshold. "You both need to grieve, and take things a day at a time. When Richard's body is returned, I can help you with the funeral and anything else that needs doing."

"Thank you."

"I must go. Constable Jenkins is waiting. Will you be alright?"

"Yes, I must be. I've a child to take care of, that isn't mine. I should also tell his parents."

"I'll come and see you tomorrow." George nodded, walked downstairs and along the hallway. Athena was still sobbing loudly. The noise only ceased once he'd stepped outside and closed the front door behind him.

FORTY

Zakynthos, Greece 1953

Eventually, the tremors had withered and become less frequent. As the days passed, the damage to the island became heartbreakingly clear. Hundreds, possibly thousands, of islanders had lost their homes. Most of Zakynthos Town was destroyed, reduced to a derelict waste ground that would take a long time to clear and rebuild.

The small house on the Sarkis land that Angelos and Maria had lived in had fared better than the main Sarkis house. Save for several small cracks, it was standing strong. It became their home after the earthquake, sharing it with Niko until it could be enlarged to give them their own space. They were lucky to still have a roof over their heads, even if it was a small one.

Angelos had avoided the Sarkis house, not wanting to see the damage. It still hurt too much. He'd found the courage, however, when Pentalis told him he'd lost almost everything, including family members, a business and possessions. It was a cruel blow to the kind man.

A NIGHT OF THUNDER

Angelos had only lost the Sarkis house; many of his possessions still lay inside the ruined building. One bright sunny afternoon, Angelos, Niko and Pantelis gathered outside the ruinous house with a plan to retrieve what they could before the olive harvest began and winter set in.

Once a beautiful home to a long line of Sarkis owners, the Sarkis house was now a ruined shell. The roof had fully collapsed, the side wall was gone, and part of the front had a gaping hole and a large crack in it. It was past saving.

With great care, Angelos, Niko and Pentalis carefully began moving rubble and stone from the front of the house. Much of the stone would be used again for olive grove walls and extending the smaller house. The unusable rubble was moved to one side to be disposed of later. It was hard work, but eventually, they cleared a path through to the main door. What was once a beautiful wooden door was now split and hanging from its hinges, now only good for firewood. A sad end for something that had welcomed so many.

Carefully walking into the house, Angelos stopped. He'd expected things to be bad, but the horror that awaited him could never have been imagined. Roof timbers lay twisted and broken. Roof tiles were smashed. Furniture was covered in dust and debris; some was salvageable, some crushed beyond repair. Pictures hung at an angle; others had fallen and been punched through with debris. Their home, their life, lay around him in tatters, and he didn't know where to start.

"Do you think it is safe to be in here, Angelos?"

"Probably not, Pentalis, but I must see it for myself. I must reclaim what I can of my life. If not for me, for *Mana* and Sophia."

"I understand. I wish I could do the same. Everything I

owned is gone. I love Zakynthos, but life here has been hard. Nature has been crueller." Pentalis shook his head. "I will help you get your belongings. Helping you will make me feel better. If not, we can go to the Kafenion for a coffee afterwards."

"I think the Kafenion is a good idea. We will need it after this." Niko patted both men on the shoulder. "Shall we start?"

Angelos nodded and the three men stepped forward. Methodically, they began to remove treasured family items, carrying them outside and piling them up in the sunshine. Just over an hour later, after searching as much of the house as they could, and narrowly avoiding another small collapse, they'd done all they could. As they walked back outside with the last of the belongings, Sophia walked up the driveway.

"*Baba!* What are you doing! Do you not know how dangerous it is to be in the house? There could be another earthquake. It could have fallen and killed you! I cannot lose you! And you, Uncle Niko and Pentalis, you should know better!"

Angelos pulled his daughter to him and placed his hands on her shoulders. "My dear daughter. Niko, Pentalis and I are brave Zakynthian men! Do you think we fear an island that shakes? No! These are my belongings. Our furniture, our clothes, our precious things. I will take them to our new home and show this island and her shaking that Angelos Sarkis is not afraid!" He laughed. "Now come, you can help us. We will continue a good life in our new house, Sophia. The old Sarkis home will stay as it is. It will remind us of our painful history. It will remind us that whilst our past may be in ruins, we can rise out of the ruins, start again and live on."

A NIGHT OF THUNDER

Angelos walked to the pile of belongings. He breathed out a big sigh. His bravery was all for Sophia. Inside, he still grieved many losses, but he needed to be strong. Sophia needed a brave father, and he didn't want her to see weakness. Lifting a pile of clothes, he turned and handed them to his daughter. "Take these to *Nonna*. They will need a clean."

Sophia did as her father asked.

"You are a good man, Angelos. You look after your family well. Much better than your own father did. Never lose that. I know you are hurting. I know your life is not how you expected it to be; mine is not either. The war ruined it all for us. But we are alive, and we must cling to that and live whilst we still can. Come, let us take this to your new home." Pentalis motioned to the piles of belongings.

"He is right, Angelos. We have all come through bad times and are stronger for it. You will be okay." Niko swung a rolled up salvaged floor rug over his shoulder.

"Thank you, my friends. Your kindness will never be forgotten."

∽

A week later, Angelos arrived at Xigia Beach and sat on a rock looking out across the sea. Breathing in the salty air, he allowed the heat of the sun to kiss his face. He always seemed to end up back here in this place.

Angelos closed his eyes, enjoying the swish, swish, swish sound of the waves as they washed back and forth on the beach. The beautiful beach, that had been a place of terror during the war, was now a place of solace and remembrance where he could sit and remember Elena and Athena. Often, he visited and just sat, listening to the sound of the waves, enjoying the sun and taking in the slight smell of sulphur that was synonymous with the beach. Remnants of the underground pitch that slid its way through small cracks in the earth, leaking out into the sea.

The silhouette of the Greek mainland sat on the horizon, reminding Zakynthians that despite being an island, they were still part of something bigger. His thoughts returned to his daughter, Athena. She would be sixteen now, and he still thought of her every day.

His biggest regret was not telling the airman who he was. He'd been so foolish, and a golden opportunity had slipped through his hands. After the earthquake, Angelos heard from Pentalis that the Englishman had been killed. Angelos wondered where Athena was and if she was grieving for the man's loss? Was Athena alone? Did she still have a roof over her head? He wished he knew.

He must keep believing she was fine and would be in the future. He had to keep believing that she would make her mark on the world. He had to keep believing that one day, life would return her to him, and when that happened, he wouldn't be such a fool. Until that day, all Angelos could do was keep her in his thoughts.

Angelos turned the bright red poppy over in his hands. Every year he marked his daughter's birthday quietly and simply, by throwing a poppy to the sea in the last place he saw her. Today felt no different to previous years, but it was. Walking to the shore, he allowed the gentle waves to lap over his shoes. This way he was completely connected to the ocean, the thing that had last held Athena and carried her away from him to a different life.

"I love you, my daughter. I have never forgotten about you. You are always in my heart. Come back to me. We need you." Angelos threw the poppy onto the rippling waves and watched as it bobbed on the water's surface until it disappeared, and his shoes were soaked through with sea water.

COMING SOON!

Coming soon, the final part of the trilogy, Hope Under Blue Skies, Book three of the Zakynthian Family series.

Author Note: Thanks for reading *A Night of Thunder*. When I decided to write the follow-up book to *Among the Olive Groves*, a request from readers, the characters took on a life of their own. The story became so big, I had to split it into two books. The third and final part of the story will be called *Hope Under Blue Skies*. It will be published very soon!

ACKNOWLEDGMENTS

There are so many people I must thank, without whom this book wouldn't have happened. Firstly, to all the readers of *Among the Olive Groves* who messaged me to request a follow up book that was never intended. Thanks for your patience as I figured out what sort of follow-up book to write, worked out the story, researched and wrote it.

Firstly, to members of my family who've helped with Bristol research including my mum for her brilliant knowledge of the area of Bristol in which Lissy's home is located and for allowing me to look at my Great Uncle Frank's incredible scrapbook containing Bristol WW2 news cuttings.

I also want to thank my Great Aunt Doreen for her memories and chats about working in the parachute factory during WW2, I wish you could have read the final book.

A massive thanks also goes out to the team at Dunkeswell Airfield Heritage Centre in Devon for answering my questions about the RAF, and the work that pilots did in WW2. I'd also like to thank M Shed Museum in Bristol, Tiverton Museum of Mid Devon Life and the Imperial War Museum in London for their excellent WW2 displays and information which were incredibly useful for my research.

To Louise Inzk, Vici Morgan and Katerina Tsekouras. You've all been so supportive, whilst I was writing this book.

You were sounding boards for characters and story points as well as early readers of the book and helped reassure me that the story worked well! Louise, thanks for double checking all my Greek and important Zakynthian facts, I couldn't have done this without your help. Thanks to everyone in the Among the Olive Groves Facebook group, who helped with the series and character names. I love being able to involve you all in the writing process, and to Rose James for doing such a great job as Facebook admin!

A huge thank you goes out to my editor Helen, who helped me pull the book into shape and tweak some important parts of the story. A massive shout out goes to Susie from Susie's Art in Greece who helped me take an idea and turn it into a beautiful cover illustration, you were such a joy to work with! I must also thank Cherie at CCBookDesign for a fantastic book cover, it looks amazing. You're a wonderful team to work with.

To Anita Faulkner and the amazing members of the Writer's Dream House. You've all been such an incredible support this last eighteen months. I must also thank fellow author Abigail Yardimci for the ongoing chats and support, see you for tea and cake soon!

Finally, to my husband T, and my family. Thank you for your continued support, I love you all very much.

Head over to **my website** to find out more about my writing.

Sign up to my newsletter here!

You can find me on social media at **@chrissieparkerauthor**

ALSO BY THE AUTHOR

Among the Olive Groves - Book One of the Zakynthian Family Series

Wind Across the Nile

A Ionian Dream Wedding - A short story

I Left My Heart in Petra – A short story

Integrate (Book one of the Moon Series)

Temperance (Book two of the Moon Series)

The Secrets: A collection of poems and short stories

Don't forget to leave a review!

Printed in Great Britain
by Amazon